PURGE

Zombie Apocalypse: The Chad Halverson Series Book 8

BRYAN CASSIDAY

BRYAN CASSIDAY

Bryan Cassiday
Los Angeles
ISBN 9798988189541
Published in the United States of America
First Edition: May 5, 2025

BOOKS BY BRYAN CASSIDAY

Chapter 1

Halverson was standing over President Mims's murdered corpse spread-eagled on his back on the desk in the president's office in the Mount Weather bunker when he heard a noise behind him.

"Drop the gun," said Purdy, a twentysomething SEAL with cropped hair and a youthful face who was pushing thirty.

His youthful face wasn't smiling.

He was standing in the doorway, training an H&K MP5 on Halverson.

B&T MP9 in hand, Halverson turned toward him.

"I said, drop the gun," said Purdy, raising his voice and jutting the muzzle of his MP5 at Halverson.

Halverson hesitated. He didn't like being unarmed, not with the way the world was—what was left of it anyway.

"Why?" he said. "I'm one of you. I'm Chad Halverson. I just got back from my mission."

"I'm Joe Purdy, and you killed the president of the United States. Now drop it."

"He was like this when I entered his office."

"I don't want to hear another word out of you till after you drop the gun," said Purdy, baring his teeth.

Halverson figured he better comply. He dropped his MP9 to the floor.

"You too," Purdy told Marta Costello.

A coder before the apocalypse rendered coding extinct, Marta dropped her knife.

"Who's running Mount Weather now?" said Halverson.

"The new president. Did you really think you would be able to take over after you killed Mims?"

"I didn't kill him. Who's the new president?"

"The secretary of state, Dean Uriah."

"Let me talk to him. I'm back from my mission. He'll want to hear my report."

"Don't kid yourself, Halverson. You're on his shit list now that you took out the president. He's not gonna be happy to see your sorry ass. I'm taking you and your coconspirator to the brig. Get moving."

"This is insane. Why would I take out Mims?"

"Tell it to the president."

"Am I under arrest?"

"I'm not a cop, but you're going to the brig for murder."

"He was already dead when I entered his office."

"Repeating something doesn't make it true."

"It doesn't make it false, either."

"You and her were the only ones in the office with his corpse. You failed your mission. He chewed you out. And you knifed him in the heart. Open-and-shut case if you ask me."

Purdy prodded Halverson's ribs with the MP5 muzzle. "Get going."

"We nearly got killed on the mission," said Marta, fuming, "and this is how you welcome us back?"

"This is how I welcome murderers, especially assassins of our president."

"What's going on here?" demanded a gravel-voiced sixtyish guy, wearing horn-rimmed glasses, their bows propped on his big ears that framed his head like seashells.

Clad in a navy blue suit and a red necktie, Secretary of State Dean Uriah stood five eleven with a gut that spilled over his belt.

"Halverson and his coconspirator assassinated President Mims. Which makes you our president," said Purdy.

"It's hard to believe Mims is dead," said Uriah, glum-faced.

"A knife through the heart, courtesy of these two butchers."

Uriah glowered at Halverson.

"Halverson left a note on Mims's chest," said Purdy.

"Note? What note?"

"It says, The purge has begun."

"I didn't kill him," said Halverson. "He was already dead when me and Marta entered his office."

"What's this about a purge?" said Uriah.

5

BRYAN CASSIDAY

"No idea. I didn't write it."

"Do you deny you were in his office with his corpse?"

"Not at all. I deny I killed him."

"If you didn't do it, who did?"

"How do I know? I just got back from my mission. The murderer was gone by the time I entered Mims's office."

His gaze intent, Uriah took a step toward him. "What about your mission? Did you accomplish it?"

"No, sir. Dr. Wheelhouse turned out to be a hoax. He lied about having the vaccine against the zombie plague in order to lure us to his lair and use us as guinea pigs for testing his vaccines—none of which worked."

"Then you don't have the vaccine?"

"Correct, sir."

Uriah clutched his forehead. "This is horrible news." He paused. "Is that why you killed the president?"

"What?" said Halverson, indignant.

"You killed him because he sent you on a wild-goose chase that turned out to be a suicide mission for nothing."

"Absolutely not."

"Where are the others?" said Uriah, looking around the hallway. "How many of your squad made it back?"

"There are no others."

"You mean to tell me you two are the only survivors?" said Uriah, baffled.

His face grim, Halverson nodded.

"You guys were well armed," said Uriah. "How could you lose your entire squad?"

"Dr. Wheelhouse poisoned most of them with his botched vaccines. He turned them into monstrosities," said Halverson, grimacing at the memory.

"They should call him Josef Mengele," said Marta.

"What a clusterfuck," said Uriah.

"What do you want me to do with the assassins, Mr. President?" said Purdy.

"That's true," realized Uriah. "I am the president. I'm next in line in succession since we have no vice president, and the speaker of the house and the president pro tempore are incommunicado."

"I heard they are at Raven Rock."

"Then why haven't they made any attempt to contact us? Until we hear otherwise, we must assume they're both dead."

"Can you make that assumption?" said Halverson with concern.

"I'm the president now," said Uriah. "Are you questioning my authority?"

"No, sir. I'm simply saying we don't know what the hell is really going on regarding Raven Rock, since comms are down."

"We're not gonna sit on our asses and wait around to hear from them. I've got a country to run. We are not surrendering to the infected ghouls simply because we lost another president." Uriah pumped his fist. "The fight goes on till the last man. I will never surrender our beloved country to the ghouls."

A tall ghoul wearing a priest's black vestment staggered toward them from the other end of the corridor, hanging his mouth open, his tongue crawling with maggots. Hundreds of pale, one-eyed nematodes wriggled out of the pores of his face like they were performing a morbid dance.

"Another security breach, goddammit," said Uriah, picking up on the ghoul.

"They're getting in through the air ducts," said Purdy, swinging his MP5 toward the ghoul and opening fire, stitching the creature's head with slugs.

The ghoul lurched to the side. His knees buckled and he collapsed on the floor, where he lay motionless.

"Maybe not," said Halverson.

Purdy whipped his MP5 back toward Halverson at the sound of his voice.

"Don't try anything," said Purdy.

"What are you talking about, Halverson?" said Uriah.

"The front door was left unguarded when we returned from our mission," said Halverson.

"Who's guarding the front door, Purdy?"

"Hmm. Romano should be there. Johnny Romano."

"Why the hell isn't he at his post?"

"Eh, he was always going on about leaving here to see his girlfriend. I thought it was just talk, you know? I never thought he'd up and leave. There's still radiation outside the bunker. And all those stinking ghouls." Purdy shook his head. "I don't like his chances."

"All right," said Uriah. "List him as AWOL and replace him. The front door must be guarded at all times. If you see Romano, throw him in the brig."

"Yes, sir," said Purdy, coming to attention.

"Is there no end to the things?" said Uriah, eyeballing the dead ghoul sprawled on the floor.

"They're all over the country, sir," said Halverson.

"Don't try anything," said Purdy, keeping his MP5 trained on Halverson and Marta. "You're both under arrest for murder."

"You take care of them," said Uriah. "I need to make an announcement over the PA system about our great leader's death and how we captured the assassins."

"What do you think that note about the purge means, Mr. President?"

Uriah thought about it. "We have to figure it means, these two assassins planned to take out the rest of the government, including me," said Uriah, cutting a glare toward Halverson. "Especially me since I was next in line to become president."

"Is it a conspiracy?"

"I don't think so. Just these two, I suspect. They wanted revenge for being sent on a suicide mission. But we can't rule anything out. We will continue our investigation into Mims's murder. By the way, have Dr. Morrow examine these two before you do anything else. I want to make sure they're not radioactive. The last thing we need is them contaminating the rest of us with radiation."

Chapter 2

Halverson found himself sitting on an examining table with paper covering it in Dr. Morrow's office.

"Take off your shirt," said Morrow, a stethoscope dangling from his neck.

Bald, clad in a white smock, Morrow was an average-sized man at five nine pushing sixty. His dolorous brown eyes took in Halverson.

Halverson took off his shirt.

"I'm surprised you made it back alive," said Morrow.

"So am I," said Halverson. "What's been going on here?"

"Our oxygen level is very low on account of the ghouls blocking our air vents."

"Yeah, I notice I've been having trouble breathing in here."

Morrow used his stethoscope to listen to Halverson's heart. He told Halverson to take a deep breath several times and listened to Halverson's lungs.

"Mims ordered me to cut back on the distribution of oxygen to the occupants of the bunker," said Morrow.

"Why would he do that?" said Halverson.

"I hate to say it, but he wanted more oxygen for himself. He was having great difficulty breathing. He had an oxygen tank, but it wasn't enough. He needed more oxygen in the air in his office. The only way to give him more oxygen was to cut back on everybody else's."

"Sounds like a motive for someone to kill him."

Morrow took out a Geiger counter and aimed it at Halverson. The machine reacted to Halverson's radioactive body by making a static-like sound.

"How long do I have?" said Halverson, expecting the worst.

He knew he had been subjected to fallout from the LGM-30G Minuteman III ICBM that had struck the bunker at ex-president Cole's behest. Cole, who had gone mad, had been the acting president before Mims had taken over. The ICBM had been equipped with a W78 thermonuclear warhead with a yield of 350 kilotons.

The Mount Weather bunker had withstood the nuclear blast, but miles of forest surrounding the bunker had been razed to the ground.

"You're not that bad, considering," said Morrow, examining the readout on the Geiger counter in his hand.

"Considering what?"

"The amount of time you were outside," said Morrow, looking up from the machine.

"The armor-plated Chevy Suburbans shielded us from the radiation when we left. It's only when we came back that we were exposed to the radiation."

"Do you want the good news or the bad news first?"

"The good news."

"The good news is you're gonna live. The bad news is you're gonna live," said Morrow, his face expressionless.

Halverson sniggered. "Yeah, the apocalypse. If you can call this living. And now they think I murdered President Mims."

"What?" said Morrow in surprise.

"They found me and Marta in his office with his corpse."

"Why did you—"

"I didn't do it. I was in the wrong place at the wrong time. I had just got back from my mission and I was reporting to his office when I found him murdered."

Morrow paced around the room, brooding.

"I'm not surprised," he said.

"Explain."

"I believe somebody found out that Mims was cutting back on everybody's oxygen in order to increase his own supply. The other occupants heard about it."

Halverson nodded.

"I tried to talk him out of it, but he wouldn't listen to me," Morrow went on. "He wanted me to keep it a secret. He didn't think the others would ever find out."

"Somebody might have overheard you two talking about it."

Morrow shrugged. "I never thought it would come to this."

"It doesn't take much to set people off now that the ghouls have overrun the country and left it in ruins."

"Mims was an arrogant man. He believed the country couldn't exist without him, which, in his eyes, gave him the right to use more oxygen than anybody else so he could be in good health while everybody else languished."

MP5 in hand, Purdy kicked open the doctor's door.

Taken aback, Halverson and Morrow watched him.

"Verdict, Doc?" said Purdy.

"He'll live," said Morrow.

Purdy snorted a laugh. "But not much longer after we find him guilty of first degree murder. Put your shirt on, Halverson, and let's go to the brig." He turned to Morrow. "Did you examine the girl."

Morrow nodded yes.

"Good," said Purdy, slewing toward Halverson and unleashing a shit-eating grin. "You and your cohort will have separate cells. You two can stare at each other's ugly faces till your execution."

Halverson put on his shirt.

Purdy prodded him in the ribs with the MP5 muzzle.

Halverson nailed him with a death stare.

Purdy laughed. "This is gonna be fun."

Chapter 3

President Uriah stood behind a lectern on a stage in the auditorium, facing the audience.

"Now that I am president I'm running a tight ship here," he announced. "A loose ship is one that sinks. We got a war on our hands. What that means is nobody steps out of line. When I give a command, I expect it to be obeyed. If you refuse to obey and flee the bunker, you will be shot in the back as a traitor."

The audience grumbled.

"I know it sounds draconian," Uriah went on. "But we live in hard times. The ghouls are systematically destroying our great country. We will not let them get away with it. We will fight till we're dead. We will never surrender."

The audience clapped.

"My predecessor, President Mims, was a good man. He would have made a great Sunday School teacher. But he was a weak president. He didn't understand realpolitik. The only way we're gonna win this internecine war is by being strong. We must never yield. All ghouls will be killed—either by a blow to the head or a bullet to the head. No ghoul in this country will be allowed to survive. It's them or us, folks. Kill or be killed. If we show no mercy toward the ghouls, we will win. I guarantee it."

The audience rose to their feet as one, cheering and clapping.

"As commander in chief I will treat all of you with respect," resumed Uriah. "And I expect all of you to treat me the same way. I will not tolerate insubordination. Any soldier who deserts his post and goes AWOL will be shot dead."

More grumbling in the audience. Concerned expressions gazed up at Uriah.

"Settle down," said Uriah. "A good soldier has nothing to fear from me. I'd stake my life on it that you're all good soldiers," he said, sweeping his gaze across the crowd. "I have your six, and I want you all to have mine. Do we understand each other?"

The audience clapped.

"We have captured President Mims's assassins and we will deal with them appropriately. They will face a firing squad—after a trial, of course. Everybody has a right to a trial in this great country. You are innocent until proven guilty. We are not a banana republic. We treat everybody with respect. After all, we are the great and the good."

Escorted by Purdy, Halverson and Marta marched past the open door at the back of the auditorium and heard Uriah speaking.

"I don't like our chances," said Halverson.

"A little better than a suicide mission?" said Marta.

Halverson cracked a brief smile. "We'll muddle through."

"We fought a million zombies. What can Captain Bligh do to us?"

"He's gonna put both of you in front of a firing squad," said Purdy, strutting behind them, gun in hand.

"'What are we talking about?' you may ask," said Uriah from his lectern. "I'll tell you what we're talking about. We're talking about loyalty. I respect loyalty in a person more than any other trait. Do you hear me?"

The audience clapped.

"What I can't stand is a traitor. Loyalty will be rewarded. Traitors will be shot. Moles and traitors can leave this auditorium right now."

Nobody moved in the auditorium. Quiet reigned.

"More than anything else we need loyalty in times like these, times of intense distress, apocalyptic times. That's right, people. You heard me right. We're in an apocalypse. Mark my words, we're in an existential fight for the survival of the human race." Uriah made a sweeping gesture with his arms. "The ghouls own our country. That's right. That's why we're in hiding. But being in hiding doesn't mean we're defeated. We have lost some battles, but we haven't lost the war. As long as we keep fighting, we will win. We will rise like the phoenix from the ashes and reclaim this great country."

The audience cheered and applauded.

"The ghouls have an advantage. There are more of them than us," said Uriah, nodding. "That's right. They have the numbers. And their numbers are increasing," he added, raising his voice.

"They can reproduce at unheard-of rates, much faster than we can. Every time they bite a human they create a new ghoul. Not only that, they are rising from their graves to attack us. You heard correctly, people. The dead are rising from their graves to destroy us. All those corpses are coming to kill us. There are *billions* of them. Maybe even trillions. Think of all of the corpses that have been buried since the human race walked the earth."

Halverson could see Uriah's face slicked with sweat as he, Purdy, and Marta stood listening to Uriah at the rear door.

"Every last one of those corpses is coming to kill us," said Uriah. "I know it's a scary thought. But the zombie plague infects the dead as well as the living. We can never let our guards down. We must remain ever vigilant. We are in the fight of our lives. If we survive this apocalypse (and we *will* survive it), we can survive anything."

Thunderous applause rocked the auditorium.

"As long as we stick together as a single fighting unit, we will prevail. The only way we can accomplish that is with absolute loyalty. I demand nothing less than absolute loyalty from every last one of you."

More plaudits.

"I'm not gonna sugarcoat this. Our mission of survival is hard. We are outnumbered millions to one. But our country has survived worse. We survived the Civil War, World War I, and World War II. We fought the British to gain our independence in the Revolutionary War. We will never surrender to our enemies. We will wipe the ghouls off the face of the earth."

The audience leapt to their feet and cheered.

"We will win all our battles, because God is on our side. This is the chosen country. It will last forever. But we must keep fighting against the worst threat to our existence that we have ever encountered in the history of this great country.

"Don't talk to me about losing. We will never lose as long as we keep fighting and never give up. Our freedom was never *given* to us. We *fought* for it. We *killed* for it. As Jefferson once said, 'From time to time the tree of liberty must be watered with the blood of tyrants.' Our tyrants are the ghouls. The living dead rule us. We must fight them every minute of the day."

"He likes to hear himself talk," said Halverson.

"Shut up," said Purdy. "Listen to our great leader, the president."

Three ghouls shambled through the front door of the auditorium, one in his seventies, the other two in their forties.

Chapter 4

All three ghouls were wearing tattered rags, dried bloodstains on their clothing, stale vomit on the fronts of their shirts, urine stains on their pants.

Suppurating buboes stippled the oldest ghoul's face. Wearing a general's uniform he clamped a smoking cigar between his carious teeth as a white worm oozed out of his tear duct. Smoke puffed out of his mouth and ears. His milky eyes flashed fiery red. He spat out the damp cigar in anticipation of feasting on warm flesh.

Uriah recoiled in shock.

"It's General Lemoyne," cried a middle-aged, ponytailed guy in the audience.

"General Lemoyne is dead," said Uriah. "Kill them. Kill them all."

The guard standing near the stage wielded his Brugger & Thomet MP9 and unleashed a long burst at the three creatures, perforating their necks. Led by the general, the ghouls kept plodding forward toward the stage. The guard squeezed off another burst, his aim better this time, peppering the ghoul heads with lead. Their occipital bones blew out the backs of their skulls. The ghouls trudged forward and collapsed on the floor in heaps of rotting flesh that emitted a congeries of foul odors.

"Where the hell did they come from?" demanded Uriah.

A guard rushed into the auditorium, his face flushed. "Security breach at the front door, Mr. President. The door's broken."

"I ordered guards to be stationed there after Romano went AWOL."

"They're there now fixing the door. Everything's under control, sir."

"Destroy the ghouls' brains and drag their stinking carcasses out of here. I can't stand the sight of them."

The two guards fired MP9 bursts into the three bullet-riddled zombie heads, pancaking them and turning them into mincemeat.

"If anybody ever sees the traitor Romano, kill him on sight," said Uriah. "I want his head on a platter." He faced the audience. "Listen up, people. There's a ten-thousand-dollar reward on the traitor Johnny Romano's head."

The crowd booed.

"Romano, Romano," they chanted. "Kill Johnny Romano."

"Let's change the subject. Have you heard the hero Chad Halverson is back with us? He returned alive from his suicide mission. I'm sure you all know Halverson."

The audience cheered and clapped their hands.

"You all think he's a hero, don't you?"

"Halverson," the crowd chanted with admiration.

"He was the only one to make it back alive except for Marta Costello, who also survived the mission."

The crowd nodded with appreciation.

"They made it back because Halverson is a bona fide hero. Right?"

"Right," cried several in the audience.

"Only a hero like Halverson could survive a suicide mission." Uriah paused. "There's only one problem. He failed his mission. He didn't bring back the vaccine against the plague. But he's a hero."

The crowd looked doubtful.

"Halverson is a hero," went on Uriah. "When he reported to President Mims to tell him the bad news about the mission, Mims read him the riot act. Infuriated, Halverson and his cohort Marta stabbed the president in the heart."

A hush fell over the audience, who were taken aback at the revelation.

"But Halverson is a hero. Therefore, he had every right to retaliate against Mims in any way he saw fit."

"No," said the crowd, becoming uneasy.

"Halverson killed our president, but Halverson is a hero."

"No," cried the audience. "Down with Halverson."

"But he's a hero."

"He's a killer. Down with Halverson and Marta. Kill them."

"Kill a hero?" said Uriah, cupping his ear to make sure he could hear their answer correctly.

"Kill Halverson," roared the crowd. "Kill Halverson and Marta."

Uriah nodded his approval of the crowd's demands. "He's a cold-blooded murderer."

"Kill Halverson," hollered the crowd.

"Settle down," said Uriah, using his hands to calm them. "We live in a free country. We don't execute anyone without giving them a fair trial. Halverson and his cohort will have their day in court."

"Kill the assassins now," screamed the crowd.

"After we find them guilty, we're gonna put him and Marta in front of a firing squad."

"Kill Halverson," the audience roared, jumping to their feet. "Kill Halverson."

Halverson was liking his chances less and less. A kangaroo court awaited him and Marta.

"Get going," said Purdy, "unless you want that mob to tear you to pieces here and now. All I do is say your name and they'll rip off your faces in a New York minute."

Knowing Purdy was right, adrenaline coursing through him, Halverson strode down the hall out of sight of the auditorium's open rear doors. He and Marta were safer in the brig at this point. Uriah had already tried and convicted them in the court of public opinion. The mob wanted blood.

Chapter 5

Marta was standing in the jail cell opposite Halverson's. She was staring at him as he sat on his bunk, brooding.

"Are you OK?" she said.

"We risked our lives to get the vaccine to save them, and now they want to kill us for committing a murder we didn't commit."

"Who do you think really did it?"

"Someone here in the bunker. Or at least someone who was in the bunker at the time of the assassination."

"What are we gonna do about it?"

"Nothing. They're gonna execute us any time now," said Halverson, hanging his head.

"I get it. You're depressed. Clear your mind of your black thoughts."

He was sick of repeatedly risking his life to carry out missions for the CIA and the government and getting treated like dirt for his efforts. Why should he care who assassinated Mims? He wasn't going to be around much longer. It was only a matter of time before he would be standing in front of a firing squad with Marta on a trumped-up charge of murder.

"We need to get outa here," said Marta. "We stay here, we're dead."

"I'm sick of busting a gut for these people. And this isn't the first time they have tried to kill me. They have tried numerous times."

"And failed."

"Because I'm a hero," muttered Halverson, his face clouding.

"That's right. We need to be heroes and keep fighting to go on living in these dark times."

"How can we fight the president? He's the head of the country."

"We've fought millions of ghouls, and we won. Why not fight the president who is falsely accusing us of assassinating President Mims."

"I'm a black ops CIA agent. I work for the current president."

"Even when he's falsely accusing you of murder?"

Halverson lifted his head. "Maybe Uriah was the one who had Mims assassinated. We don't have any way of knowing what went on here while we were gone."

He bolted to his feet.

Marta felt encouraged by his burst of energy. "Right."

Halverson paced around his cell. "The point is we don't know who killed Mims. All we know for sure is that we didn't do it."

"We need to escape."

"If Uriah killed Mims, I don't want to work for him. He should be replaced as president."

"We can't replace him now. The deck is stacked in his favor. If we stay at Mount Weather, we're dead. He feels we're a threat to him. He can't let us go on living."

Marta grabbed the bars in her cell and tried to shake them. Halverson watched her.

"I got an idea," he said.

"You really think we can escape?"

"Yeah."

"Then we better do it ASAP."

"Are your legs strong?"

"Totally. You know I do squats every chance I get."

"Good."

Marta shrugged. "We can't run away with these bars surrounding us."

"Running is the second part of my plan."

"What's the first part? You want me to kick the bars down with my strong legs? I got news for you. It won't work." She grabbed the bars. "These are high-tensile steel. They're not gonna budge a millimeter if I kick them. I'll end up breaking my feet."

"Nothing like that."

"I don't get it."

"I'll clue you in. We need to keep our voices down."

Chapter 6

Purdy unlocked the steel door to the brig and entered, carrying his MP5 in one hand and a steel plate of biscuits in the other.

"Lunchtime," he said. "I don't know why we feed you felons. It's a waste of good food if you ask me. You're gonna be dead in a few hours if not sooner."

"Did you come here to brighten our day, sunshine?" said Halverson, standing near the front of his cell.

"Shut up."

"Oh, biscuits," said Marta. "I love biscuits. I can't remember the last time I ate."

Purdy approached her.

Halverson noticed Purdy had a B&T MP9 strapped around his shoulder. Loaded for bear.

"It's your last meal so you better enjoy it," said Purdy, letting Marta pluck two biscuits off the plate as he held it in front of her.

Marta scarfed down the two biscuits as Purdy watched her.

"Hey, asshole, where are my biscuits?" said Halverson behind Purdy's back.

Purdy stiffened and scowled. "You better not be talking to me."

"Who do you think I'm talking to? You're the only asshole here."

In white heat, Purdy wheeled around.

At that same instant Marta leapt onto the bars, placed her heels against Purdy's back and shoved him as hard as she could by extending her legs between the bars. Purdy stumbled toward Halverson's cell under the impetus of Marta's shove. Halverson reached between his cell bars and latched onto Purdy's neck, spinning him around so he faced away from Halverson, who applied a chokehold.

Purdy struggled to escape but couldn't break free. He tried to train his MP5 on Halverson without success. With his free hand Halverson knocked the weapon out of Purdy's hand onto the floor. Then Halverson grabbed Purdy's head and continued to apply the chokehold until Purdy went limp in the crook of Halverson's arm throttling Purdy's throat.

Propping Purdy up with one arm, Halverson searched Purdy's body for the key to the cell.

"Is he dead?" said Marta.

"He's out cold. I don't know about dead. I didn't hear his hyoid bone crack."

Halverson retrieved two keys, stuck one in the lock of his cell door, and flung the door open. He released his hold on Purdy's neck. Purdy collapsed on the floor and didn't move.

"If he's still alive, we better get out of here fast," said Marta.

"If he's dead, the same thing. More so. Another murder rap."

Halverson unlocked her cell door, returned to Purdy, snagged the MP5 lying near him, and tossed it to her. Next, he removed the B&T MP9 strapped around Purdy's shoulder and commandeered it for himself. The SIG P226 in Purdy's holster ended up in Halverson's rear waistband.

"Let's go."

He used the second of Purdy's keys to unlock the door to the brig and peeked into the corridor. He didn't see a soul.

"Where is everybody?" said Marta.

"Hopefully they're still listening to Uriah's speech. It could last a long time. The windbag loves an audience."

"A break for us."

"Let's go."

They stole down the corridor, making for the front door.

They picked up on a guard stationed in front of it. Constructed of steel and thick enough to withstand a nuclear blast, the blast door closed vertically. There were about seven inches of opening beneath it. Halverson and Marta hid behind the hall corner.

Oblivious to everything else, the twentysomething Hispanic guard with a lantern jaw was keeping his B&T MP9 trained on the opening under the door to make sure ghouls didn't enter.

"They must not have fixed the door yet," whispered Halverson.

"The guy in the auditorium told Uriah it was fixed," said Marta.

"He lied to save his ass."

"It doesn't look like they're doing anything to fix it. Just that armed guard standing there watching it."

"The control panel on the wall has wires dangling from it. The electrician could be on a lunch break. We have to move fast."

"At least the guard's not looking over here."

Halverson stole toward the guard, grabbed him from behind, and applied a chokehold. Halverson couldn't help but notice the guy smelled like Irish Spring soap.

"You're good at that," said Marta.

"They train us well at the CIA," said Halverson. "In black ops they teach us how to kill people a hundred different ways."

He laid the slumping, unconscious guard down on the floor and relieved him of his MP9.

Chapter 7

"The question is, can we fit under the door?" said Marta.

"It's gonna be a tight fit," said Halverson.

"That blast door must weigh at least a ton. What if it closes on us while we're under it?"

"We won't have to worry about standing in front of a firing squad."

She gave him a look. "That's not funny."

He got down on his knees.

"Lucky we haven't eaten in a couple of days," she said, following his example. "No potbelly is gonna fit under there."

"You just ate two rolls."

"And that's gonna make me fat?"

Halverson peeked through the opening under the door, searching for ghouls. He picked up on several of them shambling aimlessly among the hundreds of ghoul corpses that had been nuked and machine-gunned and lay sprawled on the driveway leading away from the door, their brains decimated. The living ghouls were foraging for food without any luck.

Halverson craned his neck back toward Marta.

"They're not gonna stop us from getting out," he said. "They're too far away. Exhale before you slide under the door."

"You want me to go first?"

"Ladies first."

Marta eyed the heavy steel door and the narrow space below it.

"How thick is that door?" she said.

"About four feet, if I remember correctly."

"That's a long way to slide to get outside."

His face unsmiling, Halverson nodded.

"How long does it take to die when you're crushed by a steel door weighing over a ton?" she said.

"Not long. Your brain would turn to mush in seconds."

"I guess there are worse ways to go," she said, sliding her MP5 under the door ahead of her.

The MP5 didn't go very far because there was a rubber mat lying on the floor under the door. The mat also made it difficult for Marta to slide under the door.

"Uriah may be running out of hot air by now," said Halverson. "We'd better get going."

"See you on the other side."

She lay on her back and, turning her head sideways, commenced sliding under the door.

"Can you fit OK?" said Halverson, watching her.

"It's tight. I can hardly move. It's not easy to slide over rubber."

She froze in terror when she heard a creaking sound above her.

"What's that noise?" she said.

"I dunno. The door could be settling."

"I'm claustrophobic to begin with, and now you're telling me the door is gonna crush me?"

"You need to get out of there. Keep sliding."

"Maybe I should come back," she said, her face beaded with sweat, adrenaline surging through her body.

She reversed direction and slid toward him.

"No," he said. "The other way. You're almost out. Keep going out."

She halted. "I can't turn my head to look at you. I can only see the driveway. Are you sure I'm closer to the driveway than to you?"

"Yeah," he lied. "Keep sliding out."

She changed direction again. "This is taking forever."

He could see that she was nearing the driveway. He couldn't wait for her to get completely out. He had to get moving. He slid his machine pistols and the SIG under the door. They didn't go very far thanks to the rubber mat on the floor. About to slide under the door on his back, he heard the door creak again. If it settled just another inch, he wouldn't be able to fit under it.

His pulse racing, he slid under the massive steel blast door. Only four feet to go. She was right about it being a tight fit. He could barely move. He saw her slide out from under the door. Maybe his skull was wider than hers. His ears squeezed tight to his head, he could scarcely move. The best he could do was an inch at a time, if that.

He shoved the machine pistols and the SIG ahead of him again. They didn't quite reach beyond the door.

Getting down on her knees Marta peered under the door at him.

"Are you stuck?" she said with concern.

"I don't think so."

He heard the door creak above him again.

Christ. If it dropped even a quarter of an inch, he might be trapped here until the electricians fixed the door. And then it would crush him.

"That door's making too much noise," said Marta, staring at him.

"Can you reach my guns?"

Marta lay on her back so she could reach farther under the door. She pulled out his three guns.

His face oozing bulbs of sweat, Halverson kept wriggling on his back toward her.

"Is the door lowering?" she said, her voice tight.

The door creaked overhead again.

"I can't tell," said Halverson. "I'm still able to move."

Lying on her back, she reached toward him. "Grab my hand."

His head was the most difficult part of his body to move. He felt like he was going to shear his ears off if he kept moving toward the driveway. His face flushing, he reached toward her hand. He felt her grab his hand.

She fell to pulling his arm toward her.

"Am I pulling too hard?" she said. "I don't want to pull your arm out of its socket."

"No. Keep pulling. It's helping. Don't worry about my arm."

Even though he could see outside, he felt like he wasn't getting enough air. He was having difficulty breathing. He had to get out.

He used all the strength he could muster to squirm toward the driveway as he gripped her hand.

He could feel the air outside as it blew against his arm, which Marta had pulled outside.

"Hold on tight," she said.

He tightened his grip on her hand.

She changed her position on her back in order to find purchase for her feet against the door and use her legs for leverage to yank him out.

He felt himself sliding out.

He inhaled the sweet air as his head cleared the door's bottom, his ears throbbing.

She lay supine beside him.

They gazed at the cloud-mottled blue sky. A welcome sight, he decided, breathing deeply.

"We have no time," he said, and sprang to his feet.

He gathered his guns and commenced picking his way through the dead ghouls that littered the driveway. MP5 in hand, Marta ran alongside him.

He couldn't believe his eyes when he spotted a Jeep Wrangler Rubicon driving toward them on the driveway.

Chapter 8

"Who is that?" said Marta, watching the Rubicon crush ghoul bodies under its thick wheels.

"It could be a soldier returning to base," said Halverson, his MP9 at the ready, its fellow strapped over his shoulder.

Halverson noticed the Rubicon was having trouble driving in a straight line, perhaps because of all the ghoul corpses sprawled in front of it.

"Is he drunk?" said Marta.

"We need a vehicle to get out of here."

He and Marta sprinted toward the Jeep.

"Stop," said Halverson, waving his hand at the driver.

The Rubicon was barely moving now. Its left rear wheel had a ghoul stuffed between the tire and the fender, preventing the wheel from spinning.

Halverson halted in astonishment when he saw the driver.

His grey eyes glazed with a milky coating and staring forward without seeing, the suit sitting in the driver's seat was grabbing the steering wheel. He was wearing a navy blue businessman's suit and a turquoise necktie. He could have been a corporate raider driving home from his Wall Street office except for his entrails coiled in his lap like a water moccasin.

"Do you know him?" said Marta.

"Luckily no."

"He seems to know how to drive."

"He doesn't. He looks human, but he's not," said Halverson.

"A fucking ghoul," said Marta in shock. "They can't drive. They're too uncoordinated."

Halverson studied the ghoul. He noticed the driver's-side window was smashed with glass spalls sprinkling like jimmies the blood-streaked entrails piled on the ghoul's lap, and there was a hole in the creature's jacket sleeve. The jacket and the torn white shirtsleeve under it were dappled with bloodstains.

"A ghoul must have bitten the driver's arm and infected him with plague," said Halverson. "Then the driver turned while he was driving the Jeep."

The suit flailed his arms at Halverson, trying to grab and bite him.

"Why's he wearing a suit?" said Marta.

"He must be a politician on his way back to the bunker."

"You said you don't know him."

"I don't know a lot of politicians."

Halverson yanked open the Jeep door as the Rubicon engine continued to rumble while the vehicle remained stuck. He released the seat belt around the ghoul's lap. Freed, the ghoul tried to bite Halverson.

Halverson swung the butt of his MP9 against the ghoul's head. The ghoul didn't die. It looked stunned for a moment then tried to take a bite out of Halverson again. Halverson slammed his MP9 butt into the ghoul's temple, sending slivers of shattered bone into the creature's brain.

The ghoul slid out of the driver's seat and fell onto another ghoul that lay dead beneath the Rubicon door.

Halverson turned off the engine and took stock of the dead ghoul wedged between the rear tire and its fender.

"Get in the driver's seat and put the shifter into drive," he said.

"We better make this fast. A ghoul's headed this way."

Halverson picked up on a thirtysomething ghoul no taller than five six shuffling toward the Rubicon. An earbud was stuck in his left ear with the wire trailing down to his shoulder. Maybe the wire used to be connected to a cell phone. Not anymore.

Clad in a red short-sleeved sweatshirt and jeans, a pocket pen protector in his breast pocket, the scrawny creature had cropped ginger hair. At another time in another life he would have been considered a twerp. But now he was a grimacing, growling feral creature that would devour you as soon as look at you. The uncoordinated monstrosity wasn't making good time as he approached the Rubicon. He kept tripping on dead ghouls strewn on the bunker's frontage.

Halverson returned his attention to the ghoul stuck in the wheel well.

"We need to get that ghoul out of there," he said.

"I could shoot that sleazeball heading our way."

"No. You'll draw the attention of the bunker guards."

"Well, we're not going anywhere with that ghoul stuck there."

"I know. Accelerate slowly."

Halverson watched the ghoul remain stuck as the tire tried to rotate without success.

He latched onto one of the ghoul's arms.

"OK," he said. "Accelerate again while I pull on its arm."

"These Jeeps have four-wheel drive."

"Which should help me get the thing out of there. OK, now."

Marta accelerated slowly.

Halverson laid his MP9 on the Jeep rocker panel and yanked on the ghoul's arm. "The Jeep's starting to move. Give it more gas."

Marta did so.

Halverson yanked harder. He gave it all he had until the creature pulled free from the tire and fender and landed near him as he fell on his back on a dead ghoul that lay beneath him.

Marta pulled her foot off the gas as the Rubicon, now that its wheel was freed, was starting to move forward.

The trouble was the ghoul trapped in the wheel well wasn't dead. Its head hadn't been crushed by the tire. Squirming on its crushed ribs, it crawled onto Halverson's supine body in search of food. Revolted, Halverson kicked his leg out to get the creature off him. The creature tried to bite his leg. Halverson snagged his MP9 and, not wanting to make any noise and alert the inhabitants of Mount Weather that he and Marta had escaped, he did not pull the trigger. Instead, he swung the butt at the ghoul's head, connecting with it and fracturing it. The head which had been partially crushed by the Jeep tire became completely crushed. The ghoul sprawled motionless.

"Let's beat it," said Marta.

Halverson whipped around the front of the vehicle, flung open the passenger's-side door, and claimed the shotgun seat.

Marta executed a bumpy U-turn with the Rubicon and drove away from the bunker, crushing ghoul corpses under the vehicle's churning tires.

"Try not to get another ghoul stuck in the wheel well," said Halverson.

"How do I do that?"

"Drive on the tarmac as much as possible."

She gazed at the myriad ghoul corpses blanketing the driveway.

"What tarmac?" she said.

Halverson noticed the twerp ghoul in the red sweatshirt was within six feet of the Rubicon.

"Just head away from the bunker," said Halverson. "It's a wonder people haven't noticed we're gone yet."

"I'm dying to split that skeevy ghoul's head in half with a burst of rounds," said Marta, reaching for her MP5.

"We need to save ammo. Let's move."

Marta drove forward, the Rubicon's wheels jouncing over the slew of corpses strewn on the driveway. The ghoul schlepped after them, waving his arms and snapping at the air with his putrid, chipped teeth in frustration at being unable to keep up with them.

He stumbled on a ghoul carcass and, windmilling his arms, fell on his obscene face.

Chapter 9

At last Halverson and Marta drove onto a road clear of ghoul carcasses, though Marta had to drive around abandoned cars on occasion.

"Where are we going?" she said, at the wheel.

"Pennsylvania."

"Why Pennsylvania?"

"Raven Rock is there."

"And?"

"And that's where the speaker of the house should be holed up."

"And?"

"And if he's alive, he should be the current president, not Uriah, who was the secretary of state when Mims died."

"Do you mind if we stop off at my brother's house?"

Riding shotgun, Halverson faced her. "Where does he live?"

"Washington, DC."

"Does he work for the government?"

"I think he was working for Uber the last time I talked to him."

"Do you know if he's still alive?"

"I have no idea. I haven't heard from him since the plague started. I hope he is. He's all the family I got left," she said, her voice cracking.

"No problem."

"What about you?"

"What do you mean?"

"Do you have anybody left?"

Halverson began thinking about Victoria. She was the only one he had ever been close to, and she was dead. He got depressed every time he thought about her. They had been through a lot together. They had even survived a nuclear blast near Las Vegas.

They had endured unlivable conditions, but they had continued fighting the ghouls and their relentless attacks. Until they didn't. At least, she didn't. The ghouls had finally gotten her and turned her into one of them.

Marta glanced at him. "Are you getting bummed out again?"

"I was remembering Victoria. She was the only one I was ever close to. And she's gone. I never had much of a home life. My parents died when I was young. That's why I joined the CIA at an early age. Then my brother died in a car accident."

"If you don't mind my asking, what happened to Victoria?"

Halverson's visage became glum. "The ghouls got her."

"I'm sorry."

"There was no reason for it really. The same thing could happen to any of us any day."

"Will we ever defeat the ghouls?"

"I don't see how. There are too many of them, and they keep multiplying at a mind-numbing rate."

"We're all living on borrowed time."

"We can't give up. We have to keep fighting. Maybe one day we'll find a vaccine against the zombie plague that infected the world."

"We already tried that with the mad Dr. Wheelhouse and his cave's freak show of terrors."

"There could be another scientist somewhere working on the vaccine. The point is we don't know since comms are down. The nuclear EMP blast knocked out all electrical devices, including the Internet. I'm surprised this car works. It must have been out of range of the EMP."

As if on cue, the Rubicon started slowing down.

"Why did you have to say that?" said Marta.

Halverson craned to inspect the fuel tank gauge on the odometer. "We're running out of gas."

"Where are we, anyway? Where is Mount Weather?"

"It's about fifty miles west of Washington, DC."

The Rubicon continued to lose speed.

"I guess we could walk there, then," said Marta, feeling the Rubicon jerk to a halt.

"Sounds like a plan."

They piled out of the fuel-less Rubicon.

Halverson took out a compass, eyeballed it, and got his bearings.

"Looks like it might rain," said Marta, gazing up at the ominous clouds gathering in the sky.

Halverson looked up from the compass.

"It would help if we could find an abandoned car," he said.

"I'm sure we'll find another one."

"The problem is most of them don't work because the nuke EMP knocked out their electrical systems. Only the ones outside the range of the EMP at the time of the blast would work."

They set out walking down the road dotted with crushed zombie corpses.

"Could we get something to eat?" said Marta.

"We need to get as far away from the bunker as fast as we can. I'm betting Uriah will send out a patrol to hunt us down."

Halverson sped up his gait.

"We could go faster if we could get food," said Marta, catching up to him. "We need fuel just as much as cars do."

"If we see a diner, we'll check it out."

"Don't you figure any abandoned diners and restaurants have been looted by now?"

"Probably." Halverson glanced over his shoulder. "Nobody following yet. They're gonna have a car when they come for us, so we need to move."

"Then we should leave the road."

"We can make better time on the road, but we'll get off it if we hear a car coming behind us."

Halverson heard groaning up ahead.

"What's going on up there?" said Marta.

Chapter 10

A group of fifty-odd people were marching down the road, their backs to Halverson and Marta.

The men were bare chested. So were the women except for their bras. All members of the group were moaning as they practiced self-flagellation. Their backs were torn and bloody from lashes of their whips.

Halverson dashed up to one of them, a tall guy. "I'm Halverson. Who are you?"

"Dmitri."

"What happened?" he asked the fortyish guy with a peanut-shaped head and a furrowed, agonized face.

He hadn't gotten a haircut in a while. Parted in the middle, his curly, grizzled brown hair reached an inch below his shoulders.

"We're alive," Dmitri answered, and lashed his back again.

"I don't understand," said Halverson.

"It's Armageddon. The antichrist will rise from the ashes and rule. We're doomed."

"Who is the antichrist?"

"I haven't seen him, but this is end times, and he walks the earth."

The snapping sounds of scourges and cat-o'-nine-tails filled the air and mingled with the groans of misery of the self-flagellators.

"Why are you torturing yourselves?" asked Halverson as Marta walked up to him.

"We were born to suffer. We must suffer if we want to go on living. Life is suffering. The age of the antichrist is nigh."

"Are they talking about the ghouls?" said Marta.

"The zombies are the agents of the antichrist," said Dmitri. "They follow his orders."

"They're not following orders. They don't know what they're doing. All they care about is stuffing their grotesque faces with human flesh."

"They are the armies of the antichrist," said Dmitri, continuing to march with his comrades down the road and to lash himself like the others.

"What's the point of whipping yourselves?" said Halverson. "Life is bad enough as it is with the zombie plague infecting everybody."

"We were born in pain. We must live in pain."

"The ghouls will kill you if you don't fight them."

"Many of our members have been lost to the antichrist's soldiers. We have to keep moving so they don't kill all of us."

"They're everywhere. No matter where you go, they'll find and attack you."

"So be it. We were born in pain, and we will die in pain. There is no escape from pain. Pain is life. If you're not in pain, you're dead."

"You can kill them if you kill their brains."

Halverson was close enough to Dmitri now that he could see the thick red welts and bloody scratches crisscrossing Dmitri's back. Dmitri whipped his back again with a particularly savage thrust that spilled fresh blood that ran down his spine.

"Nobody has a chance against the armies of the night," he said. "Suffering is our fate."

"Who is your leader?" said Halverson, looking toward the front of the throng.

"We have no leader. We suffer equally."

A teenage woman standing near Dmitri screamed as she scourged her naked back.

"The smell of your freshly spilled blood will attract the ghouls," said Halverson.

"We must suffer," said Dmitri. "Don't you understand?"

"Why?"

"There is no why. Do you think life has a reason? It has no reason. It's endless suffering. You suffer till you die."

"All I'm saying is if you don't defend yourselves and kill the ghouls, they will kill you."

"It's the same to us. Either way we suffer."

"If they kill you, you won't suffer anymore."

"This isn't open for argument," said Dmitri, and scourged his back again.

Halverson heard a throaty rumble in the distance in front of the group. He picked up on a motorcycle chugging toward them. The driver of the hog was carrying a machete in one hand as he steered with the other. Wild-eyed, he drove straight for the group, accelerating. He whooped.

"Look out," Halverson warned Dmitri.

Chapter 11

As the motorcycle approached, Halverson could see it was a Harley. The driver was wearing a black leather vest, a motorcycle chain dangling from his neck. Two red-painted lines underscored each of his hazel eyes. The top of his head was as bald as a landing strip. The long beer-colored hair alongside his temples blew in the wind as he drove. Brandishing his machete he started weaving back and forth on the road. He steered straight as he approached the tall blonde woman at the head of the group.

Furiously slashing her back with her whip, gouts of blood popping from her back, she paid no attention to him.

Whooping, he skidded and screeched to a stop in front of her and lopped off her head with his machete. Her arterial blood jetted into the sky. Her knees buckling, she collapsed on the tarmac. Her head landed the better part of ten feet away from her body on the grassy verge that skirted the road.

The biker bayed at the sky with glee, flourishing his blood-streaked machete.

"Where'd that psycho come from?" said Marta.

"Aren't you angry?" Halverson asked Dmitri, who had witnessed the carnage with mounting fury.

"Why? It was fated to happen," answered Dmitri, but Halverson could tell the guy was seething.

"You're lambs going to slaughter."

"Life is suffering," said Dmitri, whipping his back and moaning.

Halverson stalked toward the biker, who was parked in the way of the self-flagellators. He straddled his motorcycle, guffawing at the dead blonde who lay at his feet.

"I guess she lost her head," he told Halverson. "A lot of chicks do that over me."

Halverson trained his MP9 on him.

"How come you're not whipping yourself?" said the biker.

"What's your name?"

"Bobby K. What's yours?"

"Halverson."

"How come you got a gun? Do you shoot yourself in the foot instead of whipping yourself?"

Bobby K. laughed at his own joke.

"I'm not one of them," said Halverson. "This gun is not window dressing."

"What's that supposed to mean?" said Bobby K., confused.

"Aren't you afraid?"

"Why should I be? These guys are dodos, and my gang's less than five miles from here."

"Do you think you'll be alive when they get here?"

Bobby K. scowled at Halverson. "Is that a threat?"

"I'm asking you a question."

"Don't you see this bloody machete in my hand? You think I won't hesitate to use it again?"

"I'm the one asking the questions."

"If you lay a hand on me, Michael K. and the High Rolerz are gonna wipe the floor with you."

"You murdered that defenseless woman. Don't you believe you deserve to die?"

"Not at all. You talk like there's some kind of law and order in this fucked-up world. I got news for you. There ain't. What you see is what you get. Chaos. The law is dead."

"Then I guess you won't be tried for murder."

Bobby K. grinned.

"I guess not," he said, licking blood off his machete blade, smiling.

Halverson shot him in the head with a single burst from his MP9. Ordinarily he would have double-tapped his foe in the head, but he needed to save ammo.

"I guess I won't either," he said, watching Bobby K. crumple to the ground dead with a puzzled expression on his warpainted face, his chopper falling on him and crushing his leg on the tarmac.

Crushed or not, Bobby K. wasn't going anywhere.

"The rest of his gang is gonna come after us," said Marta, gazing in the direction where Bobby K. had come from.

"We'll take a detour into the woods," said Halverson. He turned to Dmitri. "I suggest you and your group come with us. They're not gonna be happy when they see one of their biker buddies with a bullet hole in his head."

"We were put on earth to suffer, and that is what we'll do," said Dmitri, flogging his back and grimacing.

"Do I have to spell it out for you? They're gonna waste you."

"Why? We're not the ones who shot their pal."

"Do you think they even care? Look what Bobby K. did to your blonde member for no reason at all. They're bloodthirsty thugs. They don't need a reason to kill. They get a kick out of it. They could be on speed or crack. The point is they're killers."

"I can hear motorcycles in the distance," said Marta. "It sounds like a lot of them."

"Tell them you didn't kill their buddy," said Halverson, making a beeline for the woods with Marta. "Tell them it was someone else. Not that it's gonna matter, but who knows? Maybe you'll get lucky and they'll leave you alone."

"We were born to suffer," said Dmitri, lashing his back and screwing up his face in pain.

Chapter 12

Halverson and Marta bolted into the forest of red maples and black oaks.

"They don't understand this world," said Marta, pelting through the woods with Halverson. "It's kill or be killed with these ghouls on the loose."

"The humans still alive are even more dangerous than the infected ghouls as long as the government is in shambles. There's nothing to stop anybody from doing anything, including committing murder, torture, and mayhem."

With a sinking heart Halverson heard gunfire erupt behind him.

"I liked Dmitri," he said. "He went through a lot. He suffered and never complained."

"I'm sure Bobby K.'s friends could care less," said Marta.

"If his buddies have a single functioning brain between them, they're gonna know Dmitri didn't shoot Bobby K., because the self-flagellators don't have a gun."

Halverson heard more gunfire popping behind them. Hundreds of bullets fired. The bloodshed lasted several minutes.

"I hope they don't kill all of them," said Marta under her breath. "Maybe we should have stayed and helped Dmitri."

"I asked him to come with us, but he said no."

"I feel guilty for leaving him to be slaughtered."

"It was his choice, and he made it."

Nevertheless, Halverson felt bad for Dmitri and his group.

"Do you think he'll tell the biker gang about us?" said Marta.

"They can't follow us here. There are too many trees and underbrush for motorcycles."

"They could follow us on foot."

"Not unless they know how to track people in the woods."

"Then what?"

"Then we keep going." Halverson picked up on a ghoul shambling through the woods. "Ghoul at seven o'clock."

"Where there's one there are many."

Halverson picked his way through some underbrush, Marta in tow.

"Aren't we gonna shoot it?" she said.

"Bobby K.'s gang will hear us if we fire our pieces. If it gets too close, we'll bash its brains in. Don't worry. We're already putting distance between us and it."

"I bet there are more around here," said Marta, surveying the forest.

"One or two we can handle. It's the hordes we have to watch out for."

Halverson heard rain impinging like BBs dropping from the sky on the leaves overhead. Pitter-patter. Background music to flee by.

"Do you think the biker gang will come after us?" said Marta.

"Good question. They have no idea where we went unless one of the self-flagellators told them."

"If they get tortured, they might tell the gang."

"I wouldn't blame them. After all, I *am* the one that whacked out Bobby K."

"It's not like he didn't deserve it."

"Eventually we're gonna have to return to the road. We're not gonna make it to DC stuck in these woods."

"When will it be safe to return?" said Marta, eyeballing another ghoul wending his way through the woods with slogging steps, puking worms on his chest.

"I don't see any reason for the bikers to hang around here. After they finish with the self-flagellators, they'll move on."

"What if they send a patrol to track us?"

Halverson thought about it, rain trickling down his face as he trampled bracken.

"We'll exit the forest in a different area than where we entered," he said.

"I'm getting hungrier and thirstier by the minute. We're not gonna find any diners in the middle of the woods."

Halverson scanned the surroundings. "If we had a cup or some kind of container, we could catch the raindrops and drink them. Except . . ."

"Except what?"

"The rain might be contaminated with radiation because of the recent nuclear explosions in this area."

"Ugh."

"We'll just have to take our chances. Or we can go without water."

"For how long?"

"Three days without water will kill most people."

"Let's return to the road."

Halverson halted in the bracken and consulted his compass. "We'll head north then west back to the road. That should put us about a mile away from the site of the massacre."

"You think they're all dead?" Marta said with concern.

"Probably," said Halverson, his voice low, his face grim. "You heard all the gunshots. More than enough to wipe out fifty people."

Despondent, Marta shook her head. "Shouldn't we go back?"

"There could be hundreds of bikers. We wouldn't stand a chance."

"Such a shame."

"I thought you wanted to meet your brother in DC."

"I do. Let's get moving." Marta noticed Halverson pulling a face. "What's wrong?"

"My leg."

Chapter 13

Halverson's leg got stuck in the bracken. He struggled to free himself. He couldn't see what his leg was caught on because of the fern covering it. He pushed the large fern leaf aside with the muzzle of his MP9 in order to see his leg.

He started.

A male ghoul sprawled on his back on the ground was scowling up at him and snagging Halverson's calf with his decrepit hand, which despite its advanced stage of putrescence, exerted enough strength that Halverson couldn't break free.

Dressed in rags that had been shredded no doubt by thorns on shrubs in the undergrowth, the rawboned thirtysomething ghoul growled and, slobbering, opened his mouth, as he tried to pull his face toward Halverson's calf. Appalled, Halverson slammed the butt of his MP9 into the ghoul's forehead, attempting to smash through the skull and pulverize the brain. The ghoul jerked his head back when he saw the MP9 butt thrusting down at him.

The ghoul's sudden movement lessened the impact of the MP9's blow to his head. In short, the creature survived the blow with only a hairline fracture in his forehead.

Halverson could tell his blow hadn't wasted the ghoul, because he felt the MP9 glance off the creature's skull. Halverson lifted the MP9 and thrust it into the ghoul's open mouth, knocking out all of his rotting, jagged teeth. The ghoul growled, still alive and able to maintain his grip on Halverson's calf. But he was going to have a hard time chewing human flesh without any teeth.

"Shoot it," said Marta.

"No," said Halverson. "More ghouls will come, and Bobby K.'s gang might hear the gunfire."

The stench emanating from the creature was overpowering. Halverson felt nauseous as he inhaled the fetid odor. Grimacing with disgust, gritting his teeth, he raised his MP9 above his head and crashed its butt into the ghoul's forehead. He felt the butt crack open the creature's skull and penetrate into the brain to render it into mush. He also felt the ghoul's hand release his calf.

Halverson stamped on the ghoul's revolting worm-eaten face for good measure, making sure the brain was destroyed. It wasn't necessary. The creature was dead, never to rise again.

"We need to get out of the bracken," said Halverson. "There could be hundreds of those things concealed under the dense leaves. It's like walking into a minefield."

Halverson trampled his way out of the bracken. Marta followed his example.

"What now?" she said.

"We need to go around the ferns."

"They're all over the place."

"Maybe radiation from the nuclear fallout stimulated their growth."

Marta hiked her eyebrows. "There's still radiation in the air?"

"It's not as bad as it was. Doctor Morrow said we would live even though we had been exposed to it when we returned from Wheelhouse's cave of monstrosities."

"The rain should be helping clear the air," said Marta, gazing up at the tree branches and the clicking leaves overhead and trying to drink the raindrops that struck her face.

"Like I said before, the rain could be contaminated with radiation too."

Her face turning ashen, Marta gave Halverson a look.

"Not enough to harm us at this point," he said.

He tilted his face upward and drank scattered raindrops.

"You spoiled my appetite," she said.

Halverson consulted his compass. Raindrops blurred its plastic face. He wiped them off on his jeans and held the compass out of the rain.

"We'll walk parallel to VA 7," he said. "We should be several miles away from it. When we've gone far enough, we'll head back to it."

"What about Bobby K.'s gang?"

"They should be gone by the time we return to the road, and they were heading in the opposite direction."

"Are we gonna check if there are any survivors in Dmitri's cult?"

"We don't have time. Uriah's forces will be hunting us as soon as he finds out we escaped. We have to keep heading away from Mount Weather."

"Some of Dmitri's cult might have survived the massacre."

"They can take care of themselves."

"How? They're like children. All they do is go around whipping themselves and moaning in pain."

"They believe they were born to suffer. Who are we to tell them to change their beliefs?"

"It's just that I feel sorry for them. They live in so much pain. They're not hurting anybody. Why can't people leave them alone?"

Halverson felt responsible for their massacre at the hands of Bobby K.'s gang because he had whacked out Bobby K. But Halverson wasn't going to dwell on it. He had invited the self-flagellators to accompany him and Marta into the woods. Dmitri had refused. End of story. Halverson refused to continue his journey moping with pity and self-hatred for shooting the murdering psychopath Bobby K.

"Why did you have to *kill* him?" said Marta.

"You saw what he did. He beheaded that woman in cold blood, and nobody stopped him. He would've killed more of them and us if I hadn't stopped him. There's no telling how many people he had killed before. The man was a homicidal maniac."

"Maybe he was the gang leader."

"I doubt it. He was riding point."

"You could have arrested him."

"What good would that do? There's no law and order anymore. We're on our own."

"You could have knocked him out. You're good at doing that."

"Then he would've killed Dmitri and the others when he came to. He killed people because he liked it. I don't want to talk about it anymore."

Skirting the bracken he stalked away from her.

He didn't feel like he had won the argument, but he saw no reason to continue the discussion. They had to keep moving.

"I'm not criticizing you," said Marta, following him. "I just feel so sorry for them."

Chapter 14

When the self-proclaimed president Dean Uriah heard the news that Halverson and Marta had escaped, he blew his stack.

Joe Purdy stood in front of him in the corridor outside the brig, looking cowed. After all, the two coconspirators had escaped on his watch.

"How could you let this happen?" demanded Uriah.

"That horrible woman kicked me from behind. I had no idea she—"

"You need to find and capture them. If they offer any resistance, terminate them with extreme prejudice. They assassinated a president. Nobody can get away with committing such an egregious crime."

"Yes, sir," said Purdy, standing bolt upright, knowing he was speaking to the commander in chief.

"Shoot to kill."

"Yes, sir."

"If you bring them back here, they will be found guilty and executed. Either way they will die for committing treason."

"They will be dealt with, sir."

Uriah stepped closer to Purdy. "This is your last chance to make up for your blunder. If you fail . . ."

"I won't fail, sir."

"How many men do you need?"

"Uh—twenty."

"I'll give you ten. Why do you need twenty men to kill just two conspirators?"

"One of them is Halverson. The guy's a legend. He has a reputation as a stone killer."

"If you can't terminate two people with ten heavily armed combat-trained Special Forces soldiers, something's wrong with you."

Purdy said nothing.

"Besides, the conspirators might circle back and attempt to assassinate me while you're gone," said Uriah. "I need as much protection as I can get from these conspirators. They already killed one president. What's to stop them from killing another? They must be eliminated ASAP."

"No problem, sir. I'll take ten men in three armored Chevy Suburbans."

"They're on foot. I don't see how you can fail to catch them quickly in your Suburbans. How long ago did they escape?"

"Uh—I'm not sure, sir. They put me in a chokehold and tried to kill me. I blacked out. I don't know for exactly how long I was unconscious. I still have a headache," said Purdy, rubbing his head.

"If you want pity, you came to the wrong place."

"I don't want—"

Uriah held up his hand, signaling Purdy to stop talking.

"Did they take a vehicle?"

"No, sir. They rolled under the broken front door. They're on foot."

"The broken front door, did you say?"

"I did, sir."

"Haven't they fixed it yet?" said Uriah, apoplectic with rage. "More ghouls are gonna invade the bunker."

"Yes, sir. I mean, no, sir, they aren't. The door has been repaired."

Uriah coughed on the stale air. "We need more oxygen in the bunker."

"The ghouls continue to jam the air ducts with their stinking bodies."

"Their stench is almost as deadly as their teeth."

"Yes, it is, sir."

"Well, . . . *clear them out of the ducts*. Or do you want all of us to suffocate?"

"I'll get on it—"

"Not you. You catch and terminate Halverson and his cohort. They are the biggest threat to democracy we have ever faced."

"Yes, sir."

"They got away with one assassination. They could be plotting to kill me even as we speak."

"They're as good as dead, sir," said Purdy, his face stern.

"Bring me back their heads, and I'll believe you. I want their heads on my desk by suppertime."

"I don't think I can—"

"I'm not paying you to think. Follow orders, man. If their heads aren't on my desk tonight, you're out of a job and out of this bunker. Do you want to end up food on a ghoul's plate?"

"I will do it, sir."

Purdy hated Halverson for making him look like a fool in front of the president by escaping. Purdy would have no trouble blowing Halverson's face off with an MP9 as soon as he spotted the sonofabitch. That went double for his cohort. He might even take his time killing the two traitors just to enjoy the moment. Maybe shoot them in the stomach and let them take hours to die in agony. But then he wouldn't get back to the bunker by dinner. *Rats.*

Uriah screwed up his face and studied Purdy.

"There's one thing I need to know before you go," said Uriah. "Were you in on the assassination?"

"Sir?" said Purdy, dumbfounded.

"I'm asking you point-blank. Are you one of the conspirators?"

"Of course not. I am loyal to you, Mr. President."

"There's something I don't understand. How did Halverson and Costello get away so easily? They were locked in cells in the brig."

"I told you, they overpowered me. Halverson almost killed me. I believe he thought he *had* killed me."

"Still, you're a trained soldier in Special Forces."

"SEAL Team Six Red Squadron."

"Exactly. How could he overpower you with your special training?"

"Costello helped him."

"It sounds too easy."

"He's a CIA black ops killer, Mr. President. Those guys are killing machines. It's only by a miracle that I'm still alive."

Uriah searched Purdy's face, looking for a tell to indicate he was lying.

At last Uriah said, "If you really are one of the conspirators, I will line up your entire family in front of a firing squad."

The blood drained from Purdy's face. He fumbled for words but found none.

"Well?" said Uriah.

"I swear to you on a stack of bibles—"

"What are you waiting for?" said Uriah.

"It's—it's almost dark."

"So?"

"He's gonna be harder to find in the dark."

"Turn on your headlights."

"Yes, sir."

Purdy spun on his heel and left, visibly shaken by the threat made against his family.

He didn't see Uriah shaking his head at him.

Chapter 15

After traipsing through the dark woods for five miles, Halverson and Marta returned to VA 7 which headed toward DC.

"My arms got scratched by those bushes in there," said Marta, glancing back at the forest.

Halverson knew his arms were bleeding from contact with thorns as well. He was also shivering from the cold.

"I hope we came far enough so we don't meet up with Bobby K.'s gang," he said.

"They were going in the other direction."

"I know," said Halverson, unconvinced they would continue in that direction. He froze. "Who are those people up ahead?"

"I can hardly see in the night."

"There's a group of people up there. They're on foot."

"I thought I heard groaning and a snapping sound."

Halverson heard the snapping too.

"Let's see what they're up to," he said. "Don't make any noise. I don't want them to know we're coming until we can see who they are."

He and Marta skulked along the road, keeping to the darkest parts.

When he was near enough to them, Halverson could see it was a group of bare-chested self-flagellators who were flogging their backs and moaning in pain.

"Did Dmitri escape?" said Marta hopefully.

"I don't see him," said Halverson. "Come on."

He and Marta approached the group and greeted them. Halverson didn't recognize any of them. Granted it was dark, but none of the faces looked in the least familiar. Certainly Dmitri was not among them.

"Hello," said Halverson.

"You're very quiet," said a brunette, bare-chested save for her bra, surprised to see him appear out of the shadows.

In her late thirties she was wearing bloodstained jeans. She winced with pain as she flogged herself again. She had hollow brown eyes and high cheekbones, giving her visage the dark brooding aspect of a self-denying monk. Her back was dripping with fresh blood as she continued to flog herself.

"Aren't you cold?" said Halverson.

"Pain keeps us warm. Suffering is life."

The other members of the group continued flogging themselves.

"We weren't sure who you were. Where's Dmitri?" he said, inspecting the coterie.

There couldn't have been more than twenty of them.

"Dmitri's not with our group," she said. "I'm Vivian."

"I'm Halverson. Where did Dmitri go?"

"He's not with us. We're heading to meet him. He shouldn't be too far away," said Vivian, gazing down the dark road. "We needed to rest in the woods, because one of our members is having a baby and she got tired. Now we can catch up to him."

"I'm sorry to hear that," said Halverson, his face glum.

"What do you mean?"

Halverson didn't want to be the one to break the news to her, but he didn't see how he could avoid it. She was going to find out soon anyway.

"Dmitri was murdered," he said sotto voce.

"What?" said Vivian, taken aback. "Why would anyone want to hurt him? We mind our own business. We're not a threat to anyone."

"A bloodthirsty gang of biker thugs killed him."

"No," said Vivian, her voice faltering.

"It's true, I'm afraid," said Marta, alarmed by the thick bloody welts on Vivian's back. "You're gonna kill yourself if you keep doing that. Your wounds will get infected."

"We were born to suffer. This is our life. Suffering and pain are our fate. The antichrist has risen, and everyone must live in pain."

"What antichrist?"

"He will make his appearance. It's only a matter of time."

"There is no antichrist. There are just ghouls everywhere."

Vivian and her group kept walking. "We must meet Dmitri's group, even if he's not with them."

"The biker thugs massacred every single one of his group," said Halverson, even though he couldn't be sure of it since he hadn't seen it.

He had only heard the hundreds of gunshots coming from Dmitri's direction. Halverson doubted the bikers had left any of Dmitri's group alive. It didn't take hundreds of rounds to kill one guy. After all, the bikers thought Dmitri and his group had killed their member Bobby K.

"I refuse to believe it," said Vivian, continuing to flog her back. "None of Dmitri's group would hurt a fly."

"The gang of cutthroats was avenging the death of their member Bobby K."

"None of this makes sense."

"And they dig killing like Bobby K. did. He decapitated one of your members with a machete."

Vivian gasped. "Why, for heaven's sake?"

"Because he wanted to. You can't reason with these thugs. The law doesn't exist anymore so they do whatever they want."

Vivian fetched a sigh. "More proof the antichrist reigns on earth. The hairs on our heads are numbered."

She flogged herself with a particularly vicious snap of her wrist.

"At least the rain is letting up," said Marta, remarking a break in the thunderclouds overhead that revealed a paring of brilliant white moon.

"Are you sure you want to continue in this direction and risk meeting up with the cutthroat gang, Vivian?" asked Halverson.

"I want to see what happened with my own eyes," she answered. "What you're describing to me is hard for me to believe."

"I hope I'm wrong, but the bikers could be lying in wait to ambush you and your gang."

"Why?"

"In revenge for the murder of Bobby K. He was killed with a gun, and Dmitri's group didn't have any guns."

"Neither do we."

"Do you understand what I'm saying? Even though the gang knew Dmitri didn't kill Bobby K., they still massacred him and his group because they were near Bobby K.'s corpse. The bikers might expect additional group members, ones with guns, to hook up with Dmitri."

"Some of Dmitri's group might still be alive. Did you check to make sure they were dead?"

"No."

"Then we need to help them. If we can save one life, it will be worth the trip."

"Even if the bikers slaughter you and your group?"

Vivian whipped her spine and winced in pain. "We must help Dmitri."

"Could we bother you for some water?" said Marta.

"Herbert, help them."

A big barrel-chested bearded man with red hair in his fifties opened a leather knapsack with Velcro flaps he was carrying and withdrew a transparent plastic liter bottle full of water. He handed it to Vivian.

"Thanks," she said, accepting it.

She unscrewed the plastic cap, hoisted the bottle to her lips, and took a long pull.

"Now we must find Dmitri," said Vivian, fixing to march down the road.

"I'm the one who killed Bobby K.," said Halverson. "The bikers wants my blood."

Chapter 16

Vivian stopped and stared at him. "Why did you kill him?"

"Because he beheaded one of your people and laughed about it. I had to stop him from murdering more of your people and me and Marta."

"I don't understand you. We were born to suffer. Why kill someone?"

"Because he would have kept on killing unless somebody stopped him."

"They have nothing to fear from us. We don't kill anyone."

"Bobby K.'s gang doesn't know that. They believe one of you killed him. His death must be avenged."

"We were born to suffer, not to harm others. This gang you're talking about has nothing to fear from us."

"They believe otherwise."

"Then we will disabuse them," said Vivian, and marched with her group down the road in the direction of the massacre.

"If you see them, I urge you to avoid them and save your lives."

Marta gave the bottle of water to Halverson to drink.

None of the group paid attention to his words. They were too intent on flogging themselves and wailing in pain.

Halverson swigged water.

"Maybe we could have avoided all this bloodshed if you hadn't been so quick on the trigger," said Marta.

Halverson stopped drinking. "What do you want me to do? Apologize to the bikers?"

"Maybe you could have punched him instead of shooting him."

Halverson felt himself becoming angry. He was getting tired of explaining himself.

"He was getting ready to behead someone else, because he figured Dmitri and his group weren't going to retaliate against him so he could do whatever he wanted. And he wanted to kill."

"Why didn't you knock him out with your fist?"

"He was holding a machete. He would've cut my head off before I reached him."

Marta shrugged. "It seems like you could have waited a bit longer before pulling the trigger."

"Waited until he beheaded somebody else? He deserved to die, Marta."

"I'm not denying it. But look at all the murders that resulted from your killing him."

"We might not be here discussing this if I hadn't taken him out. Our heads could be lying on the road separated from our bodies."

"There are gonna be more murders if Vivian meets up with the bikers."

"I did all I could do to warn her to stay away from him. I also told Dmitri to come with us or have you forgotten?"

"I haven't forgotten." Marta fell to pacing around. "It's just that this is turning into a bloodbath."

Halverson watched Vivian and her group fade into the distance.

"Are you suggesting we go back with Vivian to protect her from the murderous thugs?" he said. "It sounded like there were scores of them from all the gunfire we heard. Maybe even a hundred. We have three guns between us," he said, holding up his B&T MP9, the other strapped to his back. "And we don't have any spare mags. Do the math."

Marta stopped pacing. "They can think for themselves. They made their decision." She paused two beats. "I can't help feeling sorry for them, though. This is none of their fault."

"I know. I don't like it either. If I had a squad, I'd go back and wipe those mass murderers off the face of the earth." He polished off the bottle of water and tossed the empty container on the roadside.

"You don't believe in recycling?"

"Do you really think any recycling centers are operating with the world in its death throes?"

"You don't have to bite my head off about it. I didn't make the world like this."

"We have to keep moving. Uriah's troops could catch up with us any minute."

Marta yawned. "When are we gonna rest?"

Halverson strode down the road to DC.

"I know, I'm tired too. But we don't have time. We really need to find a car," he said, picking up on an abandoned SUV in the road.

He pelted up to it and flung open the driver's-side door.

A ghoul with a disheveled blonde ponytail was sitting in the shotgun seat, blood smeared on her chin. She didn't look more than twenty. Her peaches-and-cream complexion had turned into withered parchment fit for a corpse. Wearing grime-streaked jeans she stared at him with milky eyes, which looked like they might have been blue at one time. She growled and drooled at him. She was holding a woman's bloody amputated naked forearm in her clawlike shriveled fingers. The arm had at least a dozen bites in it.

His MP9 had twenty-nine 9mm Parabellum rounds left in its magazine. He couldn't afford to waste a bullet on the revolting creature. The stock of the MP9 didn't make for a good club thanks to its thinness.

He cast around the SUV for something he could use as a weapon. Inspecting the backseat, he spotted a crowbar in the rear footwell.

Reaching over the front seat back, he scoffed up the crowbar. He clambered into the driver's seat and set to clubbing the ghoul. The ghoul put her hands up to thwart his blows. He had trouble landing a powerful blow to the creature's head because the headliner shortened his stroke and her hands kept getting in his way. None of his blows had enough force to fracture her skull.

Frustrated, Halverson changed tactics. Instead of trying to club the creature on the top of the head, he trained the chiseled end of the crowbar on her forehead and drove the tip like a spear into it. The forehead cleaved. Halverson felt the tip of the crowbar impale the pulpy brain matter. He thrust the steel tip in and out several times until she went limp.

Halverson yanked the brain-smeared crowbar out of her head. She slumped in her seat in a motionless heap of putrid, malodorous dead meat.

Halverson's eyes lit up when he spotted the key in the SUV ignition. He signaled to Marta to come over.

She flung open the passenger's-side door and recoiled in disgust as she took in the dead ghoul hunched there. She overcame her disgust, yanked the ghoul out of the car by its arm, and flung the carcass on the roadside. Wiping off her hands on her clothes, she clambered into the shotgun seat.

Halverson twisted the key in the ignition.

Nothing happened.

"Try it again," said Marta.

Same result.

He tried three more times. The car wouldn't start.

"No wonder the owner abandoned the car," he said. "The EMP from President Cole's nuke strike on Mount Weather must have knocked out the ignition."

"What kind of a world are we living in where a president goes nuts and nukes himself?"

Halverson had no answer.

He and Marta piled out of the SUV. He backed away from the vehicle and noted two bicycles mounted on the tailgate rack.

"Do you know how to ride a bike?" he said.

"I haven't been on one in years, but it's supposed to be one of the things you never forget."

One of the bikes was for a male, the other for a female.

"They must have seen us coming," said Marta.

Halverson proceeded to remove the bikes from their mounts.

"These are a lot faster than walking, and we can easily avoid abandoned cars in the middle of the road, giving us an advantage over drivers of cars."

"But cars can go a lot faster than us."

"There's that."

Marta gazed behind them. "I don't see anyone following us."

"All those massacred members of Dmitri's group should slow down anybody who's following us. The dead bodies blocking the road, you know."

"Unless the bikers threw the corpses into a ditch so they could drive their motorcycles away."

"Vivian's group is also crowding the road."

Halverson pedaled his bike around in a circle, getting the hang of it.

Marta pedaled her bike like it was second nature. She didn't bother riding in a circle. She just kept going straight.

Halverson took off after her, pumping his legs for all they were worth.

Chapter 17

Vivian was marching down the road, lashing her back, when she could hear ahead of her a faint rumbling in the distance similar to thunder. She strode around an abandoned pickup and kept heading forward, though she felt misgivings on account of the rumble. The racket was increasing, indicating it was making its way toward her.

It might be that sadistic biker gang Halverson had told her about. But then again, it could be someone else, since the noise was headed this way and Halverson had said the killer bikers were driving in the opposite direction.

She snapped the whip above her back and felt searing pain as the lash broke her skin.

"We must suffer," she told the others. "We do not run away in fear of anything. If we want to go on living, we must suffer. We must not fear pain. Pain and suffering are life."

They whipped themselves and moaned in pain as they continued their march down the road.

"We must find Dmitri," she said. "We will never abandon one of our own no matter how much trouble they are in. No matter what we do, we must suffer. Suffering gives us meaning in a world that has none."

Dressed in a skirt that covered her bulging belly, a pregnant woman flogged her naked back and grimaced in pain.

"I think I might have my baby soon," she said.

"Don't worry, Mary," said Vivian. "We will whip her when she enters this world of pain. That way she will understand like the rest of us that life is suffering."

"She's just a baby."

"We must teach them the meaning of life when they are young. She can never escape suffering if she wants to go on living."

Mary looked miserable. "Do we have to whip her right after she's born? It's cruel to whip a baby. Can't we let her whip herself when she grows older?"

Vivian stopped in her tracks. "No, Mary. Babies must be taught while they are young what it is to be alive in this world of pain. They can't avoid suffering. She must learn early the facts of life."

Vivian flogged her back, drawing blood that trickled down her spine.

"It's not fair to whip a baby," said Mary.

"When the tiger tears the jugular vein out of a zebra's throat and eats him for lunch, is that fair?"

"You're talking about animals. We're human."

"Every living creature must suffer, including humans."

"But not babies. They should be protected from suffering as long as possible."

"Spare the rod and spoil the child. I'm sure you've heard that expression many times."

"A defenseless baby shouldn't have to suffer as much as adults."

"The law of life is suffering. Nobody has the right to fight the law of life. Your baby must be broken in like the rest of us were."

"Why is life so hard to understand?"

"What makes you think you're supposed to understand it? We must suffer. That is all you need to know."

Vivian picked up on a ghoul shambling toward them from the forest. Its ripped white button-down shirt was hanging down from its waist in tatters, its naked chest rotten and infested with maggots. The creature's face was striated with scratches. Growling, the ghoul made a beeline for them. Flies swarmed around its putrescent head.

"We must keep walking," said Vivian, striding down the road away from the ghoul. "The ghoul will infect us."

"My baby is hurting me," said Mary, holding her stomach. "I don't know how much longer it will be."

"You will endure the pain. That is what we humans do."

"She might come out soon," said Mary, pulling a face.

"Not here. The ghoul is here. We must keep marching before you give birth."

"Tell somebody to kill the ghoul."

Vivian gave her a look. "You know we don't condone killing."

"But it's already dead. Look at it. It can hardly walk."

"We were meant to suffer, not to commit murder."

"Then let it kill us," said Mary in exasperation.

"No. We must save your baby. She will teach suffering to the generation that is born after us and generations to come."

Mary started waddling toward the ghoul.

"What are you doing?" said Vivian, aghast.

"I don't want my baby to grow up in a world of suffering."

Vivian grabbed Mary's arm and brought her back to the group, who continued their march down the road as they flogged themselves.

"We do not believe in suicide," said Vivian. "No matter how difficult our lives are we must continue the struggle to go on living."

"Being alive is like being cursed," said Mary, wincing in pain from stomach cramps.

"We can't choose which age we live in. We happen to live during end times. We must accept our fate of suffering and carry on."

"My baby will not thank me for being born if this is what she has in store for her."

"Don't worry, Mary. We'll teach her how to whip herself. Out of the womb and under the cat-o'-nine-tails. Flogging herself will become second nature to her."

Vivian scourged her back and ground her teeth in pain. She glanced at the ghoul making its way toward them.

"We must go faster," said Vivian. "Come on, Mary. You can do it."

Breaking a sweat Mary walked as fast as she could, given her child-bearing condition.

"You don't want that ugly ghoul to bite you and infect your baby," said Vivian.

"No," cried Mary. "No, no."

"Flog yourself so you'll walk faster."

Gasping for breath, her face sweaty, Mary lashed her back as she picked up her pace, terrified at the thought of her baby turning into a ghoul.

The self-flagellators groaned and cried out as they flogged their backs and strode away from the plodding ghoul that was flailing its arms at them and hissing.

"Mary, I promise you I'll whittle a tiny whip for your baby to use on herself when she gets older," said Vivian with a smile.

"Her flesh will be so tender. It doesn't seem right."

"It is right, because suffering is life. If she wants to live, she must learn to suffer. Whipping herself will teach her how to suffer and keep living."

"A baby whipping herself. It's dreadful to think about," said Mary, weeping.

"These are end times. Our survival depends on our willingness to suffer."

Wearing a Yankees baseball cap, a big man in his early forties bolted toward Vivian.

"Are you harassing my wife?" he said, his craggy face scowling.

His long black hair curled over his small ears. Though his ears were small, his head was big and shaped like Frankenstein's, which combined with his six-three frame, gave him an unsettling aspect. His dark beady blue eyes stared at Vivian.

Chapter 18

"Of course not, Bud," said Vivian. "I'm trying to help her."

"It looks like you're upsetting her," said Bud. "Why is she crying?"

"I'm cold," said Mary, shivering. "Can't we put jackets on?"

"We can't whip ourselves if we're wearing jackets," said Vivian. "We must continue to suffer no matter what the weather is."

"What made her cry?" said Bud.

Vivian cast a glance at the ghoul receding in the distance. "She was trying to commit suicide by ghoul."

"What? Why would she do that?"

"She didn't want her baby to be born in such an awful world."

Bud faced Mary. "Is this true?"

"We are in end times," answered Mary. "Maybe we shouldn't bear children during these dreadful days. What kind of dark future awaits our child?"

"We must remain strong. Suicide is against our beliefs, especially if you take an unborn child with you."

"We can't slow down," said Vivian. "We don't want the ghoul to catch up with us."

The group marched faster and whipped their backs with fury, whimpering and screaming.

"I don't want our child to die, Mary," said Bud.

"I don't either, but the world . . . is so dreadful and there is so much suffering. Vivian wants our baby to whip herself after she is born." Mary heaved a sigh. "Her baby flesh is so tender."

"She has to learn when she is young. It is the way. We must suffer if we want to go on living."

"Motorcycles approaching," said Vivian, gazing up ahead.

"Maybe they have seen Dmitri and his group," said Bud.

"This might be the group Halverson was talking about. The ones he said killed Dmitri."

"Why should we believe Halverson, a total stranger?"

"Or these bikers could be a different group. We don't know for sure."

"And, like I said, why should we believe anything Halverson says?"

"I don't know why he would lie."

"We're gonna find out soon enough."

Over fifty motorcycles roared down the road toward Vivian and her group. The riders were all armed. Some carried scabbards with machetes on their motorcycles. Other riders carried guns of all shapes and sizes, including handguns, shotguns, rifles, and machine pistols.

Clad in a black leather blazer with a black necktie, the leader of the pack was six feet tall with a shaved head. He was forty-three years old. He wore blue jeans and suede sepia cowboy boots. Horizontal streaks of red paint underlined his black eyes. As he steered his Harley with one hand, he gripped a Heckler & Koch MP5 in the other.

At the command of their leader the bikers came to a halt, blocking the way of Vivian and her group.

Chapter 19

"Are you planning to meet Dmitri?" said the guy with the shaved head.

"You're blocking our way, friend," said Bud, and flogged his back.

"You're gonna go blind doing that. And you're not my friend."

"We need to keep going," said Vivian. "There are ghouls following us."

"Don't worry about them. My name is Michael K. I need to ask you a few questions."

"My name is Vivian. Why?"

"Because I'm the leader of the High Rolerz USA, and when I speak, you listen."

"We need to keep going. You are in our way."

"Why do you keep whipping yourselves?" asked Michael K., bemused.

"We must suffer. We were born to suffer. Our willingness to endure pain makes us human."

"It makes you idiots if you ask me."

"What do *you* believe in?"

"We believe in doing whatever we want, whatever we can get away with. We have enough firepower that we can get away with anything. If anyone gets in our way, we whack them."

"You sound like animals, not humans."

"We're better than animals. We have weapons," said Michael K., brandishing his MP5.

"What do you do when the police bust you?"

Michael K. guffawed. "Police? There's no police. There's no law. We make our own laws. The broken-down government can't enforce any of their laws. Anarchy rules."

"Let us be on our way. We just want to be free to practice our religion."

"Your religion is for suckers. You hate yourselves so much that you keep punishing yourselves with whips."

"This is America. We're free to believe in whatever religion we want. We believe in self-flagellation."

"Self-flajuh-what?" said Michael K., amused.

"You heard me," said Vivian, dead serious.

"America is a wasteland overrun by flesh-eating ghouls. That's all America is now."

"We need to be on our way," said Vivian, lashing her back and grimacing.

Michael K. shook his head incomprehensibly. "You're gonna kill yourselves doing that."

"We don't believe in suicide."

Michael K. snickered. "Then maybe you should start running."

"I don't understand. Please get out of the road so we can be on our way to meet Dmitri."

"You're not gonna want to meet him."

"That's our decision to make. We need to get going."

"I haven't finished asking you questions. You know, you people here remind me of another group of people I met earlier. They dressed like you without any shirts, and their backs had welts and blood on them from the whips they were beating themselves with."

"Did you meet Dmitri?"

"I'm still the one asking the questions," said Michael K. He spat on the road. "Are you a friend of Dmitri's?"

"We're going to meet him and his group."

Michael K. grinned. "That's interesting that you and Dmitri are in the same group." His face clouded over. "Do you know my brother Bobby K.?"

"No. I never met him."

"And you never will."

"I don't like to say the word *never*."

"Dmitri and his group murdered brother Bobby," said Michael K., smoldering.

"I refuse to believe it," said Vivian, becoming indignant.

"Are you calling me a liar?" said Michael K., his blood boiling.

"Dmitri would never hurt a living soul."

"He said he had help."

"I don't understand."

"A guy named Halverson helped Dmitri shoot Bobby. Do you know Halverson and a girl he's traveling with called Marta?"

"No," said Vivian.

"Halverson and Marta are gonna die for what they did to Bobby."

"This has nothing to do with us," said Bud. "Let us be on our way, and we'll forget we ever met you."

"I don't want you to forget. I want some straight answers from you folks. I didn't come here to chitchat."

"What do you want to know?" said Vivian, flogging her back.

"Don't do that when I'm talking to you. I want your full attention when I'm talking."

"We mean you no harm. Let us be on our way so we can meet Dmitri."

"The only place you're gonna meet Dmitri is in hell."

Vivian stared at Michael K. "What's that supposed to mean?"

"You're gonna find out pretty soon if you don't start giving me some straight answers."

"I've answered all your questions."

"Not quite."

Vivian took a step forward. Michael K. drove his Harley in front of her, blocking her path.

Chapter 20

"Where is Halverson?" said Michael K.

"How should I know?" said Vivian. "I don't know any Halverson."

"He belongs to your group, and he whacked out my beloved brother Bobby," said Michael K., his eyes becoming teary.

"I'm sorry for your loss."

"Now all my brothers are dead. My two other younger brother Oran and Bill were slaughtered by the ghouls. It was a terrible sight to behold," said Michael K., his eyes watery. "All four of us were in a pickup, me and Bobby in the cab and Oran and Bill in the back. We drove around a turn and came face to face with a thousand ghouls who were blocking the road and trudging toward us—"

"We don't have time for this," cut in Bud.

"Shut up and listen. I'm talking about my family, my blood. Don't you care about your family?"

"I care about my wife—"

"As I was saying, we drove right at this horde of ghouls. I slammed on the brakes. I knew there was no way to go through them. They must have clogged the road for a mile. If I tried to plow through them, we would have ended up stuck and surrounded. Me and Bobby rolled up our windows good and tight. Then I shifted into reverse. We backed up around the bend and damn my eyes I couldn't believe what I saw. There was another thousand of those suckers behind us, blocking the road. I slammed on the brakes again. I don't know how they had got there so fast. They must have been in the woods that skirted the road and come onto the road after we rounded the curve—"

"We don't have time to listen to your life story—"

"As I was saying, what was I to do? I couldn't go forward or backward. The road was bordered by woods on both sides. I decided to go backwards, thinking that there couldn't be as many ghouls behind us as in front of us, since the ghouls behind us hadn't had much time to gather there. I reversed the pickup into the slobbering, growling mob of ghouls.

"'What about Oran and Bill?' said Bobby. 'They're exposed on the cargo bed.'

"'There are less ghouls behind us,' I said, sweating.

"I knew I was putting Oran and Bill at risk, but I couldn't see any other options. I plowed the rear of the pickup through the swarming ghouls. Oran and Bill both had MP5s. They blasted the ghouls until they ran out of ammo. I kept plowing the pickup through the ghouls, running them over and shoving them out of the way. In the rearview I could see a clearing behind us about a hundred yards away.

"That was when the ghouls climbed onto the cargo bed and—" Choked up, Michael K. couldn't continue. He pulled himself together. "The stinking ghouls piled into the cargo bed and attacked Oran and Bill. They both fought like mad, clubbing the ghouls with their empty MP5s. But the ghouls overpowered them, biting them and eating their flesh. Oran and Bill screamed for help—" Overcome by the memory, Michael K. had to pause. "I— I—felt like their deaths were my fault. I kept driving the pickup backwards through the ghouls even as they tore Oran and Bill apart, eating them alive. I saw no other options. The ghouls tried to get to me and Bobby, but they couldn't break through the cab's rear window. The ghouls don't have much strength, you see—"

"Does this story ever end?" said Bud.

"It does. Like your life," said Michael K., his eyes flashing daggers. "Where was I? The pickup cab protected me and Bobby as I continued to reverse through the mob of ghouls and reach the clearing, where I did a three-point turn with the pickup and drove forward. The road was free of ghouls from here on. But there were still eight ghouls on the cargo bed, feasting on Oran and Bill. When we were far enough away from the horde, I stopped the pickup. Me and Bobby piled out and plastered the ghouls with bullets from our MP5s, cursing the filthy creatures with all our might, hot tears streaming down our faces. I couldn't stand looking at what remained of Oran and Bill. Me and Bobby dragged the ghouls off the cargo bed and dumped them on the side of the road like the garbage they were. Their rotting heads were perforated with MP5 bullets. Then we had to do the hardest thing. We shot poor Oran and Bill in the head so they wouldn't turn. We left them in the pickup and drove them back to our place for a decent funeral.

"I feel a measure of guilt for their deaths. If I had gone forward instead of backward, maybe they would have survived or maybe all of us would have died. To this day I don't know. I had to make a split-second decision. My mom always said I was the eldest and I was responsible for my brothers."

Michael K. shut his eyes in agony, remembering the details of his brothers' grisly deaths.

Chapter 21

"I'm sorry for your loss," said Vivian.

Michael K. snapped open his eyes, glowering now instead of crying.

"That's not the right answer," he said. "My last remaining brother Bobby has now been taken from me. Where is Halverson?"

"There's nobody named Halverson in our group."

"Sorry to hear that. Barry, do the honors. The redheaded guy."

Sporting goggles a guy in his late twenties with stubble on his face rode his Harley toward Herbert, withdrew the machete from his scabbard, and lopped off Herbert's head. Arterial blood jetted into the sky, drenching several of the self-flagellators, including Bud.

"What'd you do that for?" cried Bud, appalled at the carnage.

"I want Halverson," said Michael K. "Where is he?"

"We met him back there—"

"Shh," cut in Vivian.

"Why? We met him back there," said Bud, pointing behind him, disconcerted. "He wanted some water. We gave him some. And he left."

"Is Halverson your leader?"

"No way. I never saw him before."

"Do you want to know what happened to Dmitri?"

"*I* do," said Vivian.

"I executed him for murdering my brother."

"You executed the wrong man," said Bud. "Halverson told us *he* killed Bobby K."

"I figured as much. Halverson's your leader then."

"He's not one of us," cried Bud. "Don't you understand English?"

"Who's this pregnant woman?"

"My wife Mary. Don't harm her. If you're gonna harm someone, harm me."

"Why would we want to harm anyone?" said Michael K., all innocence.

"We'll be on our way then," said Vivian.

"Barry, take out Mary and her child."

"No," screamed Bud.

Barry drove his Harley toward Mary. Bud ran in front of him, trying to block him. Barry kicked him out of the way and swung his machete at Mary's neck. Mary's head rode a geyser of arterial blood ten feet into the air. Mary crumpled on her back. Barry plunged his machete into her womb, impaling her baby. Blood streamed onto Mary's bulging stomach.

"Did you hear it?" said Barry, grinning at Bud. "I heard her baby screaming when my machete cut it in half."

"Monster," cried Bud in white heat.

Charging Barry, Bud raised his whip over his head to attack him.

Michael K. shot Bud in the back of the head with his MP5. Bud dropped on limp legs.

"We're self-flagellators," cried Vivian. "We don't hurt anyone."

"I guess Bud there didn't get the message," said Michael K., and shot Vivian in the head.

Vivian crumpled, blood streaming down her face.

"Kill all of them," said Michael K. "Nobody who killed Bobby gets to live another minute. Wipe out the self-flagellators or whatever they are with their perverted religion. The whole lot of them murdered Bobby. Every last one of them must die."

He revved his Harley as his followers drove into the self-flagellators and either shot or beheaded them. Whipping themselves the self-flagellators screamed in pain as they dropped to the tarmac from their wounds inflicted by the High Rolerz.

"Blood for blood," cried Michael K. "If we meet any more of these self-hating nutbags, we'll kill them too. And Halverson. I will not rest until Halverson is dead and his head is on a pike."

"Why?" screamed one self-flagellator, a middle-aged man with a tonsure who was gripping a riding crop that he was using to beat himself when Barry shot him point-blank in the chest.

Tonsure stopped whipping his back, fell on his face on the tarmac, and ceased moving, his question unanswered.

Cawing crows gathered overhead, gyring, awaiting a feast, blotting out the sky.

"It puzzles me," said Michael K, astride his Harley, surveying the massacre.

"What does, boss?" said Barry, riding up to him, his machete dripping with blood.

"How did these nutbags live so long? Instead of defending themselves they whip themselves. Not one of them made any attempt to fight us. I don't get it."

"That Bud guy tried to fight me when I wasted his wife."

"I guess he was the only of them who was normal. Not that it did him any good."

"He's as dead as the rest of them."

"And Halverson and his woman will be next."

Michael K. revved his Harley and wove his way through the blood-splattered bodies strewn on the tarmac that ran with blood, his pack of fifty strong following him.

A blanket of sable, the crows overhead commenced their descent on the massacred self-flagellators as the last motorcycle vanished in the distance.

Chapter 22

Vivian awoke to the sound of buzzing over her face, which was smeared with coagulating blood.

She managed to open her eyes which the drying blood had sealed shut. She saw a fly buzzing and hovering over her face, its metallic green body gleaming.

The dawn's blue sky blazed over her, radiant as it basked in the light of the rising sun. The storm clouds had cleared, and it looked like the beginning of a beautiful day—

Except the air reeked of blood and death.

She sat up. How could she still be alive? Michael K. had shot her in the head. She felt the side of her bloodstained head. The bullet must have grazed her. There was a lot of blood, which was why he thought he had killed her. But she knew even a scratch on the scalp could cause copious bleeding. Eventually the wound had stopped bleeding thanks to coagulation.

From her sedentary position she surveyed her surroundings and took in the stomach-turning sight. Dead bodies enveloped her, many of them missing their heads, all of them soaked in blood. She wanted to retch. She located her whip and snagged it.

She stood up, rocky on her feet, lightheaded, and fell to inspecting the corpses strewn on the tarmac to see if anybody else had survived the massacre.

"Get away," she cried, waving her hands at the crows that were pecking the corpses.

The birds fluttered their wings angrily and flew away but not far. They remained hovering over the carrion below, patiently waiting to return to their meals.

Slumped over in dejection, in a state of shock, she scrutinized the cadavers, hoping to find one that was still alive. Her search did not look promising. After the crows had abandoned their feasts, she saw no movement among the bodies. She didn't bother to inspect the headless ones. She knew they were dead. Which was why the French had devised the guillotine as a means of execution.

Now what was she going to do? Michael K. had slaughtered everyone in her group, even Dmitri and his group that she was trying to reconnect with. Half-heartedly she scourged her back and winced. She was alone in the world. She was the only self-flagellator left.

She decided she must warn Halverson and Marta that Michael K. was hunting them with the intention of killing them in revenge for Bobby K.'s death.

She couldn't stand remaining here among the carnage. All of her friends were dead for no reason at all. They had nothing to do with Bobby K.'s death, and yet Michael K. had massacred them. All part of the senseless world they were living in. A world beyond comprehension. End days. Armageddon. Pointless death and violence everywhere. And multitudes of flesh-eating ghouls roaming the earth foraging for humans to eat.

She knew she had no chance of finding Halverson before Michael K. did, since his High Rolerz had motorcycles while she was on foot. But she wasn't going to give up before she even started her search. If she had any chance at all of helping Halverson and Marta, she would try.

But there was more to it than that. She wanted to confront Michael K. with his crimes against her friends. She couldn't let him get away with killing all of them without acknowledging his guilt. She would demand an apology from him.

Flogging her back she set out on the road after the High Rolerz, who were heading in the same direction as Halverson.

Out of the corner of her eye she caught sight of a sixtysomething female ghoul shambling out of the woods toward the road. Wearing a filthy dress of rags, her grey hair tousled like a fright wig, she growled and clawed the air menacingly when she clapped eyes on Vivian. A gravedigger's nightmare with one of her feet chewed off by a ghoul when she was healthy, she still managed to slog forward, barely able to walk a straight line with only one foot. Contorting her gruesome, pustulating face she hissed at Vivian.

Vivian shivered with dread at the sight of the creature that should be inhabiting a grave.

Nevertheless, Vivian kept walking. She accelerated her pace, knowing she could walk faster than a one-footed ghoul. She wasn't worried about one ghoul. It was the others that were no doubt accompanying her, lurking in the forest, that gave her pause. They could be heading her way this very minute.

The ghoul flailed her arms in frustration at not being able to catch up with Vivian but continued to hobble after her.

Chapter 23

Riding his bicycle on the tarmac, Halverson picked up on bodies hanging by the neck from tree branches in the distance. There was also a tunnel a half mile away that had three bodies hanging from the entrance.

The bodies hanging from the tree branches were writhing even though they were hanging by their necks. Halverson figured them for ghouls. Otherwise, they would have been dead a long time ago. The bodies hanging in the upcoming tunnel were motionless. Dead humans.

Lining the road in front of the forest stood five wooden saltires with weltering ghouls nailed to them.

Halverson slowed down so Marta could catch up with him.

"Do you see what I see?" she said, riding next to him, her face pallid.

"We must be getting near somebody's hideout. These are warning signs to keep out strangers. Michael K.'s staked-out territory, I bet."

"Do you think the ghouls get scared if they see one of their own hanging from a tree limb or nailed to a cross?"

"They're too stupid to be scared of anything."

Halverson and Marta rode closer to the tunnel.

"Those bodies hanging in the tunnel aren't moving," she said.

"They're not ghouls. They're cadavers warning human strangers to stay away."

"So what do we do?" she said, slowing her bicycle.

"We know Michael K. and his biker pack are behind us."

"He could have more followers at his camp, which could be near here."

Riding his bike slowly, Halverson cast around the surrounding area.

"Sentries could be posted close by," he said. "Most of his gang are probably with him, since he's out for revenge."

"Should we go through the tunnel?"

"If we turn back, we'll ride right into Michael K.'s arms."

"We can't detour into the woods riding these bicycles."

"We're going into the tunnel."

"We can't even see what's in there. It's too dark."

Halverson stopped his bike. "Do you think the tunnel is booby-trapped?"

Marta stopped near him. "Those bikers are sick. I wouldn't put anything past them."

"It could be booby-trapped for cars, not bicycles. They could have planted landmines in the tunnel. But then they wouldn't be able to use it. I have the feeling they use the tunnel. That's why they're trying to scare people away from it with these hanging bodies." He paused. "If there are mines inside it, we could ride around them with bikes. As long as we don't ride directly over a mine, we should be OK."

"How are we supposed to see in the dark?"

"I'm betting there aren't any mines. If the mines went off, nobody would be able to use the tunnel, including the bikers."

Halverson eyed the corpses hanging from nooses above him. There were two men in their twenties and a woman in her thirties. Their heads canted, their faces masks of horror, they were sticking out their tongues and quite dead.

"I have some matches to help us see," he said.

She gave him a look. "A couple of matches?"

Halverson didn't react. "I suggest we walk our bikes through the tunnel. We have no idea what we're gonna find in there. It's pitch-dark. Best to go slow."

"Can't we take a different route?"

"This is the road to DC. I thought you wanted to see your brother."

"Can't we detour around the tunnel?"

"Michael K.'s hideout could be in the woods near here. You saw the ghouls hanging from the trees."

"We have no idea what's in that tunnel or what's on the other side."

"What do you want us to do?"

"Let's go back."

"We can't turn back. Michael K. and his gang are behind us."

Marta fetched a long sigh. "Damned if we do and damned if we don't."

"We *do* have guns. We're not totally helpless."

"We need some of those night vision goggles that you Special Forces guys wear."

"Let's go."

Halverson walked his bicycle into the total blackness of the tunnel.

Grudgingly, Marta followed him on foot, holding onto her bike handlebars.

The putrid stench that wafted out of the tunnel nauseated them.

"What if the tunnel is a graveyard?" said Marta.

"This is our only route."

"You're making this sound like a death march."

"After completing a suicide mission, why not a death march this time?"

Chapter 24

"There are abandoned cars in the road," said Halverson, keeping his voice low, guiding his bike around an SUV parked on the tarmac in the tunnel.

"I can't see a thing," said Marta, her voice fraught with apprehension.

"I can only see them when they're a few feet away. That's why we could never ride our bikes blind through here. We'd crash every few minutes."

"Do you hear something?"

"Where?"

"To our right."

Halverson listened. It sounded like scuffing. *Scuff scuff.*

"It could be rats scampering around."

"I wish we could see over there."

"Let's keep going."

Halverson walked his bike farther into the lightless tunnel. He could hear more scuffing.

"Are they following us?" said Marta.

"If we can't see them, they can't see us."

"Unless they're bats."

"Bats can't see in the dark. They use echo location to perceive things."

"Thanks, professor. But my nerves are still jittery."

"We need to press on. We could be nearing the exit."

"Then there should be light up ahead. I don't see any."

Halverson stole around an abandoned old VW bus, trying to make as little noise as possible. He craned around.

"Are you still there?" he said. "I can't see you."

"I'm coming."

He could barely see her approaching him with her bike.

"I hear more scuffing," she said anxiously.

"I do too."

He wondered if he dare light a match to see what was making the scuffing. The sudden light of the flame would attract the attention of whatever else was in the tunnel with them. And then whatever it was would see them.

Scuff scuff.

In fact, the scuffing was increasing. Perhaps shoes scraping the tarmac. More than just two shoes.

"I can smell them," said Marta, her voice trembling. "They're in here with us."

"We need to keep plowing ahead," said Halverson, ushering his bicycle forward, sweat beading above his upper lip, his heartbeat racing, "and keep our voices down."

"I have to know what's here with us."

"Rats. If we don't bother them, they won't bother us."

But he felt the same as Marta. He had to know what was in the tunnel with them besides abandoned cars. He stopped walking and propped his bicycle against the passenger's-side door of a Toyota sedan.

He withdrew a matchbook from his trouser pocket.

A lot of scuffing echoed through the dark tunnel.

He wished he could slow down his rapid heartbeat as he anticipated lighting a match. He took a deep breath.

He struck the match against the striker on the matchbook. The match didn't light. He kept striking the match against the striker. At last the match flared. He raised the smoking match near his head and peered through the darkness.

He spotted milky eyes on the side of the tunnel glowing in the weak wash of light thrown by the burning match. Turning, he checked the other side of the tunnel. Scores of milky eyes over there too. He felt his heart stop beating for a few seconds.

Marta gasped at the ocean of milky eyes glowing all around them. She felt a frisson go down her spine.

"Jesus," she said.

Halverson blew out the match.

"What did you do that for?" said Marta. "Now we can't see them."

"And they can't see us. That's the important thing. Let's get moving."

He fell to pushing his bike down the tarmac, weaving around parked cars, trying to put the eerie sound of the scuffing out of his head.

"Can they smell the smoke from the match?" said Marta, pushing her bike after him.

"We're leaving the smoke behind us so we don't have to worry about them tracking us by smelling it. For all we know, they might not be able to smell anything."

"Can they hear our footsteps like we can hear theirs?"

"We're both wearing sneakers that don't make much noise. I doubt they can hear us. We need to keep our voices down though."

"It sounds like the scuffing is coming our way."

"We need to keep going. At least I haven't seen any landmines in the road. No IEDs either. But I can't see very well in the dark."

"IED?"

"Improvised exploding device. They were used in Afghanistan and elsewhere."

"Wonderful."

They strode around a black Caddy abandoned catercorner in the middle of the road.

"Are we any nearer the exit?" said Marta.

"I don't see any light up ahead."

"This tunnel could go on for miles."

"The darkness will protect us," said Halverson, continuing to push his bike forward around stationary cars, SUVs, pickups, and vans as the ghouls continued to plod along the edges of the tunnel foraging.

He came upon a car with the blond driver's head hanging out of its open window, his mouth agape, blood coughed up from internal injuries caked on his chin, his green eyes staring into infinity, the motor of his car sitting on his bloody lap, his chest caved in. His collision with another car had killed him, but the ghouls must not have fed on him yet or he would have turned by now. Maybe the things didn't know he was there because they couldn't see him in the dark.

Halverson hurried his bike past the collision.

PURGE

He had seen hundreds, maybe thousands, of dead bodies in his life, but seeing another one didn't get any easier.

He heard Marta suppressing a scream behind him as she beheld the corpse in the driver's seat.

They kept moving. He saw no evidence of craters in the road that would indicate the presence of landmines. Nevertheless, his pulse continued to race. The sooner he got out of here the better.

He was making good time on a stretch of road empty of abandoned motor vehicles when he heard Marta scream behind him.

Chapter 25

Halverson heard another squeal behind him. It wasn't Marta's. He craned around.

"What happened?" he whispered.

Marta was holding her mouth, her face a mask of fright.

"I stepped on a rat," she said. "It scared the hell out of me."

The scuffing at the sides of the tunnel got louder.

Halverson heard the rat's claws scampering across the tarmac as it fled.

"The ghouls are coming toward us," said Halverson, keeping his voice low. "Let's move."

Marta didn't need to be told twice. She could hear the ghouls growling and trudging toward them. She hurried after him.

Halverson heard another squeal. He figured it was that of the rat being eaten by a ghoul.

"What was that?" said Marta, her voice brimming with fear.

"Forget it. Let's keep moving."

Halverson thought he felt a breeze blowing into his face. He hoped he was nearing the tunnel exit. As yet he couldn't see light ahead. He kept walking his bike, keeping up a brisk pace to avoid the agitated ghouls who knew he and Marta were present thanks to her scream.

"I can smell those dreadful creatures," said Marta, dry-heaving. "They're getting closer to us."

"Now that they know we're here they're shambling faster."

"I couldn't help it. I hate rats."

"This whole place gives me the creeps. I doubt they can catch up to us if we walk faster."

They negotiated a jog in the road. Then the road straightened out, and Halverson could see ahead of him.

"Is that light up ahead?" he said.

"I hope so. I can't stand being in this deathtrap a moment longer."

The light could be coming from a hole in the tunnel roof for all Halverson knew, but he didn't think so. He felt another breeze caress his face. He could make out the outlines of cars parked on the road in front of him. Seeing the cars enabled him to avoid them. He broke into a run.

"Come on," he said. "We're almost out."

Marta eagerly pursued him.

As Halverson came closer to the exit he saw a problem. He slowed down.

Seven ghouls were schlepping in the road at the tunnel exit.

Marta caught up with him. "Why are you stopping?"

"We're gonna have to fight our way out. Seven ghouls ahead."

"Seven is better than the hundreds of them coming toward us in the tunnel."

"I was thinking the same thing."

Drawn by their putrescence, thousands of flies swarmed around the ghouls, which ignored them. A row of decrepit faces ogled Halverson and Marta. A particularly ugly ghoul with a bulbous nose and a brown shaving-brush mustache had flesh on only one side of his face. The flesh looked like greasy wax. The other side of his face looked worse. It was skinless bone. A fly flew out of his nose and buzzed away.

Marta stood beside Halverson. She gripped her MP5 and trained it on the seven ghouls.

"Do we let them have it?" she said.

Halverson thought about it. "There could be millions more of them beyond the tunnel. Gunfire will draw them here."

"Why do we even carry these guns if we can never use them?" she said, frustrated.

"We don't know what's out there."

"The ghouls in the tunnel already know we're here so gunfire won't alert them to our presence."

Halverson commenced searching the ground in the half-light that percolated into the cave from the exit.

"What are you looking for?" said Marta.

"Anything we can use as a club. These machine pistols don't make good clubs because their stocks are too small."

"What if we just ride our bikes past them?"

"One of them could still take a bite out of us and infect us. We can't risk it."

Chapter 26

Halverson combed the ground in search of something heavy he could use as a club. All he saw were empty beer cans and discarded McDonald's wrappers littering the ground. And a crumpled Burger King bag here and there.

Marta retreated to a pickup behind them.

"Here," she said, inspecting the cargo bed.

Halverson approached her.

Empty beer bottles and a couple of empty, grease-stained pizza boxes lay strewn on the cargo bed.

Halverson snagged a Corona bottle by its longneck and brandished it in front of him like he was going to club someone.

"I was thinking of throwing them at the ghouls," said Marta.

"It's gonna be hard to crack their skulls and damage their brains by hurling beer bottles at their heads. We're gonna have to grab bottles and fight the ghouls in CQB to club their skulls and smash their brains to pulp—"

"CQB?"

"Close-quarters battle."

"The closer we get to them, the easier it will be for them to bite us."

Halverson shrugged. "You can try chucking bottles at them first if you want."

They used their kickstands to park their bikes. They wouldn't be needing rides for combat.

Marta snatched two bottles from the pickup cargo bed, approached the ghouls shambling near the entrance, and hurled the bottles one at a time at the head of the nearest ghoul, a twentysomething male ghoul wearing a ripped grey sweatshirt and dirty jeans with one leg torn off. Her first bottle missed the ghoul, who flailed away at her and growled. Her second bottle struck a glancing blow to the creature's head. The ghoul shook his head once and kept advancing on her.

"We're gonna have to move in close," said Halverson.

He started stuffing the longnecks of the Corona bottles inside his waistband until he reached ten and realized he couldn't fit any more inside.

"I figure seven bottles won't be enough," he said, making sure the bottles fit snug and wouldn't fall out of his waistband.

Baring his teeth, a bottle in each hand, he lunged toward Grey Sweatshirt and battered him upside the head. Grey Sweatshirt reeled backward but didn't go down, his skull in one piece. Halverson followed him and clobbered him twice on the crown of his head with a bottle. The first blow didn't faze the ghoul. With the second, Halverson felt the creature's skull cave in. Halverson launched another blow that penetrated the cracked skull and drove into the brain, turning it into applesauce. Grey Sweatshirt crumpled, gawping in astonishment.

A female ghoul with a brunette beehive hairdo attacked Halverson on his right flank. Maggots infested her hairdo, Halverson could see. He had to act quickly to divert his attention from Grey Sweatshirt to her. He arced the bottle toward her temple and connected with a satisfying thud. However, the bottle cracked on impact, shedding glass fragments on the ghoul's shoulder. Beehive kept coming.

She thrust her arm forward and snatched Halverson's shirt with her grimy, fungus-infested claws. Halverson yanked another bottle from his waistband and smashed the side of her head. Her towering beehive provided protection for her skull, insulating it from his blow. He changed tactics. Shifting his position he slammed his bottle into Beehive's brow. The bottle shattered. Stunned, Beehive quavered and looked like she might go down. But she didn't. She clawed Halverson's shirt and tried to draw him toward her so she could bite his neck.

Halverson jerked back from her, but he couldn't break free from her grasp. He fished out another bottle from his waistband and swung it with all his might at her forehead. He felt the bone disintegrate as a result of his blow. He needed to hit her again to reach her brain. He hit her forehead again and, not only smashed through it into the brain, but smashed the bottle as well, leaving him with the jagged, crown-shaped neck of the bottle in his hand. He jabbed the edged glass into her exposed brain. She faltered as her brains leaked out onto her face. She collapsed.

Her waistband stuffed with Corona longnecks, Marta waded into the attack. She launched a vicious, sweeping blow into a fat male fortyish ghoul with bushy eyebrows. She hit him so hard she dropped the bottle. The ghoul blinked his eyes in astonishment, but he kept grabbing at her, trying to devour her arm. She slipped his grasp, withdrew another bottle from her waistband, and clocked his head. She slammed his brow twice in rapid succession until she felt the bone crack and saw his brains ooze out.

A dwarf ghoul with long curly brown hair that stuck upward out of his scalp swiped his gnarly hand at her kneecap. He screwed up his face and growled at her, exposing his broken yellow teeth that looked like wolf fangs.

She stepped back from his hand and snagged another bottle from her waistband. She lunged at him and hammered his pate with the bottle, stunning him. Not hearing his skull crack, she delivered another blow to his scalp, shattering her beer bottle. She grabbed another bottle and smashed his head, fracturing it, as he snatched her pantleg. She kicked him in the teeth, knocking him backward, and crashed the bottle through his broken skull into his brain, destroying it. His head misshapen, the dwarf dropped and sprawled motionless on the tarmac.

Halverson engaged with Bulbous Nose. Halverson had a burning desire to kill him thanks to the creature's preternatural ugliness. Halverson clubbed Bulbous Nose in the face with a Corona longneck. Bulbous Nose growled but kept up his attack. Halverson shattered his bottle on Bulbous Nose's head, leaving the creature unfazed. Using the jagged remains of the bottle that he held in his hand, Halverson gouged out the ghoul's eyeball and drove the edged glass into the brain, where he corkscrewed the toothed glass, boring an inch-wide hole in the brain, dropping the creature where he stood.

Two ghouls remained.

Halverson shattered a beer bottle on the tarmac, keeping the longneck in his hand. He pointed the long, jagged teeth at the tall thirtyish ghoul who might have been handsome when he was human but was now as ugly as any other ghoul that ever walked the earth. He was wearing a seersucker suit that had all of its buttons torn off. His aqua necktie hung askew from his neck.

Halverson charged him and thrust the toothed end of the broken bottle through the bottom of the lantern jaw, through the tongue, through the palate, and into the brain, killing the reanimated brain. The ghoul shivered, confusion on his contorted parchmentlike face, and toppled to the ground.

"One to go," said Halverson.

"Allow me," said Marta, setting her face with determination.

Marta laid into the remaining ghoul, a blonde clad in a doctor's white smock. She could have been pushing forty, but her face was as wizened as a ninety-year-old. Marta crashed her bottle into the scowling face again and again until she felt the frontal bone yield with a thwack. Then she smashed the rotting face again until her bottle met brain and pulverized it.

"I can see hundreds of those ghouls in the tunnel closing in on us," said Halverson.

He and Marta belted to their bikes and rode them out of the tunnel, making sure to avoid any glass fragments from the broken beer bottles that strewed the tarmac.

"Next time, let's just shoot the buggers," said Marta, winded as she pedaled. "So what if anybody hears us."

"We have to conserve ammo. Our mags run dry, then what?"

Marta rolled her eyes. "The voice of reason."

They saw a figure halting toward them down the road.

Chapter 27

Halverson and Marta slowed their bikes.

"Not another ghoul," said Marta.

"He's too far away to tell," said Halverson.

"At least there's only one."

They stopped their bikes.

Marta trained her MP5 on him.

Halverson pushed her arm down.

She scowled at him. "Do we have to find another club somewhere? I don't see any Corona bottles around."

"Not a problem. We can find a tree limb in the woods. Let's get closer to him first."

"So he can bite us?"

Intent on the man, he ignored her. "He's wearing camo."

"The ghouls wear anything. So?"

"He might be human."

"No way. Look how he's hobbling. He's an uncoordinated ghoul."

"I want to check it out."

Halverson pedaled his bike toward the figure, who kept limping toward them. Halverson couldn't make out the stranger's face yet, though he could make out a wooden cane in the man's hand.

The figure waved to him.

"He's waving to us," said Halverson.

"He's flailing his arm," said Marta. "All the ghouls do that."

"I need to see his face."

Halverson pedaled faster toward the figure.

"Be careful," said Marta. "Don't get too close to him."

The guy was wearing hiking boots and camo pants with his camo jacket. His left leg looked misshapen as he dragged it along the tarmac. Bearded, the better part of six feet tall, he looked to be in his early thirties. His hair was cropped so close to his head his scalp was exposed. Halverson figured the guy shaved his head.

The guy waved at Halverson again. "Hello."

"He's human," Halverson said, craning toward Marta, who was riding a little behind him. "Ghouls can't talk."

"Hello," said Halverson, riding up to him.

Halverson kept his hand on his MP9. He had no idea who this guy was. He could be part of Michael K.'s gang of cutthroats.

"We thought you were a ghoul," said Marta, catching up to them.

"Same here. I'm Rocco," said the guy, wincing as he moved his misshapen leg.

"What happened to your leg?"

"I was riding my hog too fast around a curve. The hog crushed my leg as I slid out of control into a tree, totaling the hog. The crash knocked me unconscious. I don't know how long I was out." Furrowing his brow, his face pallid, Rocco looked at his leg. "I got a compound fracture in my crushed leg."

Since Rocco had been riding a motorcycle, Halverson figured he might belong to Michael K.'s biker gang.

"Where are you guys headed?" said Rocco.

Marta was about to answer when Halverson grabbed her arm, signaling her to keep her own counsel. She looked puzzled.

"Do you know Michael K.?" Halverson asked Rocco.

An expression of befuddlement appeared on Rocco's face.

"He owns a motorcycle like you," said Halverson, trying to get Rocco to reveal himself.

"Is his government issue like mine was?" Rocco stared at him. "Hey, wait a minute. Aren't you Halverson?"

Halverson started. "How do you know my name?"

Chapter 28

"Everybody at Mount Weather knows you," said Rocco. "You're a damned legend."

"Explain," said Halverson, wary.

Rocco loosened up and offered a brief smile. "I work for the government like you. I was on a secret mission for President Mims to contact Raven Rock to see what was going on there."

"Mims is dead."

"What?" said Rocco, taken aback.

"Somebody assassinated him."

Disconcerted, Rocco ran his hand through the stubble of hair on his head.

"Who's running the government?" he said.

"Dean Uriah."

"He's not the speaker of the house," said Rocco, bemused.

"Were you able to meet the speaker of the house at Raven Rock?" said Halverson, all ears.

Rocco gazed down at the tarmac, his face grim. "I had my accident before I reached Raven Rock. With my leg busted up I'm heading back to Mount Weather. I'll never reach Raven Rock in my condition."

"That's too bad." Halverson paused. "If you make it back to Mount Weather, don't tell anybody you saw us."

"What? Why not?"

"Uriah framed us for the murder of Mims. I'm sure he has sent a squad out to bust us or more likely whack us."

"Why would he frame you guys?"

"I'm pretty sure he was behind the assassination. He had it done to satisfy his lust for power. He set us up to take the fall."

"A lot's been going down at the bunker since I left."

"You said you don't know Michael K," said Halverson, searching Rocco's face, trying to find out if Rocco was lying.

"I don't know any Michael K."

"You're better off not knowing him."

"Bad news?"

Halverson nodded yes.

"Is there any food around here?" said Marta. "My stomach is screaming at me to feed it."

"There's a dry goods store a couple miles back," said Rocco, pointing behind him with his cane.

"Let's get going."

"It's been looted."

Slumping her shoulders Marta became dejected.

"But if you try hard enough, you can find stuff. I found an expired box of Trix. I didn't care if it was expired, it tasted good."

Marta's expression brightened. "I could care less about an expiration date."

"Are you heading through the tunnel?" Halverson asked Rocco.

"It's the only way back to Mount Weather."

Halverson eyed the tunnel behind him. "The tunnel's full of ghouls—"

"Crap."

"If you keep on the road, they won't bother you if you're quiet. They're lining both sides of the tunnel."

"Good to know. They weren't in there when I drove my hog through yesterday—or whenever it was. I've lost track of time."

"And avoid any biker gangs you come in contact with. Michael K. and his gang are on this road on the other side of the tunnel. They shoot first and ask questions later."

"He wants us dead," said Marta.

"Why?" said Rocco.

"I killed his brother," said Halverson. "The guy beheaded a woman in cold blood. I couldn't let him get away with it."

"I don't blame you. I would have done the same. What's Michael K. look like?"

"I can't say. I haven't met him."

"OK."

"Do you think you can make it back on that bum leg?"

"I don't have much choice. Mount Weather is closer than Raven Rock."

Halverson glanced at Rocco's broken leg. "It looks bad with that broken bone sticking out."

"I stanched the bleeding. That's the most important thing. Now I need a doctor to set it."

"I doubt you'll find any doctors around here."

"That's what I was thinking. I gotta head back to base."

Marta watched him hobble toward the tunnel.

"Maybe we should go back with you," she said.

"We can't," said Halverson. "We have a mission. And what about your brother?"

"Are you sure you can handle the ghouls, Rocco?"

Rocco turned around and waved his heavy wooden cane at them. "Don't worry. I'll bludgeon their brains with this. I've killed scores of them with it already." He sniffed his cane and screwed up his face. "I can smell their putrid brains on it even now." He withdrew a SIG P226 out of his waistband. "I also got this and one spare mag."

He turned around and kept halting toward the tunnel, returning his piece to his waistband.

Halverson could hear Rocco's cane ferrule tapping against the tarmac, the taps receding as Rocco reached the tunnel mouth.

"I hope he makes it," said Marta, watching him with concern.

"He's a soldier. He's trained to survive."

"I can't help thinking we're all supposed to be dead."

"We gotta keep fighting. It's the only way we're gonna make it."

Rocco disappeared into the tunnel without even pausing to have second thoughts.

Halverson started pedaling away from the tunnel. "Let's see if we can find that dry goods store he was talking about."

Marta pedaled after him.

Chapter 29

When Rocco emerged from the tunnel he came up short as he saw the three corpses hanging by their necks from the top of the tunnel. A sudden gust of wind swayed the corpses, making them look even creepier if that was possible. He didn't remember them being there when he rode his motorcycle through the tunnel toward Raven Rock.

He limped under them out of the tunnel into the sunshine. The ghouls in the tunnel hadn't bothered him, since he stuck to the tarmac and kept quiet, as quiet as he could anyway, considering he had a cane to help him walk.

The sunlight invigorated him. He halted faster down the road. His leg acted up. He felt pain shooting up it. He had run out of Tylenol. It was all he had for a painkiller. Grinding his teeth in pain, he soldiered on. He had to reach Mount Weather to see a doctor. He wasn't going to find a doctor out here in the middle of nowhere.

Maybe he could get one of these cars abandoned in the road to work. He doubted it. The ignitions and the batteries had been destroyed by the EMP generated by the nuclear blast. If he could find an old VW Bug built before the 1980s, he would be in business. Even if the battery was dead, he could still bump start the Bug. Of course, it would have to have gas in the fuel tank. The newer cars were loaded with electrical gear that was wiped out by the EMP. As well, some of these cars on the road had been abandoned thanks to empty fuel tanks.

What was he thinking? How could he drive a stick shift with this broken leg? He couldn't use a brake pedal and a clutch with only one good leg. He would have to hoof it.

He had a long walk ahead of him. Not that you could call it walking. *Gimping* was a more accurate word.

He grimaced at the pain emanating from his broken leg and banged his cane ferrule against the tarmac in frustration.

At least he didn't see any ghouls around. They were all shambling around in the tunnel for some reason. Who could understand them? They couldn't even understand themselves. Who could understand anything in these fucked-up times?

He was coming up to a hairpin turn in the road.

He could hear a rumbling like thunder in the distance and could feel it in his chest. He looked up at the clear sky. It didn't look like rain.

Motorcycles. He knew the sound of a chopper when he heard one. There wasn't just one. There were lots of them.

It could be this Michael K. that Halverson had warned him about.

Rocco had to find cover before he met up with the strangers. He cursed his leg for slowing him down as he halted out of the road toward the woods. He wasn't going to make it. Those hogs were riding fast. They would be coming around the bend any minute.

A lone biker riding point came into view.

Rocco stopped hobbling toward the woods.

The biker dressed in black leather and black boots drove toward him and braked to a halt. He gestured toward the other members of the gang as they appeared from around the curve.

Rocco saw a tall guy with a shaved head riding toward him. This must be the leader of the pack, Michael K.

Michael K. halted his motorcycle in front of Rocco.

"What happened to you?" said Michael K.

"I was in an accident," said Rocco.

"Bummer. That busted pin must hurt bad."

Rocco shrugged. He knew Michael K. couldn't care less about him. Rocco could read it from the tone of Michael K.'s voice.

"Play the hand you're dealt," said Rocco.

"We're looking for someone. Maybe you could help us," said Michael K., and revved his Harley as he sat astride it in front of Rocco.

Rocco could smell the exhaust from the Harley. He didn't say anything.

"Which direction did you come from?" said Michael K. "Beyond the tunnel?"

"Yeah."

"Did you see someone called Halverson back there? He's traveling with a woman."

"No."

"Why you packing?" said Michael K., picking up on the SIG wedged in Rocco's waistband.

"Ghouls. They're all over the place. I wouldn't go anywhere without a piece."

"Maybe you should give it to me."

"Why would I want to do that?" said Rocco, feeling his heartbeat accelerate and his palms ooze pellets of sweat.

"We're short on pistols. Are you sure you didn't see Halverson?"

"I'm sure."

"How about his woman?"

"Nope."

"I find that hard to believe, since they were headed your way. How could you miss them?"

"Maybe they went into the woods. Who knows?"

Michael K. held out his hand. "I need you to kindly hand over your piece. Guns are hard to come by. We need it more than you do."

"How do you figure?"

"You won't be needing much of anything in the near future."

"Why not?"

"Because I want you to tell me the truth. Have you seen Halverson?"

"No. What's he look like?"

"You see," said Michael K. knowingly. "You should have asked me that question before. Then maybe I would have believed you hadn't seen him."

Rocco was liking his situation less and less.

"I didn't see anyone on my way here," he said. "That's why I didn't bother asking you what Halverson—whoever he is—looks like."

Michael K. stared at the tarmac. "I've never seen him. I have only a secondhand description of him given to me by one of those self-styled self-flagellators who saw him murder my brother Bobby K."

"I can't help you."

"He's a big guy at least six feet tall. At least that's what they tell me. He's carrying a gun that he used to murder my brother Bobby."

"Doesn't ring any bells."

His face expressionless, Michael K. looked up and stared at Rocco.

"You need to hand me your SIG now," said Michael K.

"I need it for self-protection."

There was no way Rocco was going to surrender his piece to anyone. His heartbeat was thundering in his chest. He wondered if Michael K. could hear it.

Michael K.'s expression didn't change. He killed his Harley's engine, booted the kickstand, and dismounted. To a man the High Rolerz killed their Harley engines and sat astride their hogs in stone silence.

Rocco couldn't believe how silent it became. It was preternatural. It sent a chill down his spine. The deafening cacophony of revving motorcycles followed by absolute quiet.

"People always ask me why I wear a necktie," said Michael K, stroking his black leather tie. "They want to know why I dress up when I ride a hog. They think I'm strange." He gestured behind him. "None of the High Rolerz wear ties. I'm the only one."

He unfastened the knot, slid the tie through his shirt collar, and approached Rocco.

"Do you want to see my tie?" said Michael K., his expression still wooden.

"Nice tie," said Rocco through a tight throat, suspicious of Michael K. but not knowing what the guy was up to.

"A lot of people don't like wearing ties because they feel tight around the throat. But I like them. They give a person an air of dignity in this barbaric world we live in."

Rocco was thinking about pulling his SIG on Michael K. when Michael K. kicked Rocco's cane out of his hand, causing Rocco to lose his balance and fall to the tarmac on his broken leg. Rocco cried out in agony. Michael K. stomped his cowboy boot heel on the exposed fractured tibia sticking out of Rocco's leg. Rocco cried even louder.

"Asshole," he screamed, spewing flecks of spit out of his mouth.

Michael K. stepped back from him. "What did you say?"

"*Asshole.*"

Tie in hand, Michael K. jumped on the back of Rocco, who was writhing in pain on the tarmac gripping his broken leg. Michael K. wrapped his tie around Rocco's neck and fell to strangling him. His face turning red, Rocco attempted to pull the tie away from his neck. But he couldn't insert his fingers between the tie and his flesh. Michael K. applied more pressure, making it even more difficult for Rocco to pry the tie loose.

"You liar," said Michael K. "Nobody gets away with lying to me. Tell me the truth. Did you see Halverson?"

Rocco couldn't speak if he wanted to. The tie was too tight around his neck.

"The only way to rule is through fear," snarled Michael K., continuing to strangle Rocco.

Rocco's body went limp as he saw blackness.

Chapter 30

Vivian kept walking after Michael K. and the High Rolerz. She had no plans to abandon her mission of confronting him about his massacre of her people. She had to explain to the mass murderer that what he had done was wrong. The guy must be a sociopath. The taking of a person's life meant nothing to him.

Now that Dmitri and the others were gone, her life had no meaning. All of her friends and colleagues had lost their lives courtesy of Michael K. and his biker gang of mass murderers.

She continued to lash her back as she pursued him. She must catch up to him no matter how long it took. He was the evilest person she had ever met. The only reason she was still alive was because he had mistakenly thought he had killed her when he had only grazed her head with his bullet.

He would probably kill her if she confronted him, but she had nothing to live for anymore with all her friends and fellow believers gone. If he killed her, her life of suffering would end.

Not that she was going to exact revenge. The self-flagellators didn't believe in an eye for an eye. Nevertheless, she had to let him know that what he and his High Rolerz had done to her group was wrong.

No doubt he would laugh at her or shoot her in the head, but it had to be done. She could not let the murders of Dmitri and her colleagues go unatoned for. She needed an apology from Michael K.

The idea of getting a gun and shooting him came into her mind even though the self-flagellators didn't believe in killing another human being. It was her lizard brain telling her what to do. She knew she had to stifle the urge for revenge.

She whipped her back harder to get her to stop straying from her beliefs.

Her lizard brain continued to resist her.

"Instead of flogging yourself, flog Michael K.," it said. "It wasn't your fault he massacred all of your friends and colleagues."

She tried to block out the voice in her head by flailing herself harder.

Revenge will not solve anything, she told herself. Spilling another person's blood accomplishes nothing. Like everybody else she was meant to suffer. To be alive was to suffer. To suffer the loss of her friends was just more suffering, not of the flesh but of the soul, which was even more devastating. In the end it was all suffering. The essence of life was to suffer.

Screwing up her face in pain, she lashed her back.

She would confront Michael K., but she would not raise her hand against him. He must learn that what he had done to her group was evil.

There was a time when they had laws to punish criminals like Michael K., but those days were gone. The country had descended into chaos. What remained of the government was hiding in bunkers, while flesh-eating ghouls ruled the bombed-out wastelands, their only opponents militias, vigilantes, and rogue criminal gangs.

She felt weak. Maybe she had lost more blood from her head wound than she had thought. In any case, she must continue her pursuit.

She trudged ahead. She could have been a ghoul the way she plodded.

She would not rest until she confronted Michael K. and his High Rolerz with their crimes.

She flogged her back and winced. She must suffer and carry on. For as long as she lived she would suffer. She must endure the pain of being alive.

Chapter 31

Driving his bike toward a hairpin curve in the road, Halverson picked up on a wrecked motorcycle that had crashed into an oak tree and lay on its side, its handlebars bent out of shape. Skid marks streaked the tarmac behind the motorcycle.

"That must be Rocco's hog," said Halverson over his shoulder to Marta.

"Maybe we can use it," she said.

Halverson shook his head no. "The handlebars are no good." He approached the hog and slowed his bike. "The engine got knocked up bad too."

He got off his bike and stood up the Harley.

"And it's got a flat," he said.

"It's leaking oil," said Marta, noticing rainbow-colored oil leaking out of the engine and soaking into the ground skirting the side of the road.

"The key's still in the ignition."

He was going to fire the engine when he smelled gasoline.

"It's leaking gasoline and oil," he said. "A spark from the ignition might turn us into a fireball."

"What next?"

"We're not going anywhere in this thing."

He laid the Harley down on its side and got back on his bicycle.

"Maybe that dry goods store is nearby," said Marta.

They continued riding their bicycles down the road, following the curve and weaving through abandoned vehicles.

"My stomach's doing somersaults," said Halverson.

The road straightened out.

"I don't have much energy left," said Marta. "I'm running on fumes. I don't think I can pedal this bike another mile."

Halverson glanced over his shoulder at her. Her face pale, she looked wiped out. He knew how she felt. He faced forward.

"There's a building in the distance," he said, pointing ahead. He glanced back at her.

"I hope it's the store Rocco was talking about," she said, her bike starting to weave under her.

"Hold on a little longer. We're almost there. Are you OK?"

"I'm fine. All I need is a little food in my stomach."

Halverson rode past a Honda sedan with a head hanging out the window, the door half-open. In his forties he had bushy black hair. His eyes were closed. His face was drained of blood. He was wearing beat-up jeans and a faded fluorescent orange high-visibility vest.

Halverson made out the key in the ignition. He stopped his bike next to the driver's-side window, dismounted, and toed down the kickstand. Snapping open his eyes the ghoul reached out his arm to grab him. Halverson swiped the arm away.

"Watch out," said Marta.

"There's a key in the ignition," said Halverson.

"Why'd that ghoul climb into the car?" she said, catching up to him on her bike.

Halverson gazed at the shotgun seat. He saw a human foot lying on it.

"He was eating lunch in there," he said.

"Let's get out of here and get some food."

Halverson felt tempted to reach into the car past the ghoul and turn on the ignition to see if the car worked. But the creature might bite him. Instead he snagged its arm, yanked it out of the car, and slung it on the tarmac. The thing didn't weight much. It was only skin and bone.

Halverson reached into the car and fired the ignition.

Except it didn't fire. This was a new car. The EMP from the recent nuclear blast had disabled the electrical system.

"That thing's crawling toward you," said Marta.

Halverson kicked it in the head. Its head jerked back, its nose broken.

Halverson mounted his bike and made a beeline for the building up ahead, Marta in tow.

Looters had shattered the picture window of the dry goods store.

"I'll be surprised if we find much in there," said Halverson.

"I'll try anything at this point," said Marta.

They dismounted from their bicycles and entered the store through the front door, which had a broken lock. Fragments of glass from the picture window were strewn over the dirty hardwood floor. Most of the dust-mantled shelves were bare.

"I wonder where Rocco found the Trix," said Marta, wandering around the store in search of food.

"They must have a storeroom here."

Halverson noticed empty cans of dog- and cat food scattered on the floor. Had the looters eaten from the cans themselves? He saw empty cartons of cereal on several of the shelves.

"Are you finding anything?" said Marta, coughing thanks to her dry mouth.

"Empty cans and boxes."

Halverson opened several closet doors that hung ajar. The looters had raided them as well. Empty spaghetti boxes, empty soda cans, and crumbs on the floor.

"I'm getting hungry just looking at all the empty boxes I see," said Marta. "Hey, wait a minute. There's a steel door over here." She tried to open it. "It's locked."

Halverson examined the door. "It could be the door to a bomb shelter."

Marta pointed at the dents in the door. "The looters tried to kick it in."

Halverson picked up on dents in the steel near the lock. "They tried to shoot the lock open too. The bullets didn't penetrate the steel. They've been watching too many movies."

"They also tried to kick the dead bolt lock off the door, but it didn't budge."

"Good lock."

"So how do we open it?" she said, staring at him.

"It's not difficult if we can find a couple of paper clips or bobby pins."

"You're kidding."

"What? No."

"You know how to pick a lock?"

"What do you think they teach us in black ops at the CIA?"

They scrounged around the store in search of paper clips and bobby pins.

"They might not sell stationery supplies here," said Marta.

"I bet they sold a little bit of everything here when they were open."

Halverson picked up on empty shotgun ammo boxes lying on the floor.

"There's an empty Trix box on the shelf," said Marta. "That must be the Trix Rocco ate."

Halverson scoured the room for a paper clip. At last he spotted several on the floor near the store counter.

"Who would have thought?" said Marta.

"Maybe the owner used them for his accounting records," said Halverson, bending over and picking up two of the paper clips. "These are big ones. Just what I need."

He returned to the locked steel door, straightened out the paper clips, then bent them into the shapes of a tension wrench and a pick. He inserted the tension wrench into the dead bolt lock first to set it in place. Then he went to work with the pick to massage the pins.

Marta cast a glance out the broken picture window. "We got ghouls."

Three ghouls shambled along the road in the direction of the dry goods store, flailing the air with their arms, watching the store with their dead milky eyes.

Marta disappeared behind the counter, found a hammer, and returned to the storeroom.

"I don't need a hammer for this," said Halverson, concentrating on picking the lock.

"It's for the ghouls." She coughed on the dust in the store. "I'm gonna lose my voice if we don't get some water soon."

Halverson managed to open the deadbolt lock. He proceeded to work on the regular lock in the doorknob beneath it.

"You don't want us to shoot the things, so I'll use this hammer on their heads," said Marta.

"Get ready," said Halverson, swinging open the door.

PURGE

"Stay where you are," said an old guy pushing eighty, sitting in the air-raid shelter, training a double-barreled 20-gauge shotgun on Halverson's face.

Chapter 32

Adrenaline coursed through Halverson's body as he stared at the gaping eyes of the twin muzzles staring at him.

"We mean you no harm," he said.

"Then why are you breaking into my shelter?" said the man, narrowing his eyes.

Wearing wire-rim glasses, he had barely any hair on his head and patches of ragged grey stubble on his lined hatchet face. He had a mole on the left side of his jaw. Deathly pale since he never ventured out of his bunker to go outside in the sun, he could have been a corpse.

"Are you the owner of this store?" said Halverson.

"You betcha. Are you one of the looters that trashed it?"

"No. I just got here."

"Then be on your way before I let you have both barrels in the face."

"Can't you spare some food and water? We're dying of thirst."

"We?" said the geezer, squinting to see past Halverson.

"We're not here to hurt you," said Marta, shoehorning herself between Halverson and the doorjamb. "What's your name?"

"Adam."

"I'm Marta, and this is Halverson." She eyed the shelves of food lining the shelter. "You have plenty of supplies here. Can't you spare us some food and drink?"

"What's wrong with you?" said Adam, staring at her face.

"What do you mean?"

"You look like you're on your last legs."

"We haven't eaten in so long I'm becoming weak." She picked up on hundreds of plastic bottles full of water lining the walls of the shelter. "And water." She coughed with her dry throat. "We need water."

"I'm not holding a charity here. What happens when I run out of supplies? What am I supposed to do then, huh?"

"We don't want all of your supplies. Just some bottles of water and any food you can spare."

"Do you understand what's happening in the world, Adam?" said Halverson. "It's a wasteland out there with looters, militia, and vigilantes running the land—"

"I understand nobody gives a shit about me but me. That's what I understand. That's what my eighty years on this planet have told me. This is my store. I own it and run it by myself. I'm pioneer stock. I endure. And I'm gonna endure this nightmare world the ghouls and the politicians created for us."

Like most people these days, Adam hated the government, decided Halverson. He wasn't going to tell him he worked for the CIA.

"And," Adam went on, "I've been living in this shelter for—I don't really know, now that I think about it—but it's been at least a year. I've lost track of time." His voice became sad. "I lost my wife Judy just before the apocalypse or whatever this nightmare is called. She died of pancreatic cancer."

"I'm sorry for your loss," said Marta.

"My doctor diagnosed me with cancer too. Prostate cancer and kidney cancer. Take your pick. I got both of them. But I'm still alive. I spend all my days locked up alone in this bomb shelter. I know what you're thinking. It's a wonder I don't go nuts, huh?" he said, laughing. "I got food and water but this is like solitary confinement. I manage, though. I think about Judy a lot," he said wistfully. "It would be nice if she showed up at the door one day."

"Be careful what you wish for," said Halverson.

"What do you mean?"

"If she's walking around out there, she's a ghoul."

"Yeah," said Adam, disconcerted. "Well, anyway I'm still alive. And I hope things get better soon. I'm getting tired of looters coming into my store at least once a week and raiding the place. I don't see how any supplies could be left."

"It's picked clean."

"And still the looters come. It shows how desperate people are these days."

"Do they try to break into your shelter when they come?" said Marta.

"You betcha. I hear them out there all the time pounding on my door, shooting at it or trying to kick it in." Adam cut his eyes back and forth. "I'm surrounded by enemies. No telling what the looters would do to me if they managed to break open the door. That's why I got this 20-gauge to keep me company."

"We're the good guys," said Marta. "We didn't come here to rob or hurt you."

"Then why are you still here?" said Adam. "I don't give to no charity cases. Do you have any money on you?"

"Money doesn't get you anywhere these days," said Halverson. "Nobody uses it. You can't go to the store and buy something because the stores are all looted."

"This apocalypse will pass like everything else. Then we're all gonna need money again. Mark my words, money never goes out of fashion for long."

Chapter 33

"Are you open to bartering?" said Halverson.

"In a fair exchange there is no theft," said Adam, nodding.

"We'll trade you something for food and water."

"What do you have to barter?"

Not much of anything. Halverson didn't know what to say. He felt like a homeless person begging on the sidewalk. Was he going to sell the clothes on his back for food?

Adam interrupted Halverson's thoughts.

"How about one of those fancy guns you're carrying? I never seen guns like that before except in movies about spies and cartel drug lords driving Ferraris."

Halverson was careful not to react when Adam said "spies." He had the feeling Adam liked spies as little as he liked politicians. Halverson needed weapons to defend himself against the ghouls, Michael K., and the High Rolerz. But he also needed food and water, especially water. He and Marta would die if they didn't get water soon. When push came to shove, food and water were more important than guns even in an apocalypse.

"OK," said Halverson. "I'll trade one of them to you for food and drink."

He needed as much firepower as he could get to deal with the ghouls and the High Rolerz, who he figured were tracking him even now. He couldn't really spare either of his MP9s, but he and Marta needed water and food.

"At least you're not no charity cases," said Adam. "I hate charity cases. If you can't make your way in this world, you deserve to die. If I'm lyin' I'm dyin'." Adam lowered his shotgun. "I like meeting a fellow businessman. The business of America is business as someone once said."

"Calvin Coolidge."

"If you say so. Now let's get down to business. How much do you want for one of your Hollywood guns?"

"This is a beautiful piece of machinery. It's a Brugger & Thomet MP9 made in Switzerland."

"That's the thing about the Swiss. They're good at making guns and cuckoo clocks. What would we do without the Swiss? I'm part Swiss myself, my great, great, great grandfather, if I'm not mistaken." Adam looked up thoughtfully. "Maybe I added one *great* too many."

Halverson stroked the MP9 barrel. "This is one of the finest machine pistols in the world. It easily rivals the German Heckler & Koch MP5 and MP7."

"That's the thing about the Germans. They're good at making guns and cars. I'm part German myself. Let's see. My great—"

"I believe you," said Halverson, getting tired of listening to Adam's speeches about his genealogy.

"The Germans are a machine-oriented people. They're very logical about everything. Machines are exercises in logic—"

"I really would like a drink of water," said Marta, motioning to her open mouth. "Or I think I'm gonna faint."

"I believe you will," said Adam, searching her pallid face.

"We're willing to barter with you."

"Hand me that Brugger and Thomet—what's your name again?" he asked Halverson.

"Halverson."

"OK. Halverson, hand me your piece and help yourselves to some water bottles and Cheerios or whatever. I've been living off Cheerios forever. I have hundreds of boxes left."

"Do you happen to have any nine mil ammo for our guns?" said Halverson.

"Not nine mil. I got double ought buckshot for my 20-gauge Mossberg."

"That's a shame. I could use some spare mags for my piece. Her too."

"I don't run a gun shop, although I do sell buckshot."

"I'm gonna hate parting with this baby."

Halverson handed one of his MP9s to Adam, who put down his shotgun and inspected the machine pistol with fascination.

"Like I said, I never seen one of these fancy gizmos before so I don't carry magazines for it."

"Do you have another shotgun?"

"No." Adam paused and looked up from the MP9. "Do either of you know any treatments for prostate cancer?"

"We're not doctors," said Marta.

"My doctor said the cancer had metastasized to my lymph nodes and my thigh bone. I ran out of the pills my doctor gave me ages ago. There aren't any pharmacies hereabouts."

"Not any doctors, either," said Halverson.

"I wonder how long I've got left before big casino kills me." Adam thought about it for a few seconds then shrugged. "I guess it doesn't matter. We all gotta kick the bucket someday."

Halverson filled a knapsack with a large plastic jar of peanut butter, a giant box of Cheerios, and several liter bottles of water. He selected another bottle of water, and drank half of it in one gulp.

Marta filled a knapsack with food and water and strapped a hunting knife to her ankle.

"Not too fast," she told Halverson, taking small gulps from her water bottle. "You'll get sick."

"Thanks for your help, Adam," said Halverson. "We better be pushing off."

"Got somewhere to go, huh?" said Adam. "Where do people go nowadays with the world a nuked-out wasteland?"

"We're going to see my brother," said Marta.

Adam nodded. "Family. That's what it's all about. I wish I still had somebody left in mine," he said, and fell to brooding.

"We owe you our lives. We appreciate your help."

"If you meet a doctor on your trip, could you tell him to come here and check me out?"

"Of course."

"It's getting harder to pee since I ran out of my hormone pills for my prostate. I guess the cancer cells are growing. What happens when I can' t pee anymore?"

You die of uremia, thought Halverson, but held his tongue.

"When we come back this way, we'll check on you," he said.

He strapped his knapsack to his back and exited. Marta strapped on hers and followed him.

Hunched over, Adam made for the door. "When this apocalypse thing is over, let me know. Will you? I'm totally out of touch here."

"Sure thing," said Halverson, figuring Adam would be dead by the time the apocalypse ended—if it ever ended.

Maybe all three of them would be dead.

Chapter 34

"We need to get at least one of our air ducts open before we suffocate," said Uriah, standing in the presidential office in the Mount Weather bunker holding his hand up in front of the wire grid covering his air vent and not feeling any air blow against his flesh.

He coughed on the fetid air.

On the shelf behind his desk stood a bust of Ulysses S. Grant. To the right of the bust stood the American flag that hung from a pole with a gold plastic replica of a bald eagle crowning it.

The office desktop was marred with hundreds of scars etched by knives, where Mims used to play Bishop's knife game with his Secret Service agent Dakota Jones, a middle-aged Sioux Indian, who stood now in the office clad in a dark suit watching the proceedings, his hands at his sides. Mims loved the movie *Alien* and played the knife game often with Dakota.

Uriah glanced at Dakota's left hand which had only two fingers. "You must have hated Mims."

Dakota's face remained expressionless. "He was president."

"Why are we suffocating in here, Kowalski? Speak up, man."

"The ghouls keep crawling into the air ducts and blocking them, sir," said Kowalski, a thirty-five-year-old SEAL with a brush cut and ears that pressed so close to his head that they appeared to be glued to his scalp.

Stocky and musclebound, he stood five nine.

"Get the ghouls out of the vents," said Uriah like he was stating the obvious.

"As soon as we get them out, they crawl back in."

"Isn't there some kind of wire cover over the vent opening outside?"

"There used to be a steel grid, but the ghouls managed to dislodge it."

"Install a new grid in front of the vent so they can't enter."

Kowalski squirmed. "The ghouls broke the fixtures that attach the grid to the duct outside."

"Can't you attach the grid with angle irons to the steel duct? That should hold the ghouls out so we can breathe."

Kowalski thought about it. "If I could scrounge some angle irons, we could weld the grid to the duct walls."

"Do you have a welder?"

"We sure do, sir. But first we need to clear away the ghouls that are jammed inside the air duct."

"Get your squad together and clear it before we all suffocate."

"We have to kill them first then drag their corpses out."

"Do whatever you have to."

"Yes, sir."

Kowalski bolted out the office to round up a squad and obey Uriah's orders.

"Wait a minute, Kowalski."

Kowalski stopped on a dime, wheeled around, and faced Uriah. "Sir?"

"Have you heard anything about the two assassins Halverson and Marta?"

"We have no way to communicate with Purdy, Mr. President."

"Comms are still down?"

"The EMP knocked them out. The nuclear blast toppled all cell towers in this area."

"Purdy hasn't returned yet?" said Uriah, furrowing his brow with concern.

"No, sir. He's still out there hunting the assassins."

"I had hoped he would have returned by now." Uriah paused in thought. "What about that guy Mims sent to Raven Rock before he was assassinated? What's his name?"

"Rocco."

"Right. Did he ever report back?"

"No, sir."

"Send Dr. Morrow here before you work on the duct."

"Yes, sir."

Kowalski belted away.

Dakota stood with his hands behind his back, watching Uriah.

PURGE

"You can leave the room now, Dakota," said Uriah.
Dakota did so.

Chapter 35

Dr. Morrow entered the president's office ten minutes later, his face grave.

Uriah leaned against his desk, struggling to breathe.

"Doctor, I need to know how much longer we can hold out with the current oxygen supply we've got."

"Maybe a couple more hours."

"I need you to be precise."

"Three more hours, tops, under current conditions."

Uriah stroked his chin, deep in thought. "What if current conditions changed?"

"Then our time left would change."

"Suppose I ordered some of our residents out of the bunker."

"Our air supply would last longer," said Morrow, startled by the suggestion.

"Is the radiation level outside safe for humans?"

"It depends on how long they stay outside in this area. There's still radioactivity outside, but it's not nearly as strong as it was several days ago."

"So people could survive outside if they left the bunker?"

"For a while if the ghouls didn't eat them, that is."

"Or course, I wouldn't send unarmed people outside. What do you take me for?"

Dr. Morrow said nothing, his expression bleak.

"Don't you see what I'm saying?" said Uriah. "It's pointless for us all to die of suffocation in three hours. Does that make any sense?"

"Yeah."

"Kowalski can't possibly clear the main air duct of ghouls and seal it with a new steel grid in three hours."

An ineffable sadness filled Morrow's eyes. "I suppose not."

"Then you agree with me? I knew you would," said Uriah, becoming energized.

"It's not my decision to make," said Morrow, remaining noncommittal.

"No, it isn't." Uriah paused a beat. "*Uneasy lies the head that wears a crown.* Now I know what Shakespeare meant by those words."

"Do you want a sleeping pill?"

"I don't know what I'd do without you, Doctor. It was you who told me Mims was hogging all the oxygen in the bunker for himself."

"I couldn't keep it a secret. I found his actions deplorable."

"Maybe he'd still be alive today if he wasn't so corrupt."

"I never thought Halverson would kill him, though. Halverson wasn't even here when Mims was hoarding all the oxygen for himself."

"Halverson did it because he failed his mission and Mims chewed him out. Halverson retaliated with a knife. With him the only answer is violence. He thinks he can do whatever he wants because he's a CIA black ops agent."

"Maybe . . . But I think the assassin may be closer to home and is still here."

"Do you have proof?" said Uriah, taken aback.

"Just a hunch. Halverson's been through a lot—"

"We all have, Doctor."

"True—"

"He hates our democracy because it keeps him from doing whatever he wants. Our government is all that stands between us and chaos, and Halverson hates that."

Morrow frowned. "I gave him a short psychological exam when he returned from his mission to retrieve the vaccine against the zombie plague—"

"A mission he failed."

"Whatever. He passed the test with flying colors."

"He's a sociopath, Doctor. Sociopaths can beat lie detectors and psych exams."

"I'm not satisfied with his motive for assassination. Could somebody have hired him to assassinate Mims?"

Uriah chewed it over. "I guess that's possible. But I doubt it. Who hates democracy more than Halverson? I can't think of a soul. Halverson assassinated Mims on his own. He did it with his cohort Marta Costello, of course."

Morrow wasn't satisfied. "How do you explain the note about a purge that the assassin pinned to Mims's chest with a knife?"

"Halverson left it there to divert attention from himself, to make it look like the assassination was the work of a cabal of conspirators secreted inside our bunker. How better to spread fear and paranoia among us and cripple our government? The man is diabolical. There are those who think he's the devil himself."

Morrow shook his head slowly. "That's not what I hear. A lot of the men look up to him. They think of him as a legend."

Uriah pursed his lips. "A legend in his own mind." He paused. "All assassins must pay the penalty for their actions. They must be executed." He went on a coughing jag. "Hopefully, the SEALs can remove the ghouls from the air vent and seal it with a steel grid so we can start breathing real air soon. Until that time we need to conserve oxygen. Tell the residents to pick lots to find out who needs to leave the bunker for the rest of us to continue to get enough oxygen."

"Why do *I* have to do it?"

"You're a doctor. They trust you."

"We're gonna get some angry people here when the losers are picked."

"Tell them what you told me. That the air outside is not radioactive enough to kill the ones who leave the bunker."

"It's not gonna kill them, but it's not gonna do them any good, either."

"Leave out that part."

"You're not a whole lot different than the air hog Mims," said Morrow under his breath.

"What? I didn't hear you."

"Nothing."

Morrow kept his lips sealed. He didn't want to end up being one of those ordered to volunteer to leave the bunker.

Chapter 36

Halverson and Marta feasted on beef jerky, peanut butter, and Cheerios while sitting at the cashier's counter in the dry goods store. They kept gulping water from their plastic bottles to slake their thirst.

When they finished eating and were heading for the door of the dry goods store, a roly-poly, fiftyish Asian female ghoul wearing a brown dress slogged through the doorway, growling and slobbering on the floor. Spotting them with her milky eyes, she came after them.

Marta snatched a hammer from her knapsack, charged the ghoul, and smashed her in the head three times. The final blow smashed through the fractured skull into the brain and rendered it into pulp. The ghoul crumpled on the floor, her milky eyes gazing into infinity.

"I'm glad we already ate," said Marta, disgusted by the dead ghoul.

She looked away and yawned.

"I can't believe how tired I feel," she said.

"Me too," said Halverson. "This might be the best place to crash."

"I dunno," said Marta, casting around the store. "I don't feel very safe in here with the broken window and door. More looters or ghouls could walk in."

Halverson peered out the broken window. He didn't see any ghouls outside.

"We could sack out behind the counter," he said. "Nobody would see us there."

"Maybe Adam would let us into his shelter."

"I doubt he wants to be bothered by us again. If we go back to him, he's gonna think we're gonna steal his shelter from him."

"He seemed pretty nice to me. A bit eccentric but—"

"As long as we didn't plan on staying with him he was nice. If we go back there, he's gonna be suspicious of us."

"Maybe . . ."

"We have to sleep sometime. We were traveling most of last night."

"Well, this is better than sleeping on the road or in the woods."

"It'll be dark in another hour or so."

"How can we travel in the dark?"

"We just have to take it slow like last night."

"Uriah's hit squad will catch up to us while we sleep."

"That would be true if the road wasn't clogged with abandoned vehicles. They can't drive around all of them with their government Suburbans. They're gonna waste a lot of time using the Suburbans to push the vehicles out of their way."

"That's not gonna stop Michael K. The High Rolerz have motorcycles that can ride around the dumped cars."

Halverson yawned. "Maybe you're right. Maybe we shouldn't sleep now. I feel wiped out, though. If I sit down, I'm gonna crash."

"I know. I'm beat too."

"We have to sleep some time."

"I'll bring our bikes inside. I don't like leaving them on the road where anybody could steal them. Then we can hash out our next move."

Marta went outside to the road and retrieved her bicycle then Halverson's. She placed them inside the dry goods store. She surveyed the store.

"Where are you?" she said, puzzled.

She walked around the store, searching for him. She reached the counter and peeked behind it.

His eyes shut, Halverson was lying on his back fast asleep.

She thought about waking him up but decided not to. She felt more like joining him. She sat on the floor behind the counter, braced her back against the wall, and nodded off.

Chapter 37

When Halverson woke up, he didn't realize where he was at first. Then he remembered he was at the dry goods store. Scoffing up his MP9 he stood up. He hadn't intended to fall asleep, but after he had sat down on the floor he couldn't help it.

Where was Marta?

He didn't see her anywhere in the store. He saw her bike, but she was nowhere to be seen. Her H&K MP5 was lying beside her knapsack of food on the floor behind the counter. He latched onto the MP5 and slung it over his shoulders followed by her knapsack. She wouldn't have left behind her food supply and her gun voluntarily.

"Marta," he said.

No answer.

He became alert. Something must have happened to her.

He sprang to the broken window and gazed outside. She wasn't on the road.

He didn't believe that she would go off on her own without telling him. He had promised he would go with her to meet her brother in DC, and he intended to keep his promise. He glanced at her bicycle. If she had struck out for DC by herself, why had she left her bike behind? Something must have happened to her. Had a ghoul gotten her? If so, why didn't it attack him while he was sleeping?

He didn't think he could bear seeing her as a ghoul. He had already gone through that nightmare with Victoria, his friend to the end—until she wasn't. Until she wasn't human anymore. Until she was one of the living dead.

Had someone kidnaped Marta? One of the High Rolerz? But why would they take her and leave him behind? He was the one who had killed Bobby K. Marta had taken no part in it.

It was his fault. He never should have fallen asleep. If he had been awake, he could have helped her. Or could have tried.

Maybe Adam had heard something.

Halverson skirred to Adam's bomb shelter and rapped on the steel door.

"It's me Halverson," he said at the steel door.

He tried the doorknob and wasn't surprised when it wouldn't turn.

"You can't have your fancy gun back," said Adam. "We made a fair deal."

"I don't want it back."

Halverson glanced at his wristwatch, trying to ascertain how long he had been sleeping. He estimated it had been the best part of two hours.

"What do you want?" said Adam.

"Did you hear anything here in the store for the last two hours?"

"What?"

Halverson raised his voice and repeated his question.

"I can barely hear you," said Adam. "The answer to your question is no. What was I supposed to hear?"

"I dunno. I was sleeping."

"It's not safe to sleep out there. The door and the windows are broken. I hear looters in there all the time and ghouls shambling around, knocking things over."

"But nothing in the last two hours?"

"Correct."

"Marta's gone. I can't find her."

"Sorry to hear it."

"If you open your door, it will be easier for us to talk."

"I don't have anything to say. You're the one doing the talking."

"I can't understand why she didn't scream and wake me so I could help her."

"I mind my own business. I don't want to know what's going on out there. I know it's bad. The ghouls and outlaws own the land. Nobody's safe. I suggest you hole up somewhere or they're gonna get you."

"Do you have any ideas where Marta could have gone?"

No answer.

Halverson knocked on the steel door again.

"I hear you," said Adam. "You're wasting your time peppering me with questions. I can't help you. If you don't stop knocking on my door, the ghouls will hear you and come."

Halverson had a sudden thought. "Are you in there, Marta?"

"Are you nuts?" said Adam. "*I* didn't take her. There's barely enough air in here for me alone. I got a small generator pumping fresh air in the shelter. Not enough for two."

"Say something, Marta, if you're there."

"Didn't you hear what I said?"

"Give me a sign that you're there, Marta."

Halverson listened intently for any sound to emanate from Adam's bunker.

If Adam had taken her, he would have jacked her MP5 as well thanks to his fascination with machine pistols. Adam seemed like a decent guy who owned a shop and had given them plenty of food whereas a lot of other people in his place wouldn't have been so generous. Halverson believed him.

Halverson mulled it over. The ghouls wouldn't have taken Marta hostage. They would have torn her apart and eaten her in the store and then eaten him while he slept. Somebody else must have kidnaped her. But who?

Or did she get cold feet and decide to return to Mount Weather? That option didn't track. He couldn't see her returning to the bunker knowing that the sociopath Michael K. and his High Rolerz loomed in her path.

Halverson retreated to the broken front door and gazed at the road to DC. Whoever had kidnaped her must have gone in that direction—unless they didn't know the homicidal High Rolerz were patrolling the opposite direction. But Marta would know. She would have warned the kidnaper to head toward DC.

He felt forlorn. How was he going to find her in this wilderness of horrors?

Staying here would accomplish nothing. He had to find her. By now the High Rolerz must be very close indeed.

Halverson rolled the two bikes out of the shop onto the road. He would take Marta's bike with him along with her MP5 and her knapsack of food strapped on his back, making his load cumbersome and apt to cause him to lose his balance. But he believed he would find her, and she would need her food and supplies for them to continue to DC.

He felt guilty for her kidnaping, but how was he supposed to prevent himself from falling asleep while she was kidnaped? Kicking himself wouldn't solve anything. He had to get over the guilt and keep going. The strong feeling she was in danger gnawed at him.

He mounted his bike, managing with difficulty to keep his balance on account of the extra weight he was carrying. Holding onto Marta's bike he weaved down the road in the direction of DC. After a while, becoming accustomed to his load, he was able to maintain his balance and ride in a straight line while guiding her bike at his side.

Chapter 38

A lone motorcycle drove toward the High Rolerz, who were straddling their Harleys and waiting to find out what Michael K. wanted to do after he had strangled Rocco.

Tying his necktie around his neck to look neat as he stood, Michael K. signaled to the rider to approach.

His thick shoulder-length brown hair blowing in the wind, pushing thirty, the rider drove to Michael K. The rider was wearing a black leather vest. Instead of fringe hanging from the bottom of the vest, shrunken heads dangled from wires.

"What's up, Darren?" said Michael K.

"We got company behind us moving fast."

"Are they gonna be trouble?"

Darren nodded. "Three black Chevy Suburban SUVs. The lead car is flying the American flag."

"Government vehicles."

"What do we think of the government, boys and girls?" said Michael K., addressing the High Rolerz.

They booed and gave the thumbs down.

"They're the ones who nuked our country and turned it into a radioactive wasteland," cried a fortyish tattooed skinhead, straddling his chopper.

"They don't give a damn about us," said a peroxide blonde in her thirties near him, a tat of a coiled rattlesnake on her right arm, two grenades strapped across her chest. "All they care about is power—their power."

"Should we give them a taste of *our* power?" said Michael K.

The High Rolerz cheered and whistled.

"Being that there are government vehicles headed this way, we gotta figure the people inside them are armed to the teeth."

The High Rolerz grumbled and muttered among themselves.

"Are we gonna let that stop us?" said Michael K.

"No," they cried, brandishing their machetes, their AR-15s, and sundry rifles and pistols.

"How soon will they get here?" said Michael K.

"Ten minutes max," said Darren. "They can't move as fast as us because we can weave between the abandoned cars on the road."

"Kudos to you for stating the obvious."

Darren felt embarrassed.

Michael K. eyeballed the tunnel with its three corpses hanging in its mouth.

"We can get through the Tunnel of Death faster than they can," he said. "They're gonna have to plow the abandoned cars and trucks out of their way in there while the ghouls attack. Let's wait for them on the other side and see what they want." He glanced at the ghouls hanging from the tree limbs and writhing in futility. "Look at those idiots up there."

Some of the bikers laughed at the hanging ghouls.

"OK, let's get serious, boys and girls," said Michael K. "We got a powwow with government bigwigs coming up."

He mounted his Harley, fired the ignition, and rode into the tunnel with the motorcycle headlights on.

The High Rolerz followed him on their chugging hogs.

"What do they want with us?" said Darren, riding up to Michael K.

"I'm getting the feeling we might have to teach them a lesson."

"Lesson?"

"Like who runs this wasteland they made of our country. Not a bunch of cowards hiding in a bunker with their tails between their legs while we're out here whacking ghouls and getting nuked by our so-called government."

"Man, that's right."

Michael K. gave him a look. "Didn't you snort blow today?"

"I—I—"

"Kind a slow, huh?"

"I—I—"

"Never mind. I'll do the thinking for both of us."

Chapter 39

A bearded, burly man of repugnant odor was standing at an angle behind Marta wearing a coonskin cap like Davy Crockett. Marta figured him to be in his fifties. Dried snot crusted his mustache. Even though he was holding her six feet away from him, she could still smell him. His stench nauseated her. She wished she could stand farther away from him, but the snake tongs gripping her neck prevented her from going anywhere. Her hands fastened behind her back with a rope, she was forced to walk with him.

Fitfully he would squeeze the grip on the other end of the six-foot-long snake tongs, forcing the jaws to dig deeper into her throat with their serrated edges.

She grimaced in pain. He shoved her forward.

At his side walked a sad-eyed black and brown mutt that would whine every time Coonskin would kick him for no reason at all, which was often.

In fact, it was the mutt's whining that had attracted her attention back at the dry goods store. She had heard the whining right after she had noticed Halverson had fallen asleep behind the counter. She had gone outside the store with the intention of helping the poor dog, leaving her gun behind because she hadn't thought she would need it.

Which was when Stinky had jumped her, covering her mouth and preventing her from screaming. He immediately attached the snake tongs around her neck and told her he would squeeze them harder if she attempted to scream. The tongs were already hurting her, cutting her flesh. Applying more pressure on them would cause her excruciating pain. They were so tight now that several streams of blood were streaking her throat.

It was lucky he hadn't entered the store or he might have found Halverson and killed him. He probably had already looted the place and saw no need to bother doing it again.

"What do you want with me?" she contrived to say through a dry throat.

"I want a slave."

You came to the wrong place.

"Who are you?" she said.

"Gozzard."

"Is that your real name?"

"Real name, fake name. What difference does it make nowadays with the apocalypse? What's your name?"

"Marta."

The dog whined.

Gozzard kicked him in the hind hip.

The dog whined louder as the kick lifted him off the ground.

"Why are you torturing your dog?" said Marta, appalled.

"Because I can. There's no ASPCA anymore. He makes too much noise anyway."

"He wouldn't whine if you didn't kick him so much."

Gozzard waved his hand at her. "What do *you* know? Nothing."

"What's his name?"

"Buzzard."

"That's a horrible name for a dog. No wonder he's sad all the time."

"If he doesn't like it, he can leave." He glanced at Buzzard. "But he never will. He knows who his meal ticket is."

She noticed Gozzard had a rifle slung over his shoulder and a revolver wedged inside his waistband. If she could just get closer to him, she could relieve him of the revolver . . . But it was impossible with the jaws of the snake tongs gripping her neck. They forced her to stay six feet away from him at all times.

"Why do you hate everybody?" she said.

"Everybody hates me. We got no country left. All we got is ourselves. And everybody knows it. That's why everybody hates everybody else. All of us got to scrounge for food like pack rats. We're all fighting for the same food. We don't have stores anymore where you can buy food. I need you to serve as my slave to help me get food."

"I don't want to be your slave."

He gripped the handle of the tongs harder, squeezing their jaws tighter around her throat. She groaned in agony.

"I don't want to have to kill you," he said. "I had to kill my other slave. That's why I need a new one."

The blood drained from Marta's face. She knew her life was hanging by a thread. This guy would kill her with the slightest provocation.

Maybe he needed attention. A lot of people these days were roaming around the wastelands trying to process what had happened to their lives. One day they were well off with plenty of food and a place to live, the next they were prowling around the ruins searching for crumbs—if they weren't already dead and turned into ghouls. A lot of the survivors couldn't handle the drastic changes the apocalypse had wrought in their lives. This Gozzard guy could be one of them.

He sounded like he was alone all the time. Maybe he needed someone to listen to him.

"What did you do before the plague?" she said.

"I booked passengers for flights."

"You were around people all the time in your job."

"Yeah. But nobody flies anymore. The airports are closed down, overrun by ghouls."

"Maybe if you socialized, you would feel better."

Gozzard rounded on her. "Feel better? What's that got to do with anything? I'm fighting for my life trying to make ends meet. I'm doing what has to be done. If I don't do it, I die. I feel like shit, is what I feel."

"Life is hard for everyone."

"You need to shut up. You're a slave. You aren't permitted to talk unless I say so."

Gozzard kicked Buzzard in the hind hip. Buzzard yelped in pain.

"Stop it," said Marta. "You're hurting him."

"If you don't shut up, I'm gonna kick you too."

Sticking out his tongue at her and biting it, Gozzard squeezed the tongs handle, tightening the serrated jaws around her neck.

"Ow," she cried. "You could kill me with that thing. What if you cut my carotid artery?"

Gozzard put his tongue back in his mouth. "You'd die."

"Then stop squeezing that grip."

"You're my slave. You have no right to give me orders."

Gozzard squeezed the tongs handle again.

Marta cried out.

"As long as you remember you're my slave, there'll be no problems," said Gozzard.

Marta glowered at him.

"I'm gonna break you if it kills me," he said, returning her glower.

If she wasn't so exhausted, maybe she could figure out a way to escape. But the only thing she could think about was sleep. Her mind was slowing down.

"Follow my orders," he said, "and we'll be fine. I know what I'm doing. Most of the people in this country are dead, but I'm still here. Follow my orders and we'll both survive. Disobey me at your own risk."

She was sick of smelling his stench and listening to his lies. Fear-pumped adrenaline was keeping her walking. She knew if she stopped walking, he'd squeeze the tongs around her neck.

Buzzard looked at her and whined, seeming to commiserate with her plight.

They were in the hands of a monster. You couldn't reason with a monster. Marta kept her own counsel and told herself to keep walking despite her difficulty in keeping awake. Somehow she had to keep her heavy eyelids open. She yawned. She cut off her yawn when she felt the serrated edges of the tongs bite into her throat.

"You need permission to yawn like you do for everything else," said Gozzard. "Don't start thinking you're free, because you ain't. You're my slave."

"I'm nobody's slave."

Gozzard squeezed the tongs handle, applying pressure to her neck.

She grimaced in pain, barely suppressing a scream.

"Why are you slowing down?" said Gozzard.

"I'm tired."

"I didn't tell you you could slow down."

"Where are we going?"

"To find food. You're gonna find food for me. Keep looking, slave."

How she hated Gozzard. Breathing his fetid stench was bad enough, but having her ears bombarded with his delusion that he was her master was insufferable. His abhorrent treatment of his dog was in itself a crime.

She made up her mind she was going to kill Gozzard.

Chapter 40

Michael K. straddled his Harley on the other side of the Tunnel of Death.

"Get out the spike strip," he said.

A gangly guy in his late twenties with a mohawk unfurled the rolled-up spike strip with the help of two bearded men with potbellies, who latched onto the other end of the strip and pulled it across the entire width of the road.

"That's right," said Michael K. "Put the spike strip down at the mouth of the tunnel."

The three men flattened the strip against the tarmac, pulling it tight between them on either side of the road.

"What if the feds see it?" said Darren, standing next to Michael K.

"They're gonna be coming out of there like bats out of hell once they get past the last abandoned car in the tunnel. They're not gonna have time to hit the brakes and stop."

"I dunno," said Darren, scratching his long hair. "Some of these fed cars got run-flat tires the last I heard."

"You got bugs or something?"

Darren stopped scratching his scalp.

"There's something to what you say," said Michael K. "The feds spend all our taxpayers' money on state-of-the-art weapons and fancy cars. We gotta disable the first Suburban so it'll stop and trap the ones behind it in the tunnel. The object is to pin them in the tunnel and rain bullets on them."

"If they got run-flat tires, they're not gonna stop, boss."

"I don't know what I'd do without you, Darren."

Darren looked puzzled like he couldn't figure out if what Michael K. had said was compliment or sarcasm.

"Do you have any suggestions?" said Michael K.

"Uh—I—uh—"

"I do," cut in Michael K. "What if we lined a bunch of our hogs across the road after the spike strip and blockaded it?"

"The lead Suburban would have to stop or crash."

"If the spike strip doesn't stop him, the hogs will."

Darren scratched his head again. "Do you think they could run over our hogs? Those Suburbans are big and heavy with big tires."

"We'll put six rows of hogs blocking the road. What do you think the driver will do?"

"I dunno."

"Slam on his brakes. He's not gonna want to plow into six rows of hogs. Why would he risk it? He would get out of his SUV and have his men clear the hogs out of the way. Isn't that what most people would do?"

"Wouldn't he wonder why the hogs are there?"

"He would indeed. *After* he stopped his vehicle."

Darren shuffled his feet. "Are we gonna whack these guys?"

"The only good fed is a dead fed."

Darren chuckled. "Yeah, boss."

"We don't want them invading our territory. Wherever the feds move in, they take over."

"And make a mess of everything. They were the ones who nuked our country."

"To kill the ghouls. But the feds' ICBMs with nuke payloads killed more people than the ghouls did and spread radiation everywhere."

"Maybe the feds came here to whack us."

Michael K. nodded, grim-faced. "We're gonna turn the tables on them."

Darren strained his ears. "I think I can hear the motorcade approaching."

"OK. Get six rows of hogs lined up behind the spike strip."

"You got it, boss," said Darren, and made to leave.

"We still got time. The motorcade will have to slow down after it enters the tunnel with abandoned vehicles blocking the road."

Darren nodded yes.

"Wait a second." Michael K. surveyed the tree-lined mountainside that loomed over the tunnel. "I'm wondering if we could send a team over the mountainside on foot and set up an ambush on the other end of the tunnel in case the feds try to retreat."

Darren eyeballed the mountainside. "I can get a team ready in seconds."

"But tell them not to open fire on the Suburbans when they approach. Let the vehicles enter the tunnel. Then spring the trap."

"Got it, boss."

"I figure those Suburbans are bulletproof. We're not gonna be able to whack anybody till they exit their cars."

"That's what they'll have to do when they clear away the spike strip."

Michael K. mulled it over, furrowing his brow.

"We need to knock the lead vehicle over with grenades," he said. "That way it'll block the path of its followers. The feds will be trapped in the tunnel with the ghouls."

"We got plenty of grenades, boss."

"You smell like a wet dog," said Michael K., sniffing the air.

"Boss?"

"Never mind. When the first Suburban is about to exit the tunnel, lob grenades under the chassis and roll the car over with their blast. Once it's tipped over, they'll never be able to set it upright. Those things weigh tons. They would need a crane to right it."

Darren stood listening to him, hanging on every word.

"Is there something you don't understand?"

"I understand, boss."

"Then why are you standing there?"

Darren hustled away to set the plan in motion.

Chapter 41

An MP5 strapped to his shoulder, Purdy was sitting shotgun in the second Suburban when he noticed the first Suburban slowing down ahead of him. Purdy tapped the walkie-talkie perched on his shoulder.

"Angel One, this is Angel Two. Why are you slowing down? Over."

"This is Angel One," said a staticky voice. "There's a tunnel up ahead with three corpses hanging by the neck in the entrance. Over."

"Are they humans or ghouls? Over."

"Human stiffs. It looks like some kind of warning to keep out—"

"We're the United States government. Nobody can keep us out of anywhere. This is our land. Over."

"What do you want me to do, sir? Over."

"Enter the tunnel slowly because we don't know what's in it. Over."

"Roger, sir."

"Is the tunnel lit? Over."

"It's pitch-black. There are ghouls hanging by the neck from trees on the sides of the road too. Over."

"Do they scare you? Over."

"Not at all, sir. Actually they look funny writhing up in the trees. Ha ha. Over."

"There are probably abandoned cars in the tunnel so we'll have to go slow and maneuver around them, or push them out of the way if we can't. Over."

"Yes, sir. Over."

"Put your headlights on high. Over and out."

"What's that all about?" said Guevara at the wheel, a cropped, beetle-browed thirty-three-year-old SEAL with a bone frog tattoo etched on his chest that Purdy could see because Guevara's button-down shirt was open at the collar.

"Somebody's marking their territory with hanged stiffs," said Purdy. "What they *think* is their territory, anyway. This public road is the territory of the United States government. Nobody else can claim it as theirs."

"Do we go in with guns blazing, sir?"

"I want to find out what's in the tunnel first. If people are in the tunnel, why don't they have their lights on? Why would they sit around in the dark? I doubt the people that hanged the bodies are inside the tunnel."

"OK, sir."

"I want to meet the people that hanged these guys. They might have seen Halverson and Costello pass this way. If we go in guns blazing, they won't want to talk to us."

"Something tells me they're not gonna welcome us with open arms."

"We need intel. We'll get it out of them one way or the other. They want rough, we'll give them rough. We need to know if we're on Halverson's trail or whether we lost him."

Purdy watched Angel One drive slowly beneath the hanging cadavers into the dark tunnel. Angel One's high beams flooded the interior of the tunnel with light.

"Let's see what happens before we enter," said Purdy.

"Right," said Guevara, stopping the second Suburban before the tunnel entrance.

"What do you see, Angel One? Over," said Purdy into his shoulder mic.

"Abandoned cars blocking parts of the road, sir," came back the reply. "Over."

"Is that all? Over."

"Oh wait. Crap. There is a bunch of ghouls in here. They're swarming toward us, attracted by our lights. Man, they're ugly. Over."

"Don't worry. They can't get inside your vehicle. Keep your windows rolled up. Over."

"Do you want us to proceed through the tunnel, sir? Over."

"Yes. Over."

"Are you coming in behind us, sir?"

"Yes. Over and out."

"I don't like this," Purdy said, turning toward Guevara at the wheel. "What if those ghouls were put inside the tunnel by the same people who hanged these men at the entrance?"

"It wouldn't surprise me," said Guevara, stopped at the entrance. "Do you want me to follow Angel One? What if this tunnel is boobytrapped?"

Purdy thought about it. "I don't think so. The people claiming this tunnel wouldn't want to risk blowing it up with a landmine or an IED. They want it in usable condition or it's no good to them."

"I see what you mean. Do you want me to follow Angel One?"

"Not yet. Wait a bit. Just in case they run into something else in there." Purdy glanced at his wristwatch. "Give them five minutes. Then we go in."

Guevara shot him a look.

"We're not abandoning them," said Purdy. "I just want to know a little more about the tunnel interior before we enter. Are we gonna run into a conflict?"

"Yes, sir."

"Angel Two, this is Angel One. Over."

"Go ahead, Angel One," said Purdy into his shoulder mic. "Over."

"Some of these pickups abandoned in the road are gonna be hard to bypass. Over."

"Can we plow them out of the way with our bull bars? Over."

"I think so, but there's not a lot of room on either side of the road. In any case, It's gonna slow us down, sir. Over."

"As long as we can get through, we're good. I don't want us to get trapped in there." Purdy paused. "How are you handling the ghouls? Over."

"If they get in the way, we run them over, sir. Otherwise we ignore them. Over."

Purdy nodded yes. "Good."

"With all due respect, why aren't you following us, sir? Over."

"I want to make sure you can reach the other end of the tunnel. Do you think you can? Over."

"I believe so, sir, but I can't see the other end of the tunnel because there's a jog in the tunnel. When I get around the jog, I'll know for sure. Over."

"Proceed. Over and out." Purdy exchanged looks with Guevara. "Let's go inside."

Guevara fired the ignition, shifted into drive, and drove into the tunnel, flicking on his high beams. The Suburban behind them followed.

Chapter 42

Marta didn't think she could stand being with Gozzard much longer. She watched him withdraw a bottle of bourbon from a cargo pocket in his trousers and take a long pull on it. Maybe if he got drunk, she would be able to break free.

"I don't like that look on your face," he said. "Are you thinking about escaping? If you are, forget about it. You ought to be thinking about how to better serve your master."

Marta snickered.

Gozzard squeezed the grip on the snake tongs, clamping the tongs harder around her neck.

"Ow," she cried.

"I will not tolerate disrespect from my slave."

"I'm not your goddamn slave."

Gozzard shook the tongs backward and forward, the serrated jaws of the tongs digging deeper into Marta's neck, drawing more blood.

She screwed up her face in agony. "My cuts are gonna get infected with that dirty thing around my neck."

"Then stop fighting me. Obey me, and things will go easier for you. I treat my slaves well."

She wanted to scream at him she wasn't his slave, but she decided to repress it, knowing he would inflict more pain on her throat. She didn't know how this rotten creep had managed to live so long without getting himself killed. Maybe it was his very rottenness that kept him alive in a world as depraved as this one. Or maybe he was living a charmed life.

His life would soon end when she took him out. The problem was, as long as he had her trapped in these snake tongs, she couldn't do anything to get within six feet of him. Which meant she needed a gun to kill him. She couldn't throw a knife with any accuracy. No gun no way. How was she gonna get a gun while she was snared at the end of these tongs?

Halverson might be able to help her if he woke up in time. Gozzard and she were walking while Halverson had a bicycle. He could easily catch up to them depending on when he awoke.

She couldn't count on Halverson to save her, though. In the end you couldn't count on anybody but yourself. Somehow she had to get ahold of the revolver snugged in Gozzard's waistband. She couldn't do much of anything until he fell asleep. Then maybe she could find a six-foot-long tree limb and relieve Gozzard of his piece or at least club him in the head. Except she couldn't make a move without waking him up.

"Where are we going?" she said.

"To my business."

She couldn't believe Gozzard had his own business. How could anyone run their own business during the apocalypse? Who was left to buy their products?

"What do you make?" she said.

"I don't make anything. I run a service."

She couldn't figure out what kind of service he would be able to run during these dire times.

"We're almost there," he said.

Marta couldn't believe her eyes when she saw a wall constructed of human skulls cemented together blocking the road ahead.

"Here we are," said Gozzard, approaching the obscene wall.

"I don't get it."

Chapter 43

"This is my toll booth," said Gozzard, puffing out his chest with pride as he took in his wall of death. "In order to continue driving on this road you have to pay me a toll so I'll open my blockade. If you don't, you don't pass."

"What kind of toll?" said Marta. "Money's no good these days."

"They trade me food or other supplies. Clothing, ammo, whatever." He gazed down at his beat-up shoes. They looked like clown shoes thanks to their bigness. "I need a new pair of shoes, but it's hard to find somebody with the same size foot as me."

"What if they don't trade with you?"

"If they don't, I don't let them pass. The gate in the wall remains shut."

"What if they decide to ram through it?"

"You ask too many questions," he said, staring at her. "But I'll tell you because I'm proud of my work. If they try to ram my wall, they'll get blown to smithereens."

Marta eyeballed the wall of skulls. She didn't see any dynamite attached to any of the skulls.

"How?" she said. "Skulls don't blow up when they're rammed."

"These do. Every other skull has nitroglycerin in it. Jostle those babies just a tad and they'll explode and send a car flying through the air. Nitroglycerin is notoriously unstable. It doesn't take much to set it off."

"Where did you get nitroglycerin?"

"I raided one of the coal mines in West Virginia. They have coal mines all over the place. The mine I hit was deserted except for ghouls shambling around. It was easy to loot the nitro from the mine company's storeroom. The tricky part was transporting it without having it blow up in my face. I used a wheelbarrow to transport it, and I made sure I walked slow."

"How do you stay in business with the wall blown apart?"

"I have one of my slaves rebuild it. That's where you come in."

That's what you think.

"Oddly enough," he went on, "I've only had one person try to ram it. He's now lying in pieces strewn in the forest." Gozzard chuckled. "There's always a wise guy who thinks he can game the system and get away with it."

"Most people just hand over all their food and supplies to you?" said Marta, incredulous.

"Well, I'm not a hog. I don't make them give me everything they have—unless they have hardly anything to their name. Then I have no choice. I mean, business is business. I can't run this business without getting something in return."

"Your 'business' sounds like extortion."

"Extortion? There's no extortion. There's no law so how can there be extortion?"

"Where's your toll booth?" she said, casting around the forest.

"I stay behind that big oak over there. When a car screeches to a halt in front of my wall, I come out from behind the tree and tell the driver how they can pass through the gate."

"And, of course, they can see you're armed."

"There's that."

"But it's not extortion?"

"I don't force them to pay me at gunpoint. I'm not a thug. I just tell them what they have to do to pass through the barrier. If they don't agree to my terms, they back up their cars and head elsewhere. But, like I said, most of them agree. They can see I'm operating a legitimate toll road here."

Marta sniggered. "Legitimate? How can it be legitimate? This road is public property. It's not yours."

"It is now," said Gozzard, directing a glare at her.

"I'm surprised nobody's taken you out."

"Not everybody is armed. Guns and ammo are hard to come by what with the gun shops all looted a long time ago."

Gozzard strode toward a massive oak, its trunk the better part of twenty feet wide.

Marta stumbled after him, the tong jaws biting her neck. She cursed Gozzard to herself every inch of the way. Whenever she couldn't keep up with him, he wrenched the snake tongs toward him, forcing her to run after him, or the jaws' serrated edges would dig into her flesh and draw blood. She was almost always bleeding. So far he hadn't cut the carotid artery or the jugular vein.

"Where are we going?" she said, grimacing in pain.

"My digs."

When they rounded the oak, Marta clapped her eyes on a crude shack completely hidden from the road by the oak. In front of the door she picked up on a puddle of vomit that couldn't have been over a few hours' old as it was still moist.

She pulled a face in disgust.

"My stomach's giving me trouble," explained Gozzard, noting the vomit.

He took a pull on his bourbon bottle.

The oak trunk formed the rear of the shack. The three other sides of the shack were constructed of plywood with a sheet of plywood forming the roof, slanted to keep the rain from accumulating on it. Black shingles were nailed to the plywood roof. The shack had ten-foot-wide sides that were eight-odd feet high.

"Pretty cozy, I must say," said Gozzard, admiring the shack.

"It doesn't have any windows," said Marta, struggling to keep the stench of the stale vomit that she was standing beside out of her nose.

"I couldn't find any glass all in one piece around here. I don't want wind blowing into the hut. It gets cold enough in there as it is."

Gozzard kicked Buzzard in the hindquarters and tied his leash to a sapling. The dog whimpered at the pain but sat obediently next to the tree. He whimpered again as he sat tentatively on his sore hindquarters.

Gozzard pulled open the door, which had a hole in it instead of a doorknob. He maneuvered away from the door so he could push

Marta inside the shack ahead of him. He entered and closed the door behind him.

Marta noticed bottles of booze stocked the shelves that lined the walls. Piled on the floor were boxes of cereal, cannisters of orange-flavored Tang, bottled water, jars of peanut butter, canned tamales, canned ravioli, and cans of SpaghettiOs.

Gozzard took in the liquor bottles, his eyes glittering. "I'm not gonna die of thirst."

Maybe if Gozzard got drunk enough, she could overpower him.

Being shut in an enclosed, unventilated space with Gozzard concentrated his stench. At least there was one good thing about the snake pole. It kept him six feet away from her so she didn't have to endure an even stronger whiff of his noisome odor.

"You can sit on that wooden crate, slave."

Marta's legs were killing her. She sat down awkwardly but gingerly on the crate so the tongs wouldn't chew into her neck.

She picked up on a bunch of brunette hair on the ground. It looked like a woman's wig.

"That's from my former slave," said Gozzard. "She refused to obey me. I had no other choice but to scalp her and kill her. Her body's in the woods."

Marta felt sick. She looked away from the hair and fortified her resolve to kill him.

"I will tell you my story so you'll feel better about being my slave for the rest of your life," said Gozzard, taking a seat on another wooden crate.

"You wish," said Marta under her breath with a jaundiced expression.

"I can't hear you. What did you say?"

"Nothing."

"The more you understand me, the more you'll like serving me."

Marta was barely able to suppress a guffaw, squirming in discomfort.

"Are you OK?"

"Something was tickling my throat."

"I don't want any more interruptions," he said, scowling at her.

She nodded, her face blank.

"I have lived a life of endless pain," said Gozzard. "I will begin."

Marta yawned.

Chapter 44

"I had a younger brother named Greg when I was growing up," said Gozzard. "We were friends, which isn't always true about brothers, I'm sure you know. Anyway, we went swimming in a swimming hole in a muddy river when we were kids. We were the only ones there. He was only eight at the time. There was a spare tire hanging from a rope tied to a tree branch that extended over the river. To get onto the tire you had to climb the tree, climb out on the limb, and then shinny down the rope until you could sit in the tire. Then you could swing back and forth across the river and dive into it.

"Greg managed to climb the tree, crawl across the limb, and shinny down the rope till he sat in the spare tire. It was his first time, you see, and he was really happy about being able to do it. He beat his naked chest and screamed like he was Tarzan, king of the jungle. I laughed with joy at the sight.

"He was able to kick his legs back and forth to make the tire swing out over the river. He was screaming and laughing and having a great time. He was swinging higher and higher. The problem was, he swung so high that he was directly over the branch, fell straight down, and slammed his head into the branch. Then he dropped into the water, unconscious, and the current swept him away."

Despite herself Marta found herself listening intently to Gozzard.

"I dove into the river but couldn't find him because the river was so dirty. The current was carrying him downstream and I couldn't see him.

"'Greg,' I cried. 'Where are you?'

"He didn't answer.

"I dogpaddled in the river, searching everywhere for Greg. For the life of me I could not see him anywhere. Then I swam with the current because I knew it would be carrying him downriver.

"I was terrified. He was my best friend. My only brother.

"I swam a couple miles downstream from the swimming hole and searched for him for the next half hour, but I never found him. I figured he must have drowned. I knew he was unconscious when he dropped into the river because he had slammed his head into the tree limb and had made no attempt to swim after he had hit the water. If he hadn't died when he crashed his head into the branch, he must have drowned by now.

"Heartbroken, I finally gave up my search and returned home. My pulse raced like crazy when I thought about telling Mom and Dad about Greg's death. I dragged my feet, walking home. I was doing everything I could do to avoid ever reaching home. But I had to return there. I had nowhere else to go. I had to tell them," said Gozzard, his voice quavering with emotion.

"After what seemed like a year I reached home. Mom and Dan were sitting in the TV room watching the TV.

"'Where have you been?' demanded Mom. 'We've been worried sick about you and Greg. Why are you all wet?' She paused and looked around. 'Where is Greg?'

"I started crying. I couldn't help it.

"'Oh no. What happened?' she said.

"I struggled to talk. It was difficult for me to form words because I was so upset. At last I couldn't hold it back any longer.

"'He drowned in the swimming hole.'

"I stopped crying. I felt better, having told them.

"Mom started crying.

"'No, no,' she screamed, her face deep red.

"Fit to be tied, Dad grabbed my arm and marched me out of our house.

"'Show me where,' he said, his face drained of blood.

"I took him to the swimming hole and showed him where Greg had slammed his head into the tree limb supporting the hanging tire and then dropped into the river.

"He started hollering Greg's name.

"All we could hear was the river roaring like a carnivorous beast.

"At last Dad got tired of yelling Greg's name. His face clouded as the truth of Greg's death sank in.

"'Let's search downriver,' he said.

"'I already did.'

"'Then we'll do it again.'

"We strode down the river, searching the riverbanks and the river for any sign of Greg. We didn't see him anywhere. The river still must have had him in its clutches.

"We must have walked at least five miles along the riverbank, and I was getting tired. My legs were killing me. The sun had set, and it was getting dark. We could hardly see anything.

"'We can't see in the dark,' I said.

"'I refuse to believe he's dead. He regained consciousness and crawled out of the river. He'll find his way back to our house,' he said, but he didn't sound optimistic.

"It was like Dad refused to believe Greg was dead. He couldn't accept the horrible truth.

"We went back home, disconsolate. I wasn't crying anymore. I never cried again after that awful day. Nothing was worth crying about.

"Greg never came back home. Three months later Mom stuck her head in the kitchen oven and turned on the gas.

"Dad blamed me for Mom's death and treated me like dirt for the rest of my life. He got drunk all the time and beat me, blaming me for everything that went wrong after Mom died. And he never got tired of blaming me for Greg's death. He said it was my fault that I didn't save him from drowning."

"Where is your dad? Do you ever see him?"

"He opened the door to his pickup one day and a ghoul lunged out at him. It bit his hand and infected him. Six hours later he turned. I shot him in the head.

"I felt nothing when I did it. I hated my father at that point for mistreating me for so many years. To this day I still feel guilt for Greg's death and to some degree for Mom's suicide. If Greg hadn't died, Mom wouldn't have killed herself."

"Do you want to hear about my life?" said Marta.

"No. Slaves don't have lives. You are beneath me. I am your master."

How was she going to get that gun out of Gozzard's waistband? There had to be a way. He had to go to sleep eventually. Then she would make her move. He would never wake up again. She could care less about how much guilt Gozzard felt for his brother's death. If telling her his life story was his way to get her to like being his slave, he had failed. She would rather die than be anybody's slave. Soon Gozzard would end up dead like his brother. There was no way she would allow him to go on living.

Chapter 45

Dean Uriah was in his office with Dr. Morrow in Mount Weather when a black Army Ranger with a cropped haircut entered. Adriana Copper was twenty-five years old and stood just shy of six feet. She played center in basketball at high school, but she couldn't afford to go to college. Instead she joined the Army and with hard work became a Ranger.

"Mr. President, we have finished hauling the ghouls out of the air vent and have welded a steel grid over the opening," she said, standing bolt upright.

"Good work. Faster than I expected. Did you clear away the ghouls outside of the vent?"

"We did, sir. But they're all over the place. It's only a matter of time before more of them gather around the vent. Should we leave a detail outside to guard it?"

Uriah thought about it then shook his head. "It's a waste of ammo. I don't see how the ghouls can break through a steel grid. They're too feeble and uncoordinated. The only reason they got in in the first place was because the nuke that hit the bunker loosened the original grid."

"Yes, sir. I'll tell the others members of the team to come inside," said Copper, and left.

"Are we gonna have enough oxygen now?" Uriah asked Dr. Morrow and coughed on the foul air.

"It may take a while for the fresh air to reach the entire bunker, but yes, we should have enough oxygen in the near future."

"Then the members won't have to draw lots to see who has to leave the bunker so the rest of us can survive?"

Morrow furrowed his brow in thought. "I'm not sure how long it will take for the fresh air to circulate through the entire bunker. It could take a day or more."

Uriah pulled at his collar and loosened his necktie. "I can barely breathe. I swear I'm gonna be sick if I don't get fresh air ASAP."

"Does any of what I tell you go beyond these walls, sir?" said Morrow, apprehensive.

"Of course not. Our conversation is confidential."

Morrow nodded, feeling downcast. "Then you better have the members draw lots and send the losers outside. They probably won't have to stay outside long. The fact is I'm concerned for your health." Morrow scrutinized Uriah's face. "Your complexion is too pale."

"To be honest, I feel weak," said Uriah, leaning against his desk, his body limp.

"You're not getting enough oxygen. To be frank, none of us are."

"All right. You're the doctor. Have our residents draw lots to see which twenty of them have to go outside for a short while."

"Me?" said Morrow, dumbfounded. "Why me?"

"You're the doctor. You can explain to them why we have to draw lots."

"*We*? Are you and me drawing lots too?"

"Of course not. I'm the president. And you're the doctor. You're exempt from the lottery. We can't jeopardize our health by staying outside for any length of time in air that is contaminated with radiation. Of course, don't mention to the others that we're not in the lottery. It's none of their business."

Morrow shifted edgily on his feet. "I don't understand why I'm the one who has to make the announcement."

"You're the doctor. You're in charge of health in the bunker."

"But I'm not the one making the decision to hold a lottery."

"You should be proud you're the doctor in charge of health in the bunker. People look up to you. They respect your qualifications for making a medical decision."

"I thought you said earlier that what we said in this room stayed here."

"It does. Don't tell them they need to draw lots because the president isn't getting enough air. That's how President Mims earned so much resentment. People found out he was hogging the oxygen in the bunker and letting the rest of them suffocate."

"Yes, sir. I still don't know how they found out about that. We must have had a mole in the office when Mims ordered me to give him more oxygen and cut back on everybody else's."

"Look around you, Doctor," said Uriah, making a sweeping gesture with his arms. "We're the only two people in my office. Do you see any moles? Who else can hear us?"

"Maybe the office is bugged," said Morrow uneasily. "Aren't you worried about another purge like the one that put Mims in disfavor and ended up with his assassination?"

"No," said Uriah, and approached the kneehole in his desk. "And you know why I'm not worried?"

Morrow shook his head no.

Uriah leaned over and, with both hands, lifted a metal Zero Halliburton suitcase from the kneehole, grunting as he did so, because the nuclear football weighed forty-five pounds. His face flushed as he stood up and placed the football on his desktop with a loud thud. He gasped for breath as he straightened, massaging his lower back.

The football was charred and had numerous scratches and dents in it.

"Because I'm the president of the United States and I have the football," he said, tapping the top of the suitcase with two fingers. "Whoever has the football rules. I can nuke anyone any time anywhere."

"If you nuke anybody inside this bunker, you'll end up nuking yourself, sir."

Uriah fired an angry look at Morrow. "I'm talking about the twenty losers of the lottery who have to go outside. They're the ones who are gonna be angry and resentful about having to draw lots. They're the ones I can nuke. I'm getting ahead of myself. Make an announcement over the PA system that we're having the lottery—"

"With all due respect, sir, you're the president so you should be the one who makes such an important announcement."

"That's right, Doctor, I *am* the president. And I'm ordering *you* to make the announcement."

"With any luck, maybe we won't have to make an announcement because our air will become cleaner with the vent open—"

"I never count on luck. That's how I rose to the top of the greasy pole, as Disraeli called it, even if he was talking about being prime minister and not president. Anyway, we can't wait any longer," said Uriah, coughing and loosening his tie again. "I feel sick and weak. You saw me. I could hardly lift the football. Go to the comms room and make the announcement now, Doctor, before I pass out from lack of oxygen. That's a direct order."

Morrow fetched a sigh of resignation. "Yes, Mr. President. Why are there so many dents and burn marks on the football?"

"Because President Cole used it to commit suicide by nuke."

"How could I forget?" said Morrow, face gaunt.

"We were lucky to find it after the explosion. It's a little worse for wear, but it still works. It's built to withstand nuclear blasts. It's lined with lead. Frankly, it's indestructible."

"That's too bad," muttered Morrow.

"What was that? I think my hearing's going because of the foul air we're breathing."

"I was thinking about poor Cole."

"Don't waste your time on him. He couldn't handle the job. He went mad and caused a lot of damage around here like the damaged air vent. We could be dead thanks to that guy. He's the one who gave us this toxic air to breathe."

Dejected, Morrow made for the door.

"And, Doctor, I don't need to remind you that none of what was just said here goes beyond these four walls."

"Of course, Mr. President."

"If it does, I'll know who to blame."

Morrow brushed beads of sweat from his forehead as he opened the office door and paused in front of it.

"That will be all, Doctor," said Uriah in a tone that brooked no debate.

With a heavy heart Morrow struck out for the comms room.

Chapter 46

Vivian plodded down the street, her feet throbbing from so much walking.

But she expected it. Life was about pain and suffering. She flogged her back to remind herself of what it was to be alive.

Despite her aching feet she told herself she needed to keep going. She needed to confront Michael K. for killing Dmitri and all of her friends in the group.

She heard something behind her. She turned around and saw a stray, scrawny brown mutt following her. He stopped when she did. He looked apprehensive that she might attack him.

"Are you headed my way?" she said.

He stared her in the eye, asking her not to shoo him away.

"We're both going in the same direction so we might as well go together," she told him. "I could use some company."

He seemed to understand what she was saying, at least she thought he did.

She flogged her spine and grimaced.

The mutt gave her a puzzled look.

The edges of his whiskers were turning grey, she noticed.

"Are you an old dog?" she said. "You're a survivor like me. Let's go."

They walked down the road with him taking the rear. She stopped and pointed to her side.

"Walk beside me."

He looked at her with baffled eyes.

She jerked her forefinger up and down, pointing to the tarmac at her side.

Sheepishly the dog walked to her side like he thought she might strike him with her whip if he disobeyed.

"Have people been beating you?" she said. "Is that why you look afraid of me?"

He stood there.

"It's better walking together, isn't it?"

He stood beside her looking confused, feeling like he was supposed to do something but he didn't know what.

"You need a name," she said, seeing that his leather collar didn't have a dog tag.

She mulled it over. "How about Freedom?"

He looked at her with his big moist brown eyes.

"This is still a free country, right?"

Why did she think he was going to answer her? Maybe she was losing it, expecting a dog to talk.

"I'm gonna call you Freddie for short. *Freedom* is a mouthful."

She flailed her back, winced, and headed down the road, Freddie at her side.

"I wish I could feed you. You look like you need food. I know I do. Holler if you see anything to eat."

They trudged past an abandoned silver SUV parked catercorner in the road.

She flogged her back. "The flesh is meant to be mortified."

Freddie fell to barking at the SUV as he stared at it.

"What's wrong, Freddie?"

Vivian warily approached the SUV, not knowing what to expect.

She peered through the rear window at the backseat and spotted a paper bag. Meanwhile, Freddie kept barking at the SUV. She checked the rear door to see if it was locked.

It was open. A lot of people fleeing both the ghouls and the nukes had abandoned their cars when they ran out of gas. It explained why she saw nobody in the backseat. She leaned into the car interior and grabbed the paper bag in order to see what was in it. Could it be the reason Freddie was barking his head off?

As she was pulling the bag toward her, an arm reached over the front seat and grabbed a fistful of her hair.

"Ow," she cried with a start.

Freddie barked even louder than before—if that was possible.

Chapter 47

Vivian craned her neck around to see who was clutching her hair.

A sixtyish ghoul with a shock of white hair stuck his head above the front seat back and growled at her with his flyblown face. He yanked her head toward him and opened his worm-eaten lips to bite her as slivers of drool like icicles hung down from his open mouth. He had long eyelashes, which turned out to be slender black worms writhing out of his eyelids.

She struck his face with her whip. He flinched and draw away from her. She kept whipping his snarling face, trying to lash his milky eyes to blind him.

She knew she wasn't supposed to hurt another living human being, but this creature was dead and it was trying to eat her. It wouldn't allow her to run away. Dmitri had taught her group never to take a human life. But this creature wasn't human. She would do anything it took to defend herself from it.

The ghoul refused to release her hair from his grimy bony hand. Becoming frantic she flipped her whip upside down and jammed the handle into the creature's left eye, gouging it out of its socket. It hung by its optic nerve down his face. The ghoul continued to keep Vivian's hair trapped in his grasp. He kept snapping his jaws, trying to bite her face. She punched out his right eye with the whip handle. The eyeball flew out of its orbit and tumbled onto the vinyl-upholstered front seat.

Even though it was blind the ghoul managed to maintain its hold on her hair.

The stench emanating from the creature was overpowering, made more so with her trapped inside the SUV's close confines with him. She hammered the whip handle against the top of the ghoul's skull over and over. She knew she couldn't break the skull since the handle was made of leather. She needed a real hammer to destroy the ghoul's brain.

At last she broke away from the ghoul's hand, which tore out a clump of her hair. She tumbled backward out of the SUV, her whip and the paper bag in her hands.

Sitting on the tarmac she watched the blind ghoul flail away harmlessly in the vehicle.

Freddie sniffed her. Or was he sniffing the bag?

She opened the bag and smelled beef.

The bag was full of beef jerky.

"You're a smart dog," she said, smiling at Freddie, who hung his mouth open happily, exposing his pink slab of tongue.

She gave him a strip of jerky and took one for herself. She couldn't tell who scarfed down the jerky faster—her or him no matter how tough it was to chew.

She realized she was having too much fun.

She flogged her back and drew a stream of blood.

Freddie continued gobbling his jerky.

He was an animal. He didn't know that they were put on earth to suffer. But she knew. Humans had eaten from the tree of knowledge and found out the truth of their horrific condition. Animals were too stupid to understand.

Even if he was just an animal with a tiny brain, she liked Freddie. If it wasn't for him, she never would have found the jerky in the SUV. She felt lucky she had met him.

She wondered if there was any more food in this vehicle and more importantly water. They needed water. She especially needed water after eating the salty jerky. Her mouth felt more parched than ever.

"Can you find us some water?" she said.

He barked at her like he understood. Then he barked at the back of the SUV.

She got to her feet, approached the hatchback, and inspected the cargo space.

Nudged behind the backseat was a shrink-wrapped package of ten plastic liter bottles of water. How could the dog smell water? She didn't waste any time thinking about it.

She tried to open the hatchback door. It was locked.

She returned to the front of the SUV and saw the blind ghoul squirming helplessly in the front seat. No matter how helpless it was without eyes, it could still bite and infect her. She inspected the ignition in the dash. No key in it.

She remembered she had opened the backdoor to get the jerky. She could therefore climb onto the backseat and reach over it into the cargo space to retrieve the package of water. As long as the ghoul didn't climb over the back of the front seat and attack her. Even though he couldn't see her, he could hear her scrabbling around on the backseat.

The problem was she needed water. You could only go so many days without it.

Freddie started barking at the front seat to distract the ghoul. She didn't know what she would do without the dog.

She clambered into the backseat, knelt on it, and reached back into the cargo space to retrieve the package of water. She strained to lift the pack over the seat back. The water must have weighed close to twenty pounds. Grunting, she hauled the package over the seat back and plumped it down on the backseat.

Out of the corner of her eye she caught sight of the ghoul reaching his arm over the back of the front seat, having heard her grunt. He tried to grab her by listening to the sound of her movements to locate her.

She ducked away from his groping hand. She dragged the package of water across the backseat, stepped out the back door, and lifted the water out of the SUV, grimacing with the effort.

Bending her knees she lowered the package onto the tarmac.

Freddie approached her from the front of the car and barked at her and at the water with satisfaction. Withdrawing a pocketknife from her jeans, she cut open the shrink-wrap to pull out the bottles of water.

She looked at Freddie. She wished she had a bowl she could pour water into and let him drink. She peered into the car. She didn't see any bowls anywhere. The owner must not have had any pets.

She unscrewed the plastic cap on one of the bottles and took a long pull on the water. She felt better with the water inside her.

Sitting, Freddie watched her and mewled.

Noticing that it was curved somewhat like a bowl, she picked up a piece of the shrink-wrap that she had torn, laid it in front of him, and poured water into it.

He eagerly began lapping up the water.

The shrink-wrap kept sliding away from him as he lapped the water, so she held it in place while he drank. She kept pouring more water into it for him to slake his thirst. She had no idea how long he had gone without water, but it must have been quite a while.

He had his fill and walked away, looking content.

She needed to take as much of this water as she could with her. She couldn't carry the water bottles in her hands. There were too many of them, and she needed one hand to carry her whip. She needed a rope.

She cast around the road for a rope without success.

She gazed down at her hiking boots and picked up on her shoelaces. Crouching, she untied the shoelace on her right hiking boot and removed it from the grommets. She stood up and held up the lace. It was the better part of six feet long. She cut the lace in half with her pocketknife, relaced her boot with one half of the shoelace, and tied it. Though it didn't go through every grommet, half the lace would be enough to keep her boot from falling off.

She took the other end of the lace and wrapped it several times around the necks of five of the water bottles, one bottle at a time. Then she tied the five water bottles to her leather belt.

She followed the same procedure with the shoelace on her left hiking boot and hung four more bottles around her belt on her left side.

"As long as we don't do any running, this should work fine."

Energized by food and drink, the bag of jerky clutched in one hand, her whip in the other, she strode down the road, Freddie beside her.

"We got work to do. We gotta catch up with the mass murderers Michael K and his biker gang the High Rolerz."

Chapter 48

Riding shotgun in his Suburban, Joe Purdy watched Angel One driving in front of him. After they negotiated the jog in the tunnel, he could see light at the other end. Angel One increased its speed as it headed for the exit.

Purdy jumped in his seat when two explosions roared through the tunnel ahead, shaking their Suburban with the blast waves. Angel One's Suburban rolled over on its side. Two chunks of the concrete ceiling of the tunnel fell to the ground with thuds. Another chunk dropped onto the overturned Suburban, clanging against the rear driver's-side door and thudding on the tarmac.

Purdy glimpsed a woman in black leather darting across the entrance.

Purdy told his driver, Guevara, to stop.

"Angel One, come in," he said. "This is Angel Two. Give me your sitrep. Over."

No response.

"They should be OK," said Guevara. "These Suburbans have bombproof chassis."

"Why aren't they reporting back?"

"They could be unconscious. Those blasts really jolted their car."

"A woman lobbed two grenades under Angel One."

"What woman?"

"She's gone now. She was dressed in black leather."

"Then we're under attack. What do you want us to do, sir?"

"We don't have time for this," said Purdy in frustration. "Every delay gives Halverson a better chance of escaping us."

"Why would somebody be attacking us?"

Purdy ignored him. "We need a white flag."

"The SEALs don't believe in surrendering, sir."

"I'm not surrendering. I just want to find out what these people want. I want to let them know I come in peace."

"Are you sure that's a good idea, sir? These attackers whoever they are have shown they're violent."

"We can't get past the overturned Suburban."

"We could plow it out of the way, sir."

"I want our team out of the vehicle safely before we push their vehicle out of the way."

"If they try to get out, the ambushers could pick them off."

"Which is why I need a white flag so I can go outside and find out what these assholes want."

Purdy cast around the cab but didn't find anything white. He looked at Guevara.

"What about your undershirt?" said Purdy.

"Yes, sir."

Guevara removed his shirt and white wife beater from his muscular chest.

"You need to work out more often, Guevara."

"There's not enough oxygen in the bunker for me to work out in the gym very long. I had to cut back my hours. I don't have any energy when I'm there."

He handed Purdy his wife beater.

"This will have to do," said Purdy, opening his door with one hand and gripping the undershirt in his other.

"I don't think it's safe for you to go out there, sir."

Purdy slid off the front seat and stood on the tarmac.

"We need to get out of this tunnel to get Halverson," he said. "Getting stuck in a gun battle trapped in here could drag on for hours or even longer."

"But, sir—"

Purdy's mind was made up. He wasn't listening. He made a beeline for the tunnel exit, keeping his eyes peeled for ambushers who might be lurking outside.

Chapter 49

When Purdy reached the overturned Suburban, he scrabbled up the chassis, climbed onto the driver's-side front door, and peered inside at the front seat. Two deathly pale bodies were strapped in with seat belts. Neither body was moving. He figured they had been knocked unconscious by the grenade blasts. The man and the woman in the backseat were also unconscious, their seat belts holding them in place. He climbed down to the tarmac.

His palms sweaty, he looked outside the tunnel, held his jury-rigged white flag above his head, and waved it to attract the attention of the ambushers who were lying in wait out there. He couldn't see any of them yet. All he could see were six rows of motorcycles blocking the road.

He picked up on the spike strip lying just outside the tunnel exit. A trap. And here he was walking straight into it.

He had no idea who he was dealing with. His heartbeat raced as he kept waving the white tank top above his head.

"We come in peace," he said, searching for a human face, knowing he was a sitting duck out here.

Clad in black leather, a Ruger pistol in her hand, a twentysomething blonde with spiked dyed hair with an inch of black roots popped out from behind a tree.

"Throw down your gun if you come in peace," she said.

Purdy withdrew his SIG from its holster on his waist.

"Do it slow," she said.

Purdy obeyed and dropped his pistol on the tarmac.

"You're trespassing on our territory," she said. "What do you want?"

"We mean you no harm."

Purdy debated whether to tell them he worked for the government. Since the lead Suburban had an American flag waving from the roof, he got the impression it wouldn't go over well, considering the condition of the Suburban.

"What do you want?" she demanded, her face surly.

"I want to speak to your leader. Who is your leader?"

A guy in a mohawk popped out from behind a tree. "I'm Spartacus."

A guy with shoulder-length brown hair showed himself. "I'm Spartacus."

Three other gang members appeared, two women and one man. They all claimed they were Spartacus.

At last, wearing a black leather blazer and a black necktie, a man with a shaved head strode out from behind an oak.

"They love doing that with strangers," he said, chuckling. "I'm the leader. State your business."

"We're looking for Chad Halverson and his coconspirator. They assassinated the president of the United States. Have you seen Halverson?"

"We're looking for him too," said the man. "Who are you?"

"I'm Joe Purdy. And you?"

"Michael K." He made a sweeping gesture with his arm to his gang. "And these fine folks are the High Rolerz. We believe in doing whatever we want. He who dares wins. Fortune favors the bold. We believe in the luck of those who dare to do what they want in life. We gamble everything to win—"

"Why do you want Halverson?" cut in Purdy, tired of Michael K.'s speech.

"He murdered my brother."

"Then we both want him for committing murder," said Purdy. "Let's join forces and capture him."

"I'm gonna hunt him down like a rabid dog and blow his brains out after I capture him."

"Let's get him together. The more people we have in our group the better."

"Maybe."

"I assure you he's a dangerous man. He fights like a cornered rat."

"Your lead vehicle is flying the American flag."

"That's right. This is America, and we're proud to be Americans," said Purdy, avoiding telling Michael K. they worked for the government.

"You sound like you work for the government."

It was time to put up or shut up. Purdy knew if he told them the truth, Michael K. might try to whack them instead of working with them.

"We work for a militia trying to save America from the ghouls and the nukes," said Purdy. "We have the right to fly the American flag just like you and your group."

"We're not flying any flags. We don't need one."

"How do people know who you are?"

"We don't care. We got guns and machetes. That's what we care about, not flags. We don't fly flags, and we're suspicious of people who do."

"We both want Halverson. Why not join forces?"

"Why should we?"

"He'll get away if we don't join forces."

"The driveshaft is broken on your lead vehicle. It's not going anywhere."

"Fine. We still have two other SUVs in perfect working order."

"Out of curiosity, where did you get gas for them?" said Michael K., massaging his jaw.

The question caught Purdy off guard. He needed to come up with an answer fast. He felt sweat bubbling over his upper lip.

"These are government vehicles," he said. "We overpowered the soldiers driving them and commandeered them for our militia. All of the SUVs had full tanks of gas. You know the government. They hoard everything for themselves, including gas."

Michael K. chewed it over. "As long as you don't work for the double-dealing feds we might be able to come to an agreement."

Purdy nodded yes. "It's to our mutual advantage to work together."

"There's something that puzzles me."

"What's that?" said Purdy, becoming edgy.

They could start firing at him any time they wanted, and Purdy would be unable to defend himself without a weapon. He felt stupid standing alone on the tarmac holding up Guevara's wife beater in front of scores of armed ambushers. They outnumbered his squadron by over five to one. Even with their machine pistols Purdy and his team wouldn't stand a chance in a pitched battle against an opponent so superior in numbers.

"If you don't work for the government," said Michael K., "why do you care if Halverson assassinated the president?"

Purdy had to improvise. His brain whirred into action.

"Because Halverson also assassinated our militia leader," he said.

Michael K. jacked up his eyebrows. "The guy's been busy."

"He's a serial assassin. And he's not done yet, I bet."

"Is he some kind of psychotic sociopath?"

Purdy nodded. "A damn killing machine trained by the CIA."

"Shit. I heard about their Project MKUltra. Did they use drugs on him like acid and other mind-bending hallucinogens to turn him into a psycho killer?"

"They're capable of anything."

"I heard the CIA got Manson hooked on LSD. Then he used it to turn his Family into killer robots by giving them it every day during their sex orgies and destroying their wills. You trip on that shit every day, you don't know what the hell is going on. Your mind flatlines."

Purdy didn't want to work with these thugs, which was what he took them for, even if their leader sported a necktie tied in a Windsor knot like a Madison Avenue exec. But Purdy saw no other way out of his dilemma. He and his team could hide in their bulletproof and bombproof Suburbans, but he didn't see how he could get past all those hogs blocking the road, not to mention the spike strip and the armed ambushers hiding behind almost every tree. In effect, he and his team were stymied. They could not advance and track Halverson without coming to an arrangement with Michael K.

"We can catch Halverson," said Purdy. "And we can do it PDQ."

"Yeah, we can," said Michael K. He stared at Purdy. "The question is, why do we need you?"

Purdy's heart skipped a beat. He knew he had to come up with a plausible answer because his neck was on the block.

"I'm waiting," said Michael K., drawing a Colt Python .357 Magnum from the leather holster on his hip.

Purdy sensed Michael K.'s gang becoming restless, leveling death stares his way.

"Because I know where he's going," said Purdy.

"I'm listening."

"If I tell you, you might decide you don't need us."

He wished he could rain down an ICBM on these clowns this minute. But the president had the football and was the only one who could do such a thing. Purdy had no way to contact Uriah.

Michael K. snickered. "I like the way your mind thinks, Hurdy."

"Purdy."

"Do you have arms and ammo you can share with us?"

Purdy figured it would help his cause if he agreed to give the High Rolerz some of his arms and ammo even though he would rather not, since he didn't trust these Hell's Angels or whatever they called themselves. Purdy believed that whenever the enemy had the upper hand, cut a deal with them.

"Yeah," he said.

"Right." Michael K. addressed the High Rolerz. "Listen up, people. We're joining forces with these fine folks, members of a militia who want to find Halverson as much as we do."

The High Rolerz showed no sign of emotion.

"Remove the spike strip and your bikes and let these folks join our team."

Still no emotion from the Rolerz.

"What are we gonna do when we find Halverson?" said Michael K.

"Kill, kill, kill," chanted the Rolerz, pumping their guns above their heads.

Definitely thugs, decided Purdy, watching them.

Chapter 50

Purdy returned to his team. He dispatched the clean-shaven medic in his early thirties smelling of rubbing alcohol to look after the four members in the overturned lead vehicle. Then he returned to his Suburban's shotgun seat, tossing the wife beater into Guevara's face.

"I cut a deal with those thugs," said Purdy.

"Is that a good idea?" said Guevara, clutching his wife beater behind the wheel. "They tried to kill us."

"Sometimes you have to cut a deal with the devil to stay alive," said Purdy, not happy about the idea.

"Why don't we just crush their motorcycles and take off?"

"They got grenades. While we're crushing their hogs, they would be lobbing more grenades at us. They also outnumber us."

Purdy watched the medic climb into the front seat of the overturned Suburban then climb into the backseat.

"We got bombproof vehicles," said Guevara. "Grenades can't harm us."

"Look at our point vehicle lying on its side and tell me that."

Glum-faced, the medic clambered out of the overturned Suburban, jumped to the tarmac, and, adjusting his wire-rim glasses, returned to Purdy. Purdy powered down his window.

"How are they?" he said.

The medic arrived at Purdy's window. "The four of them are dead."

"What?" said Guevara. "That's impossible. These are bombproof vehicles. How could shrapnel get into the Suburban and kill the passengers?"

"Shrapnel didn't kill them. The blast wave destroyed their lungs."

"A blast wave by itself can kill you?"

"It can and does kill blast victims."

"Fuck. I thought we were supposed to be safe in these things. More government propaganda."

Slumping in his seat Purdy felt dejected. He hated losing even a single soldier. He had lost four thanks to Michael K.'s army of goons.

"We should sue the makers of these so-called bombproof vehicles," said Guevara.

"Chaos rules," said Purdy. "We don't have any more laws or courts."

"Can we salvage the point vehicle?"

"No. The grenade busted the driveshaft."

"Then why should we trust these bastards and cut a deal with them?"

"We have no other options. They could lay siege to the tunnel and keep us pinned in here forever."

"We could back out the entrance."

"We're not backing out of anything," said Purdy, straightening in his seat. "Our mission is to catch and kill the two assassins Halverson and Costello. We're not returning to Mount Weather until we complete our assignment."

"And you trust these ambushers?"

"No way. But we need to get Halverson. Staying trapped in this tunnel is not an option."

"I don't understand. Why are they agreeing to help us when they outnumber us?"

"They want Halverson as badly as we do."

"Still—"

"I told them I know where he's going."

"We gotta guard our six when we're with them, I say."

Purdy nodded yes. "They could turn on us without a moment's notice.'

Guevara eyeballed the overturned Suburban with doleful eyes. "When are we gonna hold the funerals?"

Purdy said nothing, lost in thought.

"The funerals for Ed, Gabino, Sabrina, and Moon," said Guevara.

An obese black ghoul with short hair and a crone's face scratched her hooked nails against Purdy's window. She bared her broken teeth and growled at him. He glared at her milky eyes, one of which had a maggot squirming out of the pupil. She shook her head at him.

"We don't have time for funerals," said Purdy.

He withdrew from his waistband a Cold Steel SRK knife, standard issue for SEALs. The blade was made of SK-5 high carbon steel, while the handle was rubber.

He powered down his window and thrust the SRK knife into the ghoul's forehead. The crone blew out noxious breath at him, which turned his stomach. Purdy thrust his knife farther into the crone's head and felt it slide into her brain. The crone's knees buckled. She disappeared from the window, sliding off his knife.

Purdy eyed the crone's brains coating his knife blade. In disgust he wiped the blade clean on his trouser leg and sheathed the knife.

"What were you saying?" he said.

"I said we need to hold funerals for Ed, Gabino, Sabrina, and Moon."

Purdy rubbed his brow in thought. "We should, but we don't have the time. The longer we delay catching Halverson, the farther he's gonna get away from us. If we delay too long, he could reach Raven Rock."

"They were my friends and they're human beings. They deserve to be buried like everybody else."

"In a perfect world that's exactly what we would do. But this is an obscene world, a world turned upside down and writhing in the throes of extinction. Remember, the president gave us a mission to complete." Purdy paused, trying to think of a way to appease Guevara. "We can bury them when we return from our mission."

"What if the ghouls bite the bodies and turn them?" Guevara winced. "I can't even stand the thought of it."

"The ghouls don't bite dead flesh. They bite only the living. The bodies will be safe in the vehicle. We'll lock the doors to keep out looters before we go. We'll also take their guns and ammo for ourselves."

"What about the spores?"

"Spores?"

"I'm one of those who believe the zombie plague is spread by inhaling spores emitted by infected ghouls."

"Ed, Gabino, Sabrina, and Moon can't inhale anything when they're dead."

"I'm talking about before they died. Look at all the ghouls swarming in this tunnel. They could be emitting infectious spores, and we're breathing the air in here."

Purdy shrugged. "It's true we don't know much for certain about this damn zombie plague. Better to be safe than sorry."

"Are you thinking what I'm thinking?"

Purdy nodded, his face gaunt. "We'll shoot our teammates in the head before we leave so they can't possibly become ghouls."

"What about us?"

"What *about* us?"

"What if we've breathed infected spores emitted by the ghouls?"

"I'm not gonna worry about all the ways we can die. It's counterproductive. We're never gonna get anything done if we sit around worrying about dying. Send someone to shoot Ed, Gabino, Sabrina, and Moon in the head. Collect their guns and ammo and give them to the bikers."

"What?" cried Guevara.

"It's part of the deal I cut with them."

"You're making it easier for them to waste all of us."

"It's the deal. I don't want to hear another word from you about it."

"Yes, sir," said Guevara quietly, trying to settle down.

"This stuff about spores could be a rumor. We just don't know enough about the zombie plague to know all the ways it spreads."

"What do I tell the squad about not burying our dead? A lot of our squad are religious."

"Tell them we're gonna bury them when we return from successfully completing our mission. All we're doing is delaying their funerals. Ed, Gabino, Sabrina, and Moon will definitely get funerals like every human being should."

Guevara looked ill. "I wouldn't want to be the one who has to shoot them in their heads. I mean, I knew these guys. We got drunk together. We played cards together. We . . ." Guevara faltered. "I was Gabino's best man at his marriage."

Wearing a black T-shirt that said Good Times in cursive white letters, a seventysomething female ghoul with bushy white hair schlepped in front of the windshield, glared at them, and growled. A silver spiderweb thread of drool slid down the corner of her mouth.

"I know," said Purdy. "Let's just get it over with and get out of here into the daylight."

Infuriated, Guevara flung off his seat belt, flung open his door, bolted out of the driver's seat, and shot the creature in the eye with his SIG P226. The ghoul dropped dead.

Guevara returned to his seat, still bristling.

"Michael K. better not get the idea we're shooting at his gang because of your gunshot," said Purdy.

"Fuck him. Him and his gang of thugs murdered my friends. I don't care what those bottom feeders think."

"We need to join with them. Otherwise, we're not getting out of here alive."

"I couldn't help it. Those ghouls sicken me—"

"We can't go off half-cocked."

"I know. With our point team gone, there's only seven of us left," said Guevara, casting a glance at the overturned Suburban.

"Seven against how many scores of gangbangers armed to the teeth?" Purdy said to himself.

Chapter 51

Halverson pedaled down the road, steering his and, on his right, Marta's bike and casting around for her. He didn't see any sign of her.

Could she have gone in the other direction? Why would she deliberately return to that tunnel full of ghouls? Unless somebody was taking her there.

He called out her name into the woods on either side of the road. For all he knew she could have gone into the woods. But why would she? Why would she leave him behind?

He said her name, raising his voice.

No answer.

He didn't want to yell out her name too loud or the noise would attract any nearby ghouls.

He was becoming more convinced than ever that somebody must have kidnaped her or worse. Even now she could be lying dead under a pile of leaves in the forest. He told himself not to think that way. He had to remain optimistic that she was still alive.

If the kidnaper had a car, it was going to take Halverson a long time to catch up to him. He might never catch up to the guy on this bicycle.

Halverson picked up on ghouls weaving in and out of the woods, plodding and stumbling as they foraged for food. An armless fiftyish ghoul's eyeball was hanging from its optic nerve in front of his face like a cherry on a stem, and he was trying to eat it as he trudged, but it remained out of reach of his gaping mouth, frustrating him.

If Marta had gone into the woods, Halverson didn't like her chances. Then again, why would she enter the woods? She knew the woods were infested with ghouls.

Halverson pedaled along the tarmac, escorting Marta's riderless bike with his right hand.

Somebody must have kidnaped her.

The only other explanation would be that the ghouls had gotten her. He didn't want to go there.

He couldn't believe she would have gone off on her own without telling him first.

He glanced over his shoulder.

Purdy and his team would be here any time now in their Suburbans with orders to kill him and Marta. Halverson had no doubt that Uriah wanted the two of them dead. Uriah feared Halverson would go to Raven Rock and notify the speaker of the house that the secretary of state had illegally declared himself president.

Uriah's fears were correct.

Uriah could not allow Halverson to go on living.

Chapter 52

Marta sat on an empty wooden crate in Gozzard's shack, watching him sleep.

After drinking too much bourbon he had dozed off and now slumped forward on his crate, flapping his lips as he breathed through his mouth.

Despite being asleep, he continued to hold the snake pole handle. She was afraid if she tried to move, he would feel the pole move in his hand and wake up.

She had been trying to work her rope-bound wrists free for the last hour. She had no idea if she was making any headway with the knot. She didn't feel the rope loosening. With him asleep it was the best time for her to escape.

She froze.

She thought she heard someone or something moving outside the shack. She debated whether she should yell for help. The problem was that if she yelled, the noise would rouse Gozzard from his drunken stupor.

She hated these steel tongs gripping her neck.

She was sure she heard someone crunching the underbrush. They were very close to the shack. It sounded like a person. She could hear two feet plodding along. She wanted to cry out for help, but she looked at Gozzard sleeping and held her tongue, her face sweaty.

Then she heard growling.

It was a ghoul.

She was glad she had held her tongue.

She cut her eyes to the so-called door. There was no lock on it. It was nothing but a slab of plywood hanging on hinges with a waist-level round hole cut in one side for opening and closing. She figured the ghoul could push it open.

She fancied she could see the ghoul's waist through the hole in the door.

Gozzard shifted on his crate, making it creak under his weight. Marta thought he might fall off and wake up, but he remained sleeping on the crate, flapping his lips as he breathed. His grip on the snake pole was helping him remain upright in a sitting position. She willed him not to wake up.

Maybe the ghoul would sneak into the shack and bite him. But then it would also bite her unless she could escape the tongs imprisoning her.

She had to escape somehow.

She believed she could kick the snake pole handle out of Gozzard's hand. But it would almost certainly wake him.

If she was going to do something, she had to do it now. Gozzard could wake up any minute.

She heard the ghoul growling through the hole in the door. Was the creature bending down to peek through the hole? It could be listening to Gozzard's flapping lips and trying to identify the sound.

If she kicked the snake pole out of Gozzard's hand and bolted out the door, she might stand a chance of escaping. No matter how small the chance, it was better than remaining here as Gozzard's slave.

Gozzard would wake up if she kicked the pole free from his grasp, but he might be too uncoordinated from his drunken stupor to chase her.

If she waited for the ghoul to break into the shack, she didn't think she would be able to get past the thing without it biting and infecting her.

Her best chance lay in kicking the snake pole out of Gozzard's hand and running for her life out the door.

She took a deep breath to calm herself.

The ghoul was hanging around the door outside and growling. The creature must have suspected that living creatures were hiding inside.

She thought it was trying to peek inside the hole with one of its milky eyes, but it was so uncoordinated that it couldn't bend down and level its eye with the hole. The ghoul snorted in exasperation.

Chapter 53

Uriah was sitting behind his desk wheezing in his office at Mount Weather when Dr. Morrow entered and closed the door behind him.

"Well?" said Uriah.

"Everybody drew lots like you said, Mr. President," said Morrow, keeping his voice low. "Nobody was happy about it."

"Happy? Who's happy? We're in the middle of an apocalypse," said Uriah, coughing. "We need to get people out of the bunker so the rest of us can go on living."

"The twenty losers of the lottery are standing in the hall, waiting for you."

Uriah thrust to his feet. "Why did you bring them here? Didn't you tell them to go outside and wait for you to let them back into the bunker?"

"They demanded to talk to you before they would agree to leave."

Uriah shook his head with displeasure, but he saw no way out of meeting with them.

He opened the office door and entered the hallway, where the twenty members were gathered, grumbling with surly visages.

He recognized Kowalski standing in the front row of the lottery losers with an MP9 slung over his shoulder.

"Hello, people," said Uriah, his face somber. "I understand you're not happy with your mission. I can understand your annoyance. But I commend you for doing your patriotic duty and sacrificing yourselves to save America—"

"Wait a minute, Mr. President," said Kowalski. "Who said anything about sacrificing ourselves?"

"You're right, Mr. Kowalski. You're not sacrificing yourselves. You are simply going outside until we have enough oxygen to breathe in the bunker. Then you will all be let inside."

"How long is this gonna take?"

Uriah glanced over his shoulder and saw Morrow trying to fade into the background.

"The good doctor assures me that you shouldn't be outside for more than a couple of hours. Right, Dr. Morrow?"

Morrow cleared his throat. "Uh—yes, sir. That is my estimate."

"And just what are we supposed to be doing out there other than being zombie bait?" said Kowalski.

"Keeping the ghouls from breaking the steel grill and entering the ventilation shaft."

"When they see humans outside, they're gonna come from all over hell and gone to try and eat us."

"Of course, you will all be armed. That goes without saying. Let me be clear. I'm not sending any of you outside to sacrifice your lives."

"And what about the radiation that's contaminating the air outside?"

"The good doctor assures me you won't be outside long enough for it to harm you."

"Maybe just mutate our genes or something so we can't have children. Is that it?"

"No, that's not it. What do you take me for? A monster? I believe in science. I believe the doctor. He knows what he's talking about. No harm will come to you from the low doses of radiation lingering in the air outside."

Uriah heard more grumbling in the crowd.

"This isn't fair," said Kowalski. "We're not volunteering. Why do *we* have to go?"

"Let me remind you. Everybody had an equal chance in the lottery. Nobody appreciates what you're doing more than me and the rest of the residents of the bunker. Our thanks to you will be never-ending. We will be forever grateful to you people for your sacrifices—"

"There you go again with that word *sacrifice*," cut in Kowalski. "You make it sound like we're gonna die out there."

"Yeah," chimed in several in the crowd.

The crowd became restive.

"Let me be perfectly clear," said Uriah. "You are *not* going to die out there. You will be armed and you will be able to kill any and all ghouls that attack you. If you need help, let us know and I will send out soldiers to help you fight the ghouls." Opening his arms Uriah smiled broadly at them. "You are all superpatriots here, and we Americans can't thank you enough. We owe our very lives to you. Like Winston Churchill said during the darkest hours of World War II, 'Never in the field of human conflict was so much owed by so many to so few.' You are those select few he was referring to. Your heroic acts today will be indelibly etched into the American conscience. God bless all of you."

Kowalski took in the miserable faces of the crowd around him. "We never asked to be heroes, sir. And Churchill was British, not American."

Uriah glared at him. "Are you a fucking coward, Kowalski? I don't want any cowards in this bunker."

"No, Mr. President. No way. Not me. I just . . . uh—I—I . . ."

Resigned to leaving the bunker, Kowalski held his head down and didn't offer any more objections.

"What about the rest of you?" said Uriah. "Are you all good red-blooded Americans or do we have cowards skulking in here? There's nothing I hate more than cowards. We're Americans, not cowards."

Everybody looked sheepish, feeling embarrassed about refusing to go outside.

Uriah lightened up. "I knew I could count on you people." He pumped his fist. "You're Americans through and through. Courageous heroes. God bless you. And God bless America."

Uriah retreated into his office with Dr. Morrow and closed the door behind him. Gasping for air Uriah stumbled across the room and collapsed on his chair behind his desk, his arms splayed out over the armrests, his complexion sallow.

Widening his eyes Morrow pelted to Uriah's side and, bending forward, applied his stethoscope to the president's chest.

"Heart attack?" muttered Uriah.

"No, Mr. President, you just need rest and fresh air like everybody else in the bunker," said Morrow, removing his stethoscope from Uriah's chest and straightening up, his face gloomy.

"I feel like shit. I wish you hadn't brought them here, Doctor. My blood pressure must be through the roof."

"I thought the lottery losers were gonna kill me after they were picked. They became rowdy and demanded to see you."

"They looked like they wanted to kill *me*, and *I'm* the president. I think I calmed them down with my speech. At least we didn't have a riot."

Morrow heard gunfire erupt outside the bunker. "The ghouls are attacking again."

"Our heroes are well armed. They can fend off another ghoul attack."

"But for how long? There are millions of the things outside."

"Don't you think I know that? Be thankful they volunteered to help save us."

"They didn't exactly volunteer, Mr. President."

"We all agreed to draw lots. That's what I'm talking about when I say *volunteer*."

"They're resentful the two of us weren't included in the lottery. They feel we got preferential treatment, and I can't blame them."

"Why did you tell them we didn't enter the lottery?" snapped Uriah.

"I didn't," said Morrow, all innocence. "They figured it out somehow. They're not stupid, Mr. President."

"The two of us are indispensable to the running of the government, at least I am. You not so much, but we need your medical expertise to keep our people healthy. You could have volunteered to take part in the lottery if you wanted to."

"It would be a waste of my talents to send me outside."

"Exactly. You have nothing to feel guilty about. And for sure I don't."

"Nevertheless, I can understand their resentment."

"You're welcome to go out there with them if you think it will clear your conscience. I'm not gonna stop you."

Standing motionless Morrow said nothing.

Uriah used a remote to flick on the flat-panel closed-circuit TV mounted on the wall.

Hundreds of ghouls could be seen outside stumbling and lurching across the nuked-out wasteland of detritus, cadavers, and uprooted trees toward the volunteers gathered near the air vent. The volunteers pelted the ghouls with bullets that felled the creatures in their tracks whenever a bullet blew out a ghoul brain.

Another couple hundred ghouls gathered in the distance and marched toward the bunker like an army disgorged from hell.

"We will win," said Uriah, gazing at the TV screen. "We will win with such courageous patriots sacrificing themselves in the name of our country. They're mowing down those stinking, diseased things like they're cornstalks."

Uriah fell back in his chair, exhausted. "I need more oxygen."

"I can give you Mims's oxygen tank if you want," said Morrow, angling across the office to the oxygen tank stored in the closet.

"I'll be goddamned before I use an oxygen tank like a dying ninety-year-old geezer. I don't want anything to do with Mims's oxygen tank. He was a weakling who couldn't take the heat."

Chapter 54

Marta believed it was now or never. She had to take her chance.

The ghoul was still outside the door, making gurgling sounds and trying to figure out how to enter the shack.

Gozzard remained asleep, dead to the world, flapping his lips as he breathed through his mouth.

Marta shifted her body on the crate she was sitting on so she could land a solid kick against the snake pole that Gozzard was holding.

His grasp couldn't be very strong since he was sleeping. He looked like he was going to tip over any second and fall off his crate. She had to act before he fell and woke up.

In her mind she aimed her foot at the snake pole protruding from Gozzard's hand. She figured she might get only one chance. She better make it count.

She raised her right foot off the floor and flexed her knee a couple of times, swinging her foot back and forth, limbering up to launch her kick.

Gritting her teeth she kicked as hard as she could at the snake pole and saw it shoot out of Gozzard's grasp. He moaned.

She sprang off her crate and darted for the floor, the snake pole swinging from her neck. Lowering her shoulder she crashed into the door and burst through it. Crouching, her head lowered, she butted into the sixtyish female ghoul who had a Bride of Frankenstein hairdo, a complexion like cottage cheese, and milky blue eyes full of hate. Fungus covered the sides of her cheeks like a green beard. Marta rammed her head into the ghoul's stomach and knocked her to the ground on her back. Propelled by the impetus of her lunge, Marta toppled to the ground herself.

She tried to scramble to her feet, but her bound wrists and the snake pole dangling from her neck complicated her task. The ghoul was also having a rough time standing up thanks to her poor reflexes. She rolled on the ground, growling in frustration that she couldn't stand up. Unable to stand, she crawled toward Marta to take a bite out of Marta's leg.

Marta crawled away from the ghoul on her knees. On her belly the ghoul kept inching toward Marta. The ghoul swiped at the snake pole, trying to snag the handle.

Marta realized what the ghoul was trying to do and panicked. She couldn't let the ghoul take a hold of the snake pole handle, which would allow the ghoul to control her like Gozzard had.

Struggling to stand on one leg while maintaining her balance, Marta managed to straighten her other leg until she was standing on both of them. The serrated jaws of the snake tongs kept digging into her neck.

She heard a noise emanating from the inside of the shack. She glanced at the shack, fearing Gozzard would lunge out of the door any second. She had no time to spare. She whisked through the woods, taking care not to trip on a root or outcropping.

She thought she was heading toward the road. She would try to return to the dry goods store to hook up with Halverson. She cast a furtive glance behind her as she ran, the pole extending from her neck and smacking every so often into tree trunks. She didn't see Gozzard chasing her—yet. Hopefully he was still asleep in his drunken stupor.

She cried out and came to an abrupt halt as the snake pole handle became entangled in underbrush. She felt another stream of blood flow down her neck when the tongs scratched her neck on account of her abrupt halt.

Without the use of her bound hands she had to walk toward the underbrush and away from it and shake her head from side to side to jockey the snake pole handle loose from the underbrush. She heard a sound.

Clad in a tattered navy blue suit, a middle-aged male ghoul was shambling toward her, toting a brief case like a lawyer. Most of his nose had been chewed off by the ghoul that had infected him. He was munching on a finger sticking out of his mouth. The brown hair on his head was writhing. It turned out to be earthworms, she realized with revulsion.

She didn't know why he was still carrying his briefcase. A creature of habit, she supposed. In any case, he was getting nearer to her while she was still hung up in the underbrush.

The ghoul lurched toward her. More earthworms were crawling out of what was left of the creature's nose. Having finished consuming the finger, he ate some of the worms that squirmed into his mouth.

Marta redoubled her efforts to free the snake pole handle. It was frustrating not being able to use her hands. She just had to make do, moving back and forth from the underbrush.

At last she freed the handle from the brush.

The ghoul pounced on the handle, trying to snatch it.

Marta darted away from him, the tongs ensnaring her neck, the pole dragging behind her and whipping back and forth. She stifled a scream of vexation, knowing a scream might awake Gozzard and would attract more ghouls.

She had to keep running, her mouth shut, sweat pouring from her face, her heart pounding a rataplan.

Chapter 55

Halverson was riding his bicycle slowly down the road, surveying the woods in search of Marta as he steered her bicycle beside him.

He halted his bike and craned his neck around.

He considered heading in the other direction. How did he know for sure she hadn't gone back toward Mount Weather? On the other hand, why would she? But why would she take off on her own in the first place? She must be under duress. If so, she could be heading in any direction at the whim of her captors. Could the High Rolerz have gotten her? But why would they take only her and leave him behind at the dry goods store? Maybe they couldn't see him as he slept behind the counter.

He looked straight ahead down the road. He thought he saw a wall of some sort in the distance. He decided to keep heading in this direction to find out what it was.

He pedaled past a tow truck and three cars abandoned in the road.

A large gunmetal cloud hung overhead stuck like an airship on the top of the tallest tree in the woods.

Now that he was closer to the wall, he could see it was constructed of human skulls mortared together and it blocked the road. He didn't know how he would pass it.

Suspecting a trap of some sort, he slowed down and drove to the shoulder.

He started when he heard a noise like somebody running in the woods.

He dismounted, let both of the bikes fall to the ground, reached for his MP9, and inspected the woods in the direction of the running feet thrashing through the forest. They sounded like they were near the wall of skulls.

MP9 in hand, he stole toward the wall, a clear sign of somebody marking off their territory.

With a start Halverson caught sight of a figure barreling awkwardly out of the woods, some kind of contraption locked around her blood-streaked neck, her hands tied behind her back.

Marta.

What the hell had happened to her?

He pelted toward her, gun at the ready. He didn't see anyone following her. At that moment a ghoul fell out of a tree and landed near Marta's feet. She cried out in surprise, lost her balance, and fell on her face on the ground, a steel pole clamped to her neck.

Halverson couldn't imagine what had happened to her.

The ghoul, a teenage male wearing jeans and covered with tattoos, shambled toward her, drooling at the prospect of devouring her. A faint brown mustache crowned his lips. Except it wasn't a mustache. It was mold growing on his rotting cadaver face.

Halverson didn't want to fire his gun if he didn't have to. Not only would the noise attract ghouls but it would also alert any pursuers of his presence. He whipped out a hunting knife he had procured from Adam the shop owner during their bartering session and lunged at the ghoul.

Halverson didn't have any idea how the ghoul had climbed a tree. The ghouls were notoriously uncoordinated. Unless Tattoo had tried to escape a ghoul by climbing up the tree and the creature had bitten him. Tattoo then turned while he was up in the tree.

Halverson thrust his knife at Tattoo's head. Tattoo jerked away at the last second and avoided the impact of the blade, which glanced harmlessly off his temple. In this case his uncoordinated movements had aided him. Out of the corner of hie eye Halverson picked up on another ghoul, one clad in a suit and carrying a briefcase, stumbling through the woods toward Marta, who was struggling to stand up what with the snake pole clamped to her neck and her hands bound behind her back.

Halverson concentrated on dispatching Tattoo, who was making a beeline for Marta. Halverson hurled himself at Tattoo and impaled the ghoul's brain with his knife that he thrust through Tattoo's temple, his aim true this time. Tattoo dropped to the ground and remained motionless. Halverson wiped Tattoo's brains that smeared his knife blade onto Tattoo's wizened face.

Knife in hand, carrying it low like a professional, Halverson angled toward the suit.

An American cockroach or some other kind of large bug popped out of the suit's mouth as he made his way toward Marta, who continued to welter on the ground, unable to stand up.

Halverson rammed his knife through the ghoul's left milky eye all the way into the brain. The suit staggered forward and fell on his face on the ground. Halverson watched with bemusement as the back of the ghoul's suit started vibrating. Then he saw with disgust the reason as a myriad roaches scuttled out from under the filthy material onto the ground.

Halverson helped Marta to her feet and escorted her to the road.

"Let me get that snake pole off your neck," he said, picking up the pole and analyzing the handle to see how to open the tongs that ensnared Marta's neck.

He hit a switch on the handle and unlocked the tongs. He pulled the snake pole away from her and tossed it to the ground.

"What happened to you?" he said, studying the wounds on her neck to see if any of them were serious.

"Gozzard kidnaped me while you were sleeping. I heard his dog whining. I went out to check and Gozzard grabbed me."

"Your arteries in your neck look OK. Just some superficial scratches on your neck."

"They don't feel superficial," she said, wincing.

He unbound her wrists behind her back.

She shook her arms to get the circulation going.

Halverson scanned the forest. "Where is this Gozzard bastard?"

"He was dead drunk inside his shack the last time I saw him."

"Does he have anything to do with this wall of skulls blocking the road?"

"He's the one who put it there. He turned this into a toll road."

Halverson heard a bellowing in the woods and became alert.

A fiftyish burly guy wearing a coonskin cap and wielding a 12-gauge shotgun came storming through the woods toward him and Marta. Gozzard careered onto the road in front of his wall and trained his shotgun on Halverson.

"What are you doing with my slave?" Gozzard roared, his face flushed.

Marta snagged Halverson's MP9 from his hands, wheeled around, and, baring her teeth, fired a burst at Gozzard. The bullets went wide and struck the wall of skulls, which exploded into an inferno, hurling Gozzard off his feet and blowing his head apart. His body rocketed into the woods where he slammed what was left of his head into an oak trunk. He crumpled at the bottom of the trunk, headless.

The nitroglycerin explosion blew both Halverson and Marta off their feet, but they were farther away from the wall than Gozzard so the blast didn't wreak as much damage on them as it did on him. Their backs slammed against the ground near the forest.

Dazed, they sat up on the grass verge, shaking their heads. Halverson was the first to speak.

"What the—"

"Gozzard packed nitroglycerin into the skulls in the wall. If anybody tried to ram through the wall without paying him, that was the end of them."

Halverson nodded. "Your bullets hit the nitro."

"Good."

"My ears are still ringing from the blast."

"I can hardly hear you," said Marta, pulling a face.

"Michael K. and the High Rolerz must have heard the blast. We need to get going."

Halverson stood up. He helped Marta to her feet.

He eyed the devastated wall, where a cloud of smoke billowed from the remains. In place of the wall stretched a large crater. Beyond the crater were parked several cars in the road.

"We really need a car," he said. "They must be catching up with us."

Marta took in the cars.

"Are you thinking what I'm thinking?" he said.

"Somebody might have abandoned their car instead of paying Gozzard's toll to pass through."

PURGE

They sprinted to the crater and skirted it by means of a ledge on the right side. They ran to the cars.

Chapter 56

Halverson and Marta reached the car parked nearest to the wall ruins. The windshield had a hole a foot wide. Sitting on the driver's seat was a cracked human skull that the blast had slung from the wall into the car.

"Let's check the next car," said Halverson.

They darted to the next abandoned sedan, a compact pale green Fiat 500.

A pudgy ghoul appeared from behind a van. He was wearing glasses with one cracked lens. A surgeon's pale blue mask that he had bitten through hung in halves from his ears. He hissed at Halverson and tried to grab him. Halverson used his knife to stab the cracked lens and slice into the ghoul's eye, gouging it out. It landed on the tarmac near the ghoul's feet. Halverson buried the rest of his knife blade into the ghoul's brain.

The ghoul dropped dead on the tarmac.

Halverson wiped the brain-mantled blade on the ghoul's hair then sheathed it on his calf.

Halverson returned to the Fiat and inspected the dash. A key was inserted in the ignition.

"Why would they leave their key in the ignition?" said Marta, looking through the powered-down driver's-side window with him.

"Maybe they didn't want to pay the toll this Gozzard crook was charging and took off on their feet."

"Or maybe the douchebag killed them."

Halverson tossed his knapsack into the backseat, clambered into the driver's seat, and turned the key. The car didn't start.

"Then again, maybe they abandoned the car because it broke down," he said.

"Try it again."

Halverson complied.

"The battery sounds like it's working," she said.

"It's working, but maybe it doesn't have enough juice to start the engine."

"If the car has been sitting here a long time, the battery could easily have lost some of its charge."

Halverson cranked the ignition again.

"How much gas does it have?" said Marta, standing near the driver's-side window but unable to read the odometer.

"Half a tank. An empty fuel tank isn't holding it back."

"What do you want to do?"

"Cross your fingers. Maybe that'll help."

Marta rolled her eyes and made a show of crossing her fingers.

Halverson cranked the ignition again. It took a while but the motor turned over. Halverson let the car idle for a few minutes.

"What was wrong with it?" said Marta.

"I'm not a mechanic. Let's just get out of here before the High Rolerz turn up."

Halverson gazed past the broken skull wall at the road that petered into the distance.

"I don't see them," said Marta, following his example.

"Not yet anyway. Get in."

Marta hustled to the passenger's-side door, flung it open, threw her knapsack onto the backseat, and scooched onto the shotgun seat.

"Do you think Gozzard will turn and come after us?" she said.

"How could he? His head was pulverized. You can't have a zombie without a head. He's out of it."

"Maybe he's the lucky one," she said under her breath, watching ghouls constellating at the edge of the forest.

Halverson executed a three-point turn and drove toward DC.

Drawn by the deafening noise of the explosion, the ghouls emerged from the woods and clustered near the roadside, the milky eyes in their gruesome faces trained on Halverson and Marta like gun muzzles.

"As long as they don't block the road we're good to go," said Halverson.

"Don't let them hear you," said Marta, eying the ghouls with trepidation.

The Fiat puttered down the road, jerking fitfully. He wondered if there was something wrong with the engine. Maybe it just needed a tune-up. The engine should be getting enough gas with the fuel tank half full.

"What's wrong with this thing?" said Marta.

Halverson shrugged. "It's either this or the bicycles. On bicycles we'll never outrun the High Rolerz on their Harleys."

The Fiat started handling better. Maybe it hadn't been driven in so long that it needed warming up to function properly.

They drove in companionable silence for a while.

Halverson smelled a faint pine odor emanating from an old, sun-faded green cardboard air freshener in the shape of a three-inch-long pine tree that hung from the rearview and swayed as he drove.

"What did Gozzard do to you?" he said.

"Never mind."

"I could go back there and sodomize his corpse with a stick."

"Forget it. He's not worth the trouble."

Marta brought her hand down her forehead as if she could blot out the memory of Gozzard with a stroke of her hand.

"I hope his dog is OK. Gozzard used to kick the poor thing."

"I hate people who mistreat dogs," said Halverson, tempted to turn back and run over Gozzard's corpse ten times.

"It's pointless to remember evil people. Forget them and move on."

"If only there weren't so many of them."

"He'll probably haunt my dreams forever." She paused. "Let's get as far away from this place as we can."

Halverson stepped on the gas. "The good thing about this car is it's small and we can maneuver it around cars abandoned in the road."

Marta stared out the windshield, alone in her thoughts.

Chapter 57

Trudging along the road, Vivian flogged her blood-streaked back and winced.

"Put not your faith in the princes of this world," she said.

Freddie barked in agreement.

"Look what they did to the world," she said, gesturing to the nuked-out devastation of the woods pocked by bomb craters and inflicted with many broken and fallen trees.

"You know we're breathing radioactive waste polluting the atmosphere courtesy of our government."

Freddie glanced at her and looked serious.

"It's like this all over the country."

Vivian's feet felt sore. She wished she could stop and rest them, but she must complete her mission. She must continue her journey until she reached Michael K. and his murderous gang of barbarians. She must confront him with the enormity of his crime of the mass murder of her friends and associates.

She scourged her back.

Would she ever be able to catch up with Michael K. on her feet or was she deluding herself? She needed some kind of transportation. The cars abandoned in the road had no keys in their ignitions. She continued to inspect the cars without success.

She picked up on a scooter lying on the side of the street.

She strode over to it. She could make much better time riding it. She inspected it for damage and saw none. She lifted its handlebars, mounted the deck, and scooted down the street, feeling like a kid again.

Freddie barked and trotted after her.

"Now we can catch up to him," she said.

Eventually, anyway. They had motorcycles that could make a lot better time than she could on a scooter. For sure, it beat walking.

She picked up on ghouls prowling along the edge of the forest, foraging. They reared their putrescent heads when they saw her.

She knew they'd love to sink their moldering teeth into her. Too bad for them. She would never let them.

Growling and salivating, they stumbled and lurched after her. Pus streamed out of the lanky lead ghoul's nose. He had a peculiar bowlegged gait that made him look like he was riding an invisible horse. The other ghouls followed him.

They were all part of this world of endless suffering. Humanity must suffer. If it wasn't the ghouls, it would be something else to make life on earth miserable. Pain was humanity's lot. But she didn't believe in suicide. She believed in suffering. There was something cleansing about it, as Dmitri had once told her. She missed Dmitri and the others. They were her friends, and they were all taken away from her by Michael K., the evilest person she had ever met, even eviler than her father. Maybe Michael K. was the antichrist that Dmitri kept talking about. But he looked just like anybody else. Then again the antichrist *would* assume the form of a human so as not give himself away. *The Devil hath power To assume a pleasing shape.*

Her jaw set with determination, she scooted faster. She must confront him.

Freddie ran to catch up with her.

She glanced behind her at him. "Let me know when you're tired, boy, and I'll slow down."

Freddie woofed as if in acknowledgment. For the time being he kept pace with her and seemed happy to do so.

"You're the best dog in the world."

She could have sworn he was grinning at her.

Holding onto the handlebars with one hand, she flailed her back with her whip and continued pushing herself forward on the scooter with her foot.

Chapter 58

"Did you take care of Ed, Gabino, Sabrina, and Moon?" said Purdy, riding shotgun.

He watched the bikers roll up the spike strip in front of the tunnel.

"The other men refused to carry out your order," said Guevara at the wheel of the Suburban. "I took care of it personally." He contorted his face with distaste at the memory. "One bullet in each of their foreheads."

Guevara drove forward out of the tunnel.

"They refused to obey your order?" said Purdy.

"I can't blame them, sir. The only way I could pull the trigger was by imagining the four of them as ghouls. I couldn't stand the idea of it so I shot them."

"Let me remind you, Guevara, they were already dead. You didn't kill anybody."

"Yes, sir. I keep telling myself that," said Guevara, continuing to be upset by his shooting of fellow squad members. "But a bullet to the head of a friend is still a bullet to the head of a friend."

Purdy started when he heard a thunderous blast in the distance. "Did you hear that explosion up ahead?"

"Yeah," said Guevara, straining his eyes trying to make out the source. "I can't see anything. We're too far away."

"Slow down. We could be heading into a trap."

Guevara eased up on the gas.

The Harleys that flanked him drove past him toward the source of the blast.

"The idiots should be slowing down," said Guevara. "Somebody could be waiting for them with sticks of TNT in their hands."

A skinhead on a Harley knocked on Purdy's window as he chugged by.

"Move faster," said the skinhead, glowering over his shoulder at Purdy as he passed the Suburban.

Purdy glared back at him.

"Keep it slow," Purdy told Guevara.

"No problem, sir."

Purdy got on his walkie-talkie.

"Angel Three, this is Angel Two. Over."

"This is Angel Three, sir. Come in. Over."

"There was an explosion up ahead. We're slowing down while we figure out what happened. Over."

"Yes, sir. Over."

"We'll get back to you when we know what's going on. Over and out."

"You think that blast had something to do with the High Rolerz?" said Guevara.

"I don't know why they would set off a bomb in the direction we're heading. Something else must be going on."

"I see black smoke pluming in the distance."

"I can see it too."

"Maybe an abandoned car on the street blew up."

"A car wouldn't make such a loud noise. That was a military-grade explosive."

"What do you want me to do, sir?"

"Keep driving. We need to check this out."

"Could it have been a landmine? Maybe Halverson got blown up."

"Hmm. Possible. But somehow I don't think we're that lucky."

They approached the crater in the street, a segment of a wall of skulls standing on either side of it. The motorcycles that had passed Purdy were parked in front of the crater.

"What the . . . ?" said Guevara, pulling to a halt.

Purdy studied the situation. "It looks like a wall constructed of human skulls was blocking the road here. Somebody wanted to pass so they blew up the wall."

"Where's the person who blew it up?"

"If they were heading toward us, they're long gone."

"Like in *wasted*?"

"Like in *blown to bits*, or we would have encountered them on the road."

Guevara frowned in thought. "Why would someone block a public road with a wall made of human skulls?"

Purdy shrugged. "Maybe they were marking their territory."

He saw Michael K. standing near an oak staring at a body lying on the ground without a head.

"It looks like the blast claimed a life," said Purdy.

Guevara followed his gaze. "Someone was standing too close to the wall."

Purdy caught sight of Michael K. gazing at him.

"What's he want?" said Guevara. "I don't trust that guy."

"Neither do I." Purdy looked at the crater in the road up ahead. "We got a problem, and I think he knows it."

"The crater?"

"It's too deep. We're not gonna be able to drive the Suburbans through it."

"Maybe Halverson blew up the road, knowing we were following him."

"Could be. The problem is we can't go after him in these things."

"Neither can the Harleys."

"I'm not so sure. They might be able to drive around the crater rim."

"You think they'll fit?"

Purdy scrutinized the crater. "It looks like there might be enough room over there on that ledge on the right side of the crater."

"Then we'll go around it too."

"There's not enough room for an SUV. And we can't go through the woods around the crater because there are too many trees growing close together."

"Are you suggesting we abandon our vehicles?" said Guevara in surprise.

"We don't have a choice unless we turn back."

"The president won't be happy if we do that."

"I know. I've already rejected that option. We're going ahead one way or another."

"Like how?"

"Maybe Michael K. will lend us some of his Harleys."

"Do you really think so, sir?"

"No. The only reason he didn't kill us before was because I convinced him I know where Halverson is headed."

Darren dismounted his Harley and strode toward the Suburban. He made a winding motion with his hand to power down the driver's-side window.

Guevara looked at Purdy to see what he should do.

"We better find out what he wants," said Purdy. "Lower the window.

Guevara powered down the window.

Crouching, Darren gazed at Purdy sitting in the shotgun seat. "The boss wants a powwow."

"What about?" said Purdy.

"We need to discuss our future plans."

"Fine. Bring him here."

"He wants to meet you and your militia out here in the open."

"Why can't we talk through the window like you're doing?"

"I don't question his orders. I just relay them."

"I would prefer to stay in our vehicle when we powwow with your boss."

Darren shook his head. "Unacceptable. Don't you understand we have a problem up ahead." He gestured at the crater.

"Why can't he talk to me through the window like you?"

"Because he doesn't like standing next to your car looking like a hooker trying to pick up a john on the Sunset Strip," said Darren, becoming angry.

He spun on his heel and stalked away.

"I don't trust those guys, sir," said Guevara.

"Neither do I. But we need an alliance with them. We need to negotiate."

"Why do we have to get out of our vehicle?"

"We're unprotected if we go outside. At least we have protection staying in this bulletproof vehicle."

"You think he's planning to attack us?"

"He knows we can't get past the crater in our Suburbans so he wants us to leave them. We're gonna have to do it eventually."

"But how do we go after Halverson if we leave our vehicles?"

"On our feet, it looks like. Or maybe we can commandeer an abandoned car on the other side of the crater."

"I don't get why Michael K. wants to talk to us only if we leave our vehicles."

Purdy scoped out the High Rolerz mounted on the Harleys surrounding the two Suburbans.

"I don't like it," he said. "But we need to keep them as allies. They got too much manpower. You know the old saying. Keep your friends close but your enemies closer."

Guevara cracked a half smile. "*The Godfather*. My favorite movie."

"Let's find out what Michael K. wants."

Chapter 59

His SIG in his holster, Purdy stepped out of the Suburban, strode around the hood, and made for Michael K., who was standing next to his Harley, watching him.

"Stop," said Michael K.

Purdy froze in his tracks. "What's the problem? We have an alliance."

"Throw down your gun. Since we have an alliance, you don't need a gun."

"Why don't you toss down your gun too?" said Purdy, not happy about being unarmed while all the High Rolerz had guns.

"This alliance is gonna rapidly deteriorate if you don't cooperate."

Despite his misgivings Purdy didn't see any way around it. He threw his SIG on the tarmac.

"Tell the rest of your men to leave their vehicles and throw down their weapons."

Purdy felt sweat dripping from his armpits.

"Why?" he said, frowning.

"I want to talk to all of you."

"They can hear you fine from their vehicles."

"No, they can't. I don't plan on raising my voice for their sakes."

"Is this really necessary?"

"If you want to continue our alliance."

Purdy said nothing, trying to figure a way out of his dilemma.

"If you want to break our alliance, you're going about it the right way," said Michael K.

Purdy didn't like the idea of leaving all of his team vulnerable to attack.

"What exactly is the point of this powwow?" he said.

"I'll tell you after your crew members leave their vehicles and throw down their guns. This is taking too long. Either shit or get off the pot."

Purdy spoke into his shoulder mic. "Everybody get out of your vehicles without your weapons."

He saw Guevara's questioning face eyeing him with disbelief from the driver's seat of their Suburban.

"Everybody out," said Guevara. "Do you copy?"

Leaving their guns behind, Guevara and the two soldiers in the backseat slowly exited their Suburban. Led by Richard, the three soldiers in Angel Three also climbed out of their vehicle unarmed.

Five eleven, clad in camos, the SEAL leader of Angel Three, Richard was a black man in his midtwenties with cropped hair and a large nose that skewed to the right thanks to its having been broken several times in fights when he was growing up in Harlem.

He held his SIG P226 in his hand as he exited the Suburban and didn't drop it.

"Are you sure this is right, sir?" he asked Purdy. "Throwing down our pieces?"

"We're here to negotiate with Michael K., Richard," answered Purdy. "You don't need a weapon for negotiating."

"A SIG can be pretty convincing in negotiations."

"Tell him to drop it," said Michael K., eyeballing the SIG in Richard's hand.

"Get rid of the SIG," said Purdy against his better judgment.

Richard hesitated.

"If you don't drop it, you're in violation of our alliance," said Michael K.

Richard surveyed the High Rolerz. "Why don't you guys have to toss your pieces? Why is it only us?"

"Because if you don't do as I say, your heart will stop beating."

"That sounds like a threat."

Richard searched the surly faces of the High Rolerz, most of them mounted on their Harleys.

"These guys are getting ready to take us out, sir," he told Purdy.

"Toss down your piece, and I'll explain the problem we have as allies," said Michael K.

Richard kept the SIG in his hand.

"Darren," said Michael K.

Darren shot Richard in the head with a Browning Hi-Power. Richard's knees buckled. He was dead before he hit the tarmac, a nine mil buried in his brain.

His blood boiling, Purdy exploded with rage. "You had no call to do that. We are your allies."

He ached to blow away Michael K. on the spot, but his gun lay on the ground.

"Now that we got that settled, let's get down to business," said Michael K., casting a baleful glance at Richard's lifeless body. "As it may have come to your attention, there is a bomb crater in the road ahead of us. That bomb crater has rendered your Suburbans useless to us as they cannot cross it. We have no need of an alliance with you."

"Lend us some motorcycles."

"Why should we waste our hogs on you and your team?"

"Because I know where Halverson's going. I thought I made that clear to you before."

Michael K. inspected his fingernails. "The problem is you've been lying to us."

Purdy's heartbeat raced. He swallowed tensely.

Michael K. stared at Purdy. "Do you admit you lied to us when you became our allies?"

"No."

"You told us you weren't feds. You said you commandeered those Suburbans from feds."

"Right."

"If that's true, why are you champing at the bit to capture Halverson who you say assassinated the president?"

"What don't you understand?"

"Your story doesn't hold water."

"Everything I told you is true," said Purdy, adrenaline coursing through him, sweat stippling his face.

"Let me put it to you in words you can understand. If you're not feds, why do you give a flying fuck about who assassinated the president?"

Purdy deliberated. "Because we're Americans and we love our country. Every American should care who assassinated the president."

"I don't. The current government in power doesn't represent us. It tried to destroy the entire population by nuking the country."

"They nuked the country to destroy the infected ghouls."

"All we, the people, are to the politicians is collateral damage? Is that it? The entire population of the country as collateral damage is OK with the feds?"

"I'm with you," said Purdy, reversing tactics. "I hate the feds too. Look what they did to our great country."

"You were just defending their actions a minute ago. You're getting caught in your own web of lies. I believe you are all feds, and those government vehicles are yours." Michael K. turned to his gang. "Open fire."

The High Rolerz raised their weapons and obeyed his command. A barrage of bullets cut down Purdy's team.

Outraged and appalled, Purdy watched his team fall to the tarmac.

Guevara dove to the tarmac to retrieve his SIG but was perforated with twenty bullets before he could put his hand around the grip. He lay bleeding on his stomach, gouts of blood spewing from his mouth.

Purdy eyed Guevara's SIG.

"Tsk-tsk," said Michael K. "Not a good idea."

"You psycho. You're all a bunch of sociopaths. Thugs with guns."

"You shouldn't have lied to us. There's nothing I hate more than a liar."

Chapter 60

"What are you waiting for?" said Purdy, realizing he was the only one of his squad still alive, his body unscathed.

"You said you know where Halverson is going," said Michael K. "Tell me now and I might let you live."

"I doubt it."

"A tiny chance I'm telling the truth is better than no chance."

Whipping his .357 Magnum Colt Python revolver from the leather holster on his hip, Michael K. stalked toward Purdy.

Purdy stiffened.

"I call my gang the High Rolerz because we love to gamble. We gamble on everything, because that's what life is all about. It's a gamble from the day you're born to the day you die. In the end what happens to you in life is all luck. It's all about taking your chances."

Michael K. flipped out the Python's loaded six-round cylinder. He withdrew five of the rounds from their chambers and deposited them in his trouser pocket as Purdy watched with a sweaty face.

"I'm sure you've heard of Russian roulette," said Michael K. "It's a game of chance just like life. That's why I like it so much. The lucky ones go on living in this world, and the unlucky ones don't. Do you think you're lucky or unlucky?"

"Get to the point."

"We're gonna play a variation of Russian roulette."

Michael K. spun the cylinder with one bullet loaded in it then snapped it shut.

He trained the Python on Purdy's sweat-gleaming forehead. "The odds are in your favor. There's only a one-in-six chance that you will die when I squeeze the trigger. If a bullet comes out, you would have to consider yourself unlucky, I'm afraid. Let's look at it this way. You have about an 84 percent chance of living when I shoot at you."

Purdy stared at the gaping muzzle leveled at his face.

"Where is Halverson going?" asked Michael K.

Purdy gnashed his teeth. He said nothing. Out of the corner of his eye he saw members of the High Rolerz laying down bets on the tarmac, wagering with bullets instead of dollars as they watched him with greedy fascination.

Michael K. squeezed the Python trigger.

Click.

"You see, the odds were in your favor, and you won," said Michael K., grinning. His grin vanished as quickly as it had appeared. "But you didn't tell me what I want to know. It looks like the game will continue—unless you want to give me the answer now."

"I have nothing to say."

Michael K. smiled. "I'm glad you said that. Our game will continue. Russian roulette is so unpredictable. You never know what's gonna happen. It's all about the odds. And I can change the odds any time I wish, for instance when I think your chances of living are too great—like now."

He fished out another round from his trouser pocket. "Should we make this more interesting?"

Purdy said nothing, his face frozen.

Michael K. flipped open the cylinder, found an empty chamber, loaded it with the round, spun the cylinder, and snapped it shut.

"Let's see. The odds have changed now. Your chances of survival have been reduced to around 68 percent with this second bullet in the cylinder. But the odds are still in your favor—"

"Get on with it."

"Where is Halverson going?"

Purdy raised his eyebrows, said nothing.

Facing Purdy, Michael K. said, "I just realized something. You can see the chambers in the cylinder from where you're standing."

"It doesn't matter. I'm not talking."

"We'll see."

Michael K. opened the cylinder, and, spinning it, stepped behind Purdy. When the cylinder stopped moving, he slammed it shut, and trained the Python on the back of Purdy's skull, touching the bone with the steel muzzle.

"Talk," said Michael K.

Sweating, Purdy worked his mouth back and forth, dreading the sound of the gunshot.

"Where is Halverson going?" said Michael K.

No answer.

Michael K. squeezed the trigger.

Click.

"You see," he said. "The laws of probability were on your side, and you won. Now I'm gonna make the game more dangerous. I'm adding two more bullets to the cylinder. Your odds of survival are now about 32 percent."

Michael K. spun the cylinder and slammed it shut.

"Do you ever stop talking?" said Purdy.

He heard the nerve-shattering click of the Python cocking behind his head.

"I don't like your chances this time," said Michael K.

Purdy saw the High Rolerz eagerly gambling on the outcome of the next gunshot as they watched him, betting several handfuls of bullets each.

The fact was, he didn't know for sure where Halverson was going. Purdy had guessed it might be the Raven Rock bunker, because the rightful president, the speaker of the house, was taking refuge there.

"Where's Halverson going?"

"Raven Rock."

Purdy wondered if it would make any difference if he told Michael K. what he wanted to know. Once Michael K. found out Halverson's destination, he would have no use for Purdy. Purdy figured he was screwed no matter what he did. If he refused to talk, Michael K. would kill him. If he talked, Michael K. would kill him. In the end Purdy wanted Halverson dead, and he didn't care who killed him. It might just as well be the High Rolerz who whacked Halverson. If Purdy talked, he figured he had at least a smattering of a chance that Michael K. would let him live.

"Where is Raven Rock?" said Michael K.

"It's a government bunker also known as Site R."

"I asked you where it is, not what it is."

"The bunker tunnel's east opening is near the Route 16 intersection with Jacks Mountain Road in Pennsylvania right on the border with Maryland."

"Now how would you know that if you're not a government agent?"

Purdy said nothing.

"There's only one problem with your answer," said Michael K. "This is the road to DC, not to Pennsylvania."

Purdy thought about it.

"They're detouring to DC," he said.

"Why?"

There was only one reason Purdy could think of. "Costello has a brother in DC."

"How can I tell if you're telling me the truth?"

"What difference does it make? You're gonna kill me anyway."

"Like I said before, everything in this thing called life is luck. The laws of probability usually rule. Like Dirty Harry once said, 'Do you feel lucky?'"

Michael K. squeezed the Python trigger and blew Purdy's skull apart.

The High Rolerz who won their bets cheered as Purdy's body crumpled on the tarmac, his skull scattered in bloody shards around him like pumpkin pips.

"Your luck ran out," said Michael K., leering down at Purdy's corpse.

Darren ran up to Michael K. "Why'd you whack him out, boss?"

"Because he's no use to us anymore."

"He could have been lying about Halverson's destination."

"It didn't do him much good," said Michael K., holstering his Python. "Did it?"

"Where's Raven Rock?" said Darren, puzzled.

He had been too far away to hear Purdy's answer.

"'Over the Mountains of the Moon, Down the Valley of the Shadow. Ride boldly ride, the shade replied, if you seek for Eldorado.'"

"What?"

"Poetry, Darren. Edgar Allan Poe. There's more truth in poetry than in a hundred encyclopedias."

Darren continued to look confused.

"Poetry *and a gun*," said Michael K., patting his Python snug in its holster.

Darren nodded in understanding.

Michael K. started when a gunshot rang out. Drawing his Python he cast around for the source of the shot.

"This stinking fed was still alive," said a fortyish, slender blonde with a mohawk, her black leather vest hanging open as she continued to train her pistol on a man dressed in camos sprawled motionless on the tarmac.

Her face bore sharp features and blazing blue eyes.

"Good work, Gayle," said Michael K., holstering his Python.

"Thank you, sir," she said, grinning with edged lips, baring her small, even teeth.

"Let's move out," said Michael K., mounting his Harley. "Darren, you ride point."

Darren hopped onto his hog and drove over the four-foot-wide strip of earth that bordered the crater on the right. He rode onto the road and waited for the others.

Michael K. watched him, making sure the earth didn't give way under the weight of Darren's hog.

"Follow me," Michael K. told his gang as he rode over the earthen strip.

They followed him Indian file and gathered on the tarmac on the other side of the crater.

"Who killed my brother Bobby K.?" he asked.

"Halverson," they answered.

"What's our mission?" said Michael K.

"Kill Halverson," they roared in unison. "Kill Halverson."

Michael K. grinned. "Let's do it."

Whooping, they followed Darren down the road on their chugging motorcycles.

Chapter 61

Weaving between abandoned cars, Vivian scooted down the road, Freddie trotting behind her, his tongue hanging out. She glanced behind her at him and slowed down. He looked tired.

"We need a water break," she said, coming to a halt next to a stake truck.

She lowered the tailgate, sat on it, opened her water bottle, and slaked her thirst. The bottled spring water felt refreshing.

Freddie sat next to her, his tongue hanging out as he watched her.

She raised the water bottle over his head. He tilted his head upward to watch it, hanging his mouth open.

"Open wide," she said, pouring water into his mouth.

He sat there, drinking the water.

"Too bad we don't have a bowl for you," she said, looking behind her into the stake truck.

She didn't spot a bowl, just tools scattered among empty beer cans.

She capped the bottle. "That's enough for now. We need to conserve water."

She flogged her back suddenly as though she had been negligent in her self-flagellation routine while she had been riding her scooter. The burning pain of the flogging brought tears to her eyes. She couldn't imagine how messed up her back must look from all the scars and welts and cuts inflicted by her constant flogging. She would need a mirror to find out. She figured she was better off not knowing.

"We are born in pain, and we will die in pain."

Freddie barked in agreement.

"I bet you know all about pain, about starving out here in the wasteland, huh, Freddie?"

She heard mewling nearby. Tilting up her head she looked toward the source of the sound.

A black and brown dog lurked at the edge of the woods, looking toward her and Freddie. The dog continued to whine.

"Is this a friend of yours, Freddie?"

Freddie looked puzzled.

"I guess not. Maybe he's hungry. Come here, boy," she said, gesticulating to the dog.

Continuing to mewl, the dog gazed at her.

"Want something to eat," she said, holding up a strip of beef jerky.

The dog looked wary of her and Freddie. Vivian didn't understand it.

"Let's go over there and show him we're his friends."

Freddie barked in agreement.

She and he strode toward the stray dog.

Terrified, the dog bolted into the woods.

"Don't run away. We want to help you. Come back."

Buzzard slinked back toward them out of the woods.

"That's better. We're your friends," said Vivian, holding the beef jerky toward him.

His brown eyes wide with fear, he wheeled around and scampered back into the woods. Vivian picked up on his scared eyes peering out of the bushes at her.

"He must be scared of people. I can't say that I blame him. No telling what kind of people he's been dealing with. Whoever it was, they abused the poor dog."

Buzzard continued whining from the bushes and eying Vivian.

"Freddie, see if you can bring him over here."

Freddie walked toward Buzzard and, the better part of ten feet away from him, barked softly. Buzzard looked at him. Freddie turned around and walked toward Vivian, glancing behind him to see if Buzzard was following him. Buzzard watched him with lugubrious brown eyes.

Vivian whistled softly to Buzzard. "Come over here, boy. Time to eat."

Hungry, Buzzard skulked after Freddie to Vivian.

"Did somebody abuse you, boy?"

Buzzard slouched toward her, smelling the jerky in her hand.

"I won't hurt you. We're all a bunch of outcasts here, trying to get by on our own."

Buzzard came close enough to her to sniff her. He seemed satisfied with her scent. He snatched the jerky in his jaws and scarfed it down.

"Whoever abused you should be ashamed," said Vivian, watching Buzzard eat. "But what can you expect in this brutal world? Nothing but suffering."

Skittish, Buzzard expected to be kicked any minute while he ate.

"Calm down."

He looked ready to bolt any second despite her admonition.

She flailed her back, grimacing as the lash bit into her tender flesh.

After Buzzard finished eating, Vivian reached circumspectly toward his neck. When he saw her hand coming toward him he wanted to scram.

"I'm not gonna hurt you," she said.

Fearing he might bite her she reached by degrees toward his collar. She didn't hear him growl so she latched onto his dog tag and inspected it for his name.

"Buzzard," she said. "Glad to meet you, though I think your master gave you a horrible name."

Buzzard stood his ground and eyed her morosely.

"I don't know what happened to your master, but you're welcome to join us. I need to get an apology from someone who murdered my friends in cold blood." She turned to Freddie. "Come on, Freddie. We need to resume our trek."

Freddie followed her to her scooter.

She mounted her scooter and looked back at Buzzard, who was standing watching them, trying to make up his mind what to do. She thought he was looking at the whip in her hand with fear.

She wiggled the whip. "This isn't for you. Don't be scared. I'll never whip you. This is for me alone."

Head cocked, Buzzard stared at her as if trying to understand her.

Vivian flogged her back and pulled a face. "See."

Buzzard looked confused by her actions.

Vivian heaved a sigh. "You're an animal. You don't understand what life has in store for you. You're lucky, actually. We humans know. That's our lot. Too much knowledge."

A mewl issued from Buzzard's throat.

"You prefer going it alone? You're a lone wolf. Is that it? I can understand that, but most dogs need companionship. Anyway, you're welcome to come with us. If you change your mind about staying here, sniff out our trail. We want you to join us."

Vivian shoved off on her scooter.

His eyes forlorn, Buzzard watched them leave.

Trotting away, Freddie looked back at him.

His master must have been a real creep to make him so distrustful of her, decided Vivian. She thought there was still a chance he might follow them. She slowed her scooter, hoping he would run after them.

Buzzard was staring at them with longing. At last he woofed and broke into a run after them.

"Good boy," said Vivian, smiling, waiting for him to catch up. "You're better off with us than all by yourself in this wasteland."

Holding his head up high, feeling wanted, Buzzard jogged alongside them.

"You're not gonna like where we're going, boy, but I got to set things right with a mass murderer."

Chapter 62

When Halverson drove up to the White House front yard in his commandeered Fiat, he was disheartened by the sight of the decimated structure. The four Ionic columns and the triangular pediment lay in rubble on the ground. The house itself was in charred ruins. The fountain in the bomb-cratered front yard had long since stopped flowing. He halted the Fiat and gaped at the destruction.

He knew the postapocalyptic presidents had fired ICBMs with nuclear warheads at all of the most populated cities in the US in an attempt to wipe out the millions of infected ghouls that infested them foraging for living human flesh. The presidents had seen the cities as breeding grounds for the ghouls and therefore had decided those cities must be nuked into oblivion regardless of the cost to human lives who populated the cities.

If he wasn't seeing it with his own eyes, Halverson would never have believed an American president would ever nuke the White House, the iconic symbol of the United States. It just showed how desperate the presidents were to save the country from the hordes of flesh-eating ghouls.

Despite the nukes, ghouls still shambled through the White House ruins and across the front lawn, their clothes hanging from their dead bodies in charred tatters as they negotiated the detritus scattered helter-skelter. A knapsack strapped to her back, a twentyish woman wearing blue-tinted sunglasses and a navy blue wool knit watch cap had drool dripping from her mouth. A joint wedged between her shriveled lips, she scratched her hair, plucked a maggot out, and flicked it onto the lawn like it was a marble. Her eyes glowed alternately milky and scarlet as she blew smoke out of her mouth. She was slogging across the lawn toward the Fiat.

"Do those things know how to get stoned on weed?" said Marta.

The stoner ghoul continued trudging toward them, exhaling smoke and managing to keep the joint wedged between her lips at the same time. Her eyes burned like red-hot coals as she stared at them.

Halverson kept tooling down the road.

The chain-link fence surrounding the White House was no more. It too had been blasted apart and torqued by nukes.

"What have they done to us?" said Marta, riding shotgun, taking in the heartbreaking devastation.

"Supposedly they were nuking the ghouls."

"You sound like you're not surprised."

"I knew they nuked New York and Las Vegas. But this, I really didn't expect to see the White house in ruins, not from a nuke anyway. Ghouls yes. I expected to see ghouls overrunning the place. They're everywhere, and nobody can stop them."

"The White House is destroyed, but the ghouls still live."

"Radiation has little effect on the ghouls. The impact of the nuclear blast kills them by annihilating their brains, but the radiation does them no harm. It doesn't kill their brains."

"Isn't there some way we can kill these things without killing ourselves in the bargain?"

Halverson faced her. "Do you really think your brother could have survived this holocaust?"

"I hope so," she said, her voice tight. "I had no idea DC would look like this. I thought it would be the one place safe from nukes."

Halverson halted the Fiat and killed the engine.

"The politicians' lives were never at risk," he said. "They're all hiding in nukeproof bunkers in Mount Weather and Raven Rock. They have another bunker in the Cheyenne Mountain Complex in Colorado. The presidents saw DC as superfluous. Killing ghouls was more important to them than saving human lives and architecture, and they knew DC was infested with ghouls."

"I don't want to tour all the destruction here. Let's head straight for my brother's apartment." Marta paused a beat and narrowed her eyes. "What's going on over there?"

Halverson looked in the direction she was eyeballing.

Twenty-odd ghouls were surrounding a black Volkswagen Jetta sedan and trying to break into it. They couldn't get in because the car had all of its windows rolled up.

"Somebody's in trouble," said Halverson.

He fired the ignition in the Fiat and drove toward the Jetta.

"What are you gonna do?" said Marta.

"Somebody must be trapped inside the car. We gotta help them."

"There are too many of those things."

Halverson stopped the Fiat and sprang out the door, his MP9 in his hand. He advanced on the ghouls that were attacking the Jetta. Marta clambered out of the Fiat and followed him, cradling her MP5.

Halverson fired a burst into the backs of the skulls belonging to the nearest ghouls. Six of the ghouls crumpled, their brains blown out. Marta took out four more with her MP5. Stepping over the ghoul corpses at his feet, Halverson approached the driver's-side window of the Jetta. He peered through the window.

A blonde woman pushing thirty was sitting in the driver's seat and craning toward another woman, who was sitting motionless in the shotgun seat staring blindly ahead, the top of her skull broken off, exposing her brain, which the blonde was feasting on with relish, grey glop oozing out of the corners of her mouth.

Revolted, Halverson shot open the driver's-side window and blew apart the skulls of the blonde ghoul and her victim.

He scoped out the rest of the interior of the Jetta. Nobody else was inside.

Meanwhile, what was let of the knot of ghouls that had been surrounding the sedan commenced advancing on Halverson and Marta.

"We're too late," he said. "Let's get out of here."

Marta raced after him to the Fiat. The ghouls trudged after them, flailing their limbs and grunting in frustration at their inability to catch up to them.

Halverson and Marta piled into the Fiat. Halverson fired the ignition and peeled away from the curb, running over two chasing ghouls in the process.

"Do you know where your brother lives?" said Halverson, feeling the Fiat bounce up and down over the two ghouls being crushed beneath the wheels.

"A mile or so from here, according to him," said Marta. "Follow Pennsylvania Avenue, and we'll reach his apartment."

"If it looks like it does around here, I don't like his chances."

Marta stared out the windshield as if in a trance. "We need to think positive."

"Is he older than you?"

"Yeah."

"What's his name?"

"Declan."

"Didn't you say before that he drove an Uber?"

"Yeah."

"I bet he's out of work—"

"Like everybody else," cut in Marta.

Halverson nodded yes. "The only people working are guys like the slimebag Gozzard who kidnaped you—and he's a thug."

"He *was* a thug."

Halverson smiled with half his mouth.

Marta scoped out the neighborhood. "Declan's apartment is near here." She locked her gaze on an apartment house on the upcoming corner. "There. I think he lives there."

"I don't see that many ghouls around here," said Halverson, checking out the neighborhood.

He parked the Fiat near the curb and killed the engine.

Chapter 63

The apartment house was a rectangular four-story brick building that reminded Halverson of the Texas School Book Depository where Oswald had assassinated JFK, except the depository had more floors.

"It looks like a lot of these apartments could be deserted," said Halverson, inspecting the apartment house windows. He saw no one in any of the rooms.

"Don't say that. I know he's here. He has to be."

"Which apartment is he in?"

"Number 220."

They piled out of the car and made for the entrance to the apartment house, taking their weapons with them.

As they stole down the hallway of the first floor, they saw many apartment doors ajar. MP9 at the ready, Halverson checked out several of the unsecured apartments.

"Why are all these doors open?" he said.

"Something's not right," said Marta.

Halverson poked his nose into one of the apartments that had its door open. The room was deserted, save for upended furniture, and books and papers strewn on the floor. Shafts of sunlight lancing into the room highlighted swirling dust motes in their beams. The faint acrid odor of wine staining the carpet wafted to his nose.

"Looters must have rifled this one."

Marta became concerned for Declan's safety. She belted to the elevator and pressed the black plastic button at its side. She waited for the elevator. Halverson strode over to her.

"Not all of the rooms were looted," he said.

"Where's the elevator?" she said, pressing the button again and again.

Halverson looked at the unlit annunciator above the elevator door. "It must be broken. Let's take the stairs."

They found the stairs at the corner of the building and ascended them.

Out of the corner of his eye Halverson caught sight of movement as he exited the stairwell onto the second floor.

Wearing a moth-eaten yellow dress a short female ghoul with red bangs sneered at him and lunged toward him, her freckled face a mask of hatred. He whipped his hunting knife out of his belt and thrust it through her milky eye into her brain. She crumpled on the carpet, her face sneering even in death.

Marta kept her MP5 at the ready.

Halverson didn't see any more ghouls in the hallway. He wiped the ghoul's brains off his knife onto her bangs. He smelled the knife, looked sick, and returned it to his waistband.

He and Marta stole toward room 220.

The door was closed.

"At least his room wasn't looted," he said, holding his voice down in case there was another ghoul lurking about.

Marta knocked lightly on the door.

Nobody answered.

"Are you sure this is the right apartment?" said Halverson.

"Yes."

She knocked again on the door, more firmly this time.

Pressing her mouth close to the door, she whispered, "Declan, it's me, Marta."

Halverson thought he heard somebody stirring inside the apartment.

"Stand back from the door," he said.

"Why?" said Marta.

"I heard movement inside."

Marta stepped back.

The occupant cracked the door. Halverson noticed a chain-lock on it. He saw an eye peeking out from under the chain-lock.

"You're not Marta," said an unshaven guy, who was in his late twenties.

His paranoid green eyes looked world-weary. Although he had not yet reached his thirtieth birthday, his dark hair was beginning to show hints of grey.

Marta pushed Halverson out of the way and stood in front of the man as he unlocked the chain-lock and opened the door. Marta slung her MP5 over her shoulder and burst into the room to hug Declan.

"I didn't believe I'd ever see you again," said Declan, hugging her with one arm.

Marta picked up on his amputated limb immediately. His forearm and hand were missing on his left arm. Taken aback, she stepped away from him.

"What happened to your arm?"

Halverson entered the room and closed the door behind him. "We better keep the door shut in case more ghouls show up."

"Who's he?" said Declan.

"Halverson," said Marta.

"Hello," said Halverson with a brief smile.

"I wish we could be meeting under better circumstances," said Declan.

Halverson nodded.

"What happened to your arm?" Marta asked again.

Halverson saw dried bloodstains on the shredded remains of Declan's shirtsleeve on his upper arm. The shirtsleeve looked like it had been half torn off and half cut off with a dull pair of scissors. A blackened stump peeked through the rag of sleeve that partially covered it. Halverson figured the stump had been cauterized to prevent infection.

Declan became hesitant.

"What's wrong?" said Marta.

"I don't know if I should tell you," he said, gnawing his lower lip.

"I'm your only living relative. I want to know what happened."

"It will make you sick."

"No way. You can't believe what I've been through, *what we've all been through*. We're all part of this catastrophe. I was

223

kidnaped by a creep named Gozzard. He put me through hell. Nothing you can say will upset me."

"Who is this asshole Gozzard? Want me to take care of him?" said Declan, doing a slow burn.

"Forget him. He's dead."

Declan relaxed after a fashion. "I would've made him take a flying leap off a high mountain with a bat shoved up his ass."

"Your arm?" persisted Marta.

Chapter 64

Recalling the event with discomfiture, Declan paced around his apartment.

"I always keep my door shut when I go to sleep because of the ghouls," he said. "I don't want them sneaking into my room and attacking me while I sleep. When it's really hot, I keep my window open though, because I can't sleep in the heat. I have no A/C.

"A week ago it was hot here—you know how weird the weather is these days with global warming and nuke radiation. I lost my train of thought. Where was I? Oh, I know. I was sleeping in my bed during the heatwave when I felt horrible pain in my forearm," he said, glancing at his missing arm. "I jackknifed up in bed, screaming. My eyes were blurry with sleep, but I could make out in the darkness a ghoul chewing my arm. I kicked the stinking thing away, leapt out of bed, and grabbed a hammer that I kept as a weapon on an end table near the foot of my bed. I hammered the male ghoul's head with all my strength until the skull fractured and his brains oozed out. He dropped dead on the spot. I flung the brain-smeared hammer down on the floor and sprinted to the kitchen.

"I flicked on the overhead fluorescent light, which blinded me. When my eyes became accustomed to the light, I found the meat cleaver hanging from the wall. I snatched the cleaver. My face was covered with sweat as I thought about what I was about to do. But I saw no other choice. I had to do it. My forearm was bleeding all over the linoleum floor.

"I placed my bleeding forearm on the island Formica counter and raised the meat cleaver over my head, preparing to amputate my arm. My heart was racing like crazy from all the adrenaline coursing through my body. If it wasn't for the adrenaline, I would have fainted. I was wide awake now and I could see my wounded arm clearly in the fluorescent light that flooded the kitchen. I saw the blood pulsing out of the bite mark. But it wasn't the blood that worried me or the loss of my arm. It was knowing that I would turn because a ghoul had bitten and infected me. I ground my teeth. I knew I had to act quickly. Any hesitation on my part would lead to my turning. Hollering, I brought down the meat cleaver on my arm and severed it at the elbow. The forearm skittered a few inches across the counter.

"Blood gushed all over the floor. I screamed in agony and wrapped a towel around the wound to stanch the bleeding. But that wouldn't be enough, I knew. I needed to cauterize the wound to disinfect it. I turned on one of the coils on my gas range to high and held my bleeding stump of arm over the flame. Despite gritting my teeth, I couldn't help yelling from the pain. I thought I was gonna pass out any minute. Nevertheless, through sheer determination, I kept my arm stump over the flame until the bleeding stopped. The stench of my burning flesh was nauseating. It was difficult to keep from puking—especially when I spotted my gnawed amputated forearm lying on the island counter. I put on my right hand a purple Playtex rubber glove that I kept under my sink.

"My eyes wild, I scoffed up the infected forearm and dashed to the open window in my bedroom. I hurled the arm out the window onto the street below. I didn't want that thing anywhere near me. The blood dripping from it was sure to be infected.

"Looking out the window I wondered how the ghoul had gotten into my room. I cut my eyes to the front door. It was locked with the chain-lock secure. The ghoul hadn't entered there. It must have entered through the window. But I'm on the second floor. How did it get up here without a ladder? My gaze fell on the dead creature sprawled on the floor next to my bed. I couldn't stand the sight of it. The stiff was emitting a fetid odor of decay. Yet another reason for me to vomit.

"With my gloved hand I dragged the thing to the window by its necrotic hand. The creature wasn't that heavy. He was thin and not very tall. Holding my breath I lifted the carcass to the windowsill then shoved it through the window onto the street where it landed next to my amputated forearm.

"I still couldn't figure out how it had gotten through my window. It couldn't possibly have jumped from the street more than twenty feet into the air to reach my window. Craning my body around I gazed up toward the roof and noticed a cable hanging down from the eaves. Probably a cable from one of the TV satellite dishes mounted on the roof.

"Could the ghoul have climbed down the cable to my window? It seemed an impossible explanation, knowing how uncoordinated the creatures are. But I saw no other explanation. The ghoul must have slid down the cable, kicked his dangling legs through my window, and fallen feet first into my apartment.

"To this day, I find it hard to believe that a ghoul could shinny down a cable."

"Maybe some of the creatures are better coordinated than others," said Marta.

"Or maybe it didn't turn until after it had entered your room," said Halverson. "Were you awake when it fell through your window?"

"No. I was out cold. I have no idea when the thing entered my room."

"It could have been in your room as a living human being for several hours and during that time turned from having been bitten by a ghoul on the roof before it managed to crawl through your window."

"I never thought of that," said Declan. "That makes more sense than any other explanation. A human was hiding on the roof when a ghoul attacked him. He slid down the cable to escape the ghoul, but not before the ghoul had bitten him. The guy turned in my room and bit me. Yeah. Makes sense."

"Did you notice if the ghoul had bite marks on his body?"

"No. I just wanted the carcass out of my room."

"Let's not think about it," said Marta, feeling squeamish.

"I told you you wouldn't like it," said Declan.

"At least you stopped the infection by chopping off your arm," she said uncertainly, exchanging glances with Halverson.

"How long after you were bitten did you cut off your arm?" said Halverson.

Declan massaged his brow. "A matter of minutes after I killed the ghoul. I knew I had no time to waste. As soon as I was awake I knew what I had to do. I never stopped to think about it. I just did it."

"How long has it been since the ghoul bit you, Declan?"

"Last night."

"Pretty recent."

"How can I ever forget it?"

Chapter 65

"How do you feel?" said Halverson, inspecting Declan's face, which looked pale, but it could have been from loss of blood due to his amputation.

"Tired," said Declan. "That creature interrupted my sleep and gave me nightmares for the rest of the night after I tried to go to sleep again."

"I can imagine," said Marta, looking pained.

"What are you doing in this neck of the woods?"

"I wanted to see if you were OK. The world's such a mess these days with these infected, flesh-eating ghouls running amok."

"I know what you mean. I gave up working for Uber. People are scared. Nobody wants to hire a ride, because they don't want to go anywhere. They're too scared they'll run into ghouls."

"It's not only ghouls you gotta worry about. There are looters and militias all over the place. And psycho sadists like Gozzard."

Declan sighed. "My life will be more difficult with only one arm."

"We're all struggling to stay alive."

Halverson noticed that the veins in Declan's face were pulsing under his skin.

"Are you running a fever?" said Halverson.

Declan felt his forehead with the back of his hand. "I dunno. I don't think so."

"Your veins are breaking through your skin."

"Did you pick up a cold or something?" said Marta.

Declan felt his face. With anxiety he could feel the veins breaking through his flesh.

"I hate to say this," said Halverson, "but you might not have gotten all of the plague infection when you chopped off your arm."

"Am I turning?" said Declan, his eyes bugging out in horror. He grabbed Marta. "Don't let me turn into one of those things, sis."

"It's probably just the flu," she said.

"Promise me you'll kill me if I start to turn."

"You're worrying for no reason. It's the flu. You need plenty of fluids and rest."

"You gotta promise to kill me."

"You're my only living relative. I'm not gonna kill you," said Marta, appalled at the prospect.

Screwing up his face Declan fell to salivating uncontrollably.

"I gotta fight," he said as if to himself.

He leered at her cheek.

"Why are you looking at me like that?" she said, becoming apprehensive.

"He's turning," said Halverson, his MP9 at the ready.

"He just has the flu, is all," said Marta, terror mounting inside her.

The flesh withered on Declan's face. As he gazed at Marta's cheek, his irises lost their color and became milky.

Halverson trained his MP9 on Declan's forehead.

"Don't kill him," cried Marta.

Opening his mouth wide, growling, Declan lunged at her face.

Halverson double-tapped Declan between the eyes. Declan fell toward Marta. He fell against her, slid down her body, and sprawled lifeless at her feet.

"No," screamed Marta, staring in anguish at Declan's body.

She began weeping.

"He wanted us to do it," said Halverson. "The disease had already spread into his system before he cut off his arm."

She glowered at Halverson. "You killed my brother."

"He wasn't your brother anymore. He was a ghoul. He was getting ready to bite your face."

"Fuck," she cried, tears streaming down her cheeks. She gazed upward. "What kind of a fucked-up world is this?"

Shaking her head in despair, she sat on Declan's unmade bed.

"He forgot to make his bed. Do you see?" she said in a daze, smoothing his crumpled blanket with her hand. She stood up. "I'll make his bed for him."

She began pulling the sheet and blanket over the bed then fluffed his pillows.

"There. That looks much better. Help me lift him onto his bed."

"He's dead, Marta."

She approached Declan's corpse and struggled to drag it to his bed.

"Don't touch that thing," said Halverson. "It's riddled with infectious plague."

"Help me put him in bed. At least we can make him comfortable," she said, refusing to believe he was dead.

Halverson latched onto her wrist and yanked her away from Declan's corpse.

"What are you doing?" she said, fighting to free herself. "Let me put him in bed."

"We need to leave. Ghouls might have heard my gunshots and could be heading here this very moment."

She continued to eye Declan's cadaver in a daze. She made no effort to leave the room.

"I don't understand," she said.

Halverson didn't know what to say. He could imagine how she felt, losing her only brother. He remembered Victoria turning into a ghoul and the anguish that had overwhelmed him when he was forced to kill her . . . But they couldn't stay here.

"We can't help him now," he said.

He snagged Marta's elbow and ushered her to the door. In a funk she stumbled with him. She acted like she had had the life sucked out of her. She could have been a doll at his side.

"Why?" she muttered, her mind gone.

He had learned the hard way that there were no answers in this world, only more suffering. The more you cared about people the more you suffered. There was nothing you could do about it. All you could do was keep going until it was your turn to push up daisies.

Chapter 66

His face flushed, reeking of sweat, Kowalski stormed into the president's office, flinging the door open, a smoking MP9 in his hand.

"There are too many ghouls," he cried. "We need more ammo."

Uriah, who had been sitting behind his desk, bolted to his feet at the unexpected interruption.

"I couldn't stop him, sir," said Dakota Jones, a SIG P365 in his hand, charging into the office after Kowalski

"Never mind, Dakota," said Uriah. His face stern, he turned to Kowalski. "What's this all about, Kowalski? First, lower your gun. Or you will be shot where you stand. Do it now."

His body tense, Dakota was aiming his SIG at Kowalski, fixing to shoot him in the head if he attempted to assassinate the president.

Kowalski lowered his MP9 and pointed it at the floor. "It's empty anyway."

"Go on," said Uriah, waving at Dakota to lower his pistol.

"We're getting slaughtered out there by the ghouls. There are thousands of them. There arc only twenty of us. Waves of them keep coming at us, and we keep running out of ammo."

Uriah settled down, his tone becoming solicitous. "As I told you after the lottery, I will provide your group with as much guns and ammo as you need. We in the bunker appreciate the sacrifice your group is making for us."

"We're not sacrificing our lives," said Kowalski, still fuming. "That was never part of the agreement. You said we would need to stay outside until the bunker became more oxygenated. Don't you have enough oxygen in here yet?"

Uriah turned to Doctor Morrow, who was standing on the other side of the room.

"Eh, not quite," said Morrow, picking sleep out of his eye and flicking it across the room. "We are constantly monitoring the air in the bunker to see if it has enough oxygen in it. It still doesn't have enough oxygen for us to function in a healthy manner."

"Are you kidding me?" said Kowalski. "How much longer are we gonna have to stand outside fighting off ghouls? We have zero chance of winning out there. We kill a hundred, and two hundred take their place."

"Patience is a virtue," said Uriah. "Be patient. The bunker is almost at the appropriate oxygen level as long as the air vent remains open."

"Can we come inside when the oxygen level is healthy in here?"

"Of course."

"Then who's gonna keep the ghouls from coming through the air vent?"

"The air vent will hold this time. It's solid steel and it's welded into place. The only reason the ghouls were able to loosen the grid and climb into the vent before was because the bunker was hit by an ICBM with a nuclear payload which damaged it."

Kowalski's expression turned grim. "We've already lost three people, sir. You never told us we were gonna die out there."

"Absolutely not. *Nobody* is supposed to die. Good heavens, what do you take me for? Get more guns and ammo. I want all of you to be safe. Your heroic sacrifice is not going unnoticed."

"My people are terrified. They want to return to the safety of the bunker."

"Just hold out a little longer. If it wasn't for the valor of your heroic group, we would all be dead from asphyxiation by now."

"We're at the end of our rope, sir."

"Dakota, get more magazines for Kowalski and his group."

"How many, sir?"

"How many do you need, Kowalski?"

"As many as I can carry, Mr. President. Even that's probably not enough."

"You heard him, Dakota."

"Yes, sir," said Dakota, and dashed out of the office.

"There are just too many of the ghouls," said Kowalski, dejected.

"I know," said Uriah, stepping toward Kowalski and giving him an encouraging pat on the shoulder. "We are fighting the most powerful and evil enemy that this country has ever faced. It is only because of men like you and your valorous group that we will be able to withstand their assault. Make no mistake, this enemy will take every ounce of our energy and determination to defeat."

"What about our dead, sir? Do we just leave them out there? They were bitten and will turn."

"You need to destroy their brains," chimed in Dr. Morrow. "Otherwise, they will turn and attack you. You must do it immediately."

"They were our friends."

"You don't have a moment to lose. You must do it now."

Dakota bustled into the office, carrying a crate full of magazines.

"There are about fifty MP5 and MP9 mags in here," he said, offering the heavy crate to Kowalski.

"You must shoot the three fallen heroes in their heads, Kowalski," said Uriah.

Kowalski ejected the spent magazine from his MP9, latched onto a fresh mag, and slammed it home. He slung his MP9 over his shoulder and snatched the crate from Dakota.

"God bless you," said Uriah.

Kowalski nodded, slewed around, and, straining, hunching over, barreled out of the office with the heavy crate of mags.

"How much longer can they hold out?" Uriah asked Dakota.

"Not long, I fear, sir. The ghouls are thick as flies around them. I don't know how Ski was able to make his way back here engulfed in that endless swamp of flesh-eating corpses."

"I will give each of the volunteers medals for their heroism. Where do such brave people come from? We would be dead without them. It was people like them that created this great country."

"And people like you," said Morrow with an inscrutable visage.

PURGE

He produced a pair of sunglasses and put them on, shielding his eyes form Uriah's direct gaze.

Chapter 67

Vivian was scooting past a white Tesla and scoping out its interior when she came to an abrupt halt.

Freddie and Buzzard stopped beside her.

"Can you see it, boys?"

The two dogs sat down watching her.

"I guess not."

Vivian tried to open the Tesla passenger's-side door, but it was locked. She looked around for something hard. She spotted a rock the size of a loaf of bread lying on the grass that skirted the road. She retrieved the rock and returned to the Tesla, where she smashed the rock through the passenger's-side window.

The car alarm sounded, startling her, Freddie, and Buzzard.

"I didn't think of that. The noise will attract the ghouls."

She dropped the rock, reached through the broken window, and unlocked the door. She withdrew her hand from the car interior, grasped the door handle, and flung open the door. She seized the object of her desire that lay in the footwell.

It was an empty red plastic bowl for a pet.

She set the bowl on the tarmac, twisted open one of her water bottles, and poured water into the bowl.

"All right, Freddie, you first."

Freddie approached the bowl and fell to lapping the water, slurping noisily with his tongue.

Buzzard watched him enviously.

"Your turn next, Buzz."

Freddie drank all of the water in the bowl.

Vivian poured water for Buzzard, who sniffed the bowl then commenced lapping the water.

The Tesla burglar alarm kept blaring.

Watching Buzzard, Vivian flogged her back and gnashed her teeth, reminding herself she had become too happy watching the dogs drink. It was never a good idea to become too happy. Life was about suffering, not about happiness. To go on living you needed to suffer.

She scourged her back again, hard. She could feel warm blood flowing down her spine. The way of the whip was the way of life.

"I want to be sure you two are hydrated," she said, watching Buzzard finish his bowl of water. "We need to take this with us."

She lifted the empty plastic bowl, irritated by the constant keening of the alarm. She cast around the area for signs of ghouls attracted by the commotion. She picked up on two lurching out of the woods toward her. One of them was tall, the other short. They were both wearing silver hardhats and faded fluorescent yellow vests. A construction crew of ghouls besetting her.

She bent over and withdrew a hunting knife from a leather sheath strapped around her ankle. Knife in hand, she stood up. Killing humans was taboo in her religion. But there was nothing about killing flesh-eating corpses.

There was a time before the apocalypse when she would never have dreamed of killing anything. She had had qualms about killing her first ghoul. But then it got easier and she felt nothing when she killed them, because these ghouls were something spewed out of hell. They were an abomination of nature. They resembled humans, but they weren't human. They needed to be killed. Or they would kill every human being on earth.

In any case, they weren't living. They were reanimated corpses. You couldn't kill something that was already dead. She was simply stopping the corpses from moving and consuming humans. It wasn't committing murder to stop a corpse from moving.

The alarm blasting behind her, she charged the hardhats and thrust her knife under the shorter one's jaw, through his tongue, through his palate, and into his brain, which she sliced in half like butter. She thrust the knife to its hilt, mortally wounding the brain. The construction worker crumpled.

Snarling, the taller one rounded on her, drooling in anticipation of a fulfilling meal.

She retreated from him, swiping her knife back and forth in front of her to ward off his advance. She knew stabbing him anywhere else other than the brain would do no damage. She needed to kill the infected brain.

He was much taller than she was, but she believed she could impale his brain by jumping up in front of him. Holding her knife up, she jumped at his lower jaw, but fell short of it. Instead her body slammed into the ghoul's chest. The ghoul snapped his jaws at her, trying to bite her with his putrescent teeth. He got a mouthful of her hair for his troubles. She shoved his chest away from her and took two steps backward to be clear of him. Her scalp hurt thanks to all the hair the creature had torn out of her head.

It was too dangerous to lunge at the underside of his jaw again. She had to come up with another plan of attack.

Freddie and Buzzard came to her rescue. They growled and tried to bite the ghoul's legs. Freddie bit the ragged cuff of the ghoul's jeans and yanked the ghoul toward him. The ghoul growled back at him.

"Be careful, Freddie," said Vivian. "Don't let him bite you."

Freddie kept pulling the ghoul's jeans.

The ghoul stumbled forward and fell on his face, knocking his hardhat off. Flailing on the ground, he tried to turn over and stand up.

Vivian seized her chance. She leapt onto his back, straddled it, and thrust her knife into his temple. The ghoul stopped moving.

Gagging on the ghoul's stench Vivian wiped her brain-smeared knife blade on the grass, snugged her knife in its sheath strapped to her ankle, and stood up.

"Good work, Freddie."

Freddie sniffed at the prone hardhat and, cringing, slinked back from him, baring his teeth in fear and hostility.

During her scuffle with the hardhats, Vivian had dropped the red bowl. She located it on the tarmac and picked it up. She noticed a hole in its rim.

She approached the tall dead ghoul, squatted down, and untied the shoelaces on his right foot. She removed the shoelace, cut it with her knife, and inserted it through the hole in the plastic bowl. She looped the lace around her belt and tied a knot in it so the bowl hung now from her belt between two of her water bottles.

Buzzard sniffed at the dead ghoul and thought about biting its leg to taste its flesh.

"No, Buzz," cried Vivian.

Buzzard backed away and ran toward her.

"Good boy."

Vivian lifted her scooter from the tarmac and drove down the road, Freddie and Buzzard in tow.

She knew Michael K. and his bikers were getting farther away from her every moment because they were riding much faster motorcycles. But she would never give up trying to confront him. He must apologize for the horrific massacre that he had ordered.

Chapter 68

Halverson and Marta drove through DC. He could make out the Washington Monument lying on the ground, having been upended by an ICBM carrying a nuclear warhead. So much destruction was dispiriting. Yet they had to go on. He had to know. He needed to see everything. He glanced at Marta, wondering if she was taking in the annihilation of DC.

She was staring out the windshield in a funk, seeing nothing.

"Are you all right?" said Halverson.

Her expression blank, she didn't answer.

He wished he could shake her out of her depression, but he had no idea how to proceed. Maybe it was best to let her recover her senses without any help. Bringing her back to reality too soon might be bad for her health. But staying depressed wasn't any good for her, either.

Three ghouls roamed around the fallen Washington Monument.

In the end he wondered who was worse—the infected ghouls or the politicians who had nuked most of the country and rained devastation down on the country in order to kill them. The politicians had a lot to answer for. They were the ones who had authorized the creation of the zombie plague bacteria in a government-funded lab while searching for a bio weapon, the source of the funding concealed in a slush fund owned by a CIA/DIA shell company.

Halverson kept driving, observing the decimation of DC.

The Lincoln Memorial was a congeries of debris.

Saddened by the sight, Halverson drove to it. He wanted to see Lincoln's statute.

He parked the Fiat near the ruins. He didn't see any ghouls nearby.

"Do you want to go inside?" said Halverson.

Marta looked blank, her mind lost.

"Will you be all right here?" he said.

No response.

He didn't see any ghouls around. He thought she would be OK. He wasn't planning on being away for long.

He killed the engine, parked the car, got out, and wended his way through the broken chunks of concrete in search of the statue. He knew he couldn't waste much time here, but he had to know. At last he found the stature lying on its side, its head broken off and lying three feet away from its neck. The man most responsible for the current form of the country was beheaded.

His curiosity sated, his spirits dampened, Halverson bopped back to the Fiat and clambered into the driver's seat.

At once he noticed Marta was missing. Dumbfounded, he wondered what had happened to her.

Where had she gone? She couldn't have gotten too far.

He noticed her wandering through the ruins like she was sleepwalking. He bolted out of the Fiat to her side.

"We have to go back to the car," he said.

Not only didn't she see him, she didn't hear him. She kept wandering through the broken slabs of concrete with rebar sticking out of them. Out of the corner of his eye he caught sight of a ghoul in a suit lurching toward them. The navy blue suit was missing both of its sleeves. The ghoul's red tie hung loose about his neck. He had a wrinkled version of the movie actor Omar Sharif's face. Gurgling, his mouth hanging open, he plodded toward them, flailing his arms at his sides. Giant maggots like boiled shrimp tumbled out of his ears, bounced off his shoulders, and fell to the ground.

Halverson grabbed Marta's elbow and steered her through the catastrophic ruins back to the Fiat. She didn't want to leave, but, her mind blank, she couldn't muster enough energy to resist.

He ushered her to the shotgun seat, shut the door, whipped around the Fiat hood, and slid into the driver's seat, where he fired the engine. He shut his door. Every minute they stayed here was another minute Michael K.'s bikers gained in catching up to them. Halverson knew the government squad hunting him and Marta was still out there as well and hot on his trail.

He backed the Fiat away from Sharif and pulled a U-turn to head in the opposite direction. He had seen enough of DC.

He glanced in his rearview mirror in dismay one last time at the DC obliteration.

Marta remained lost in the void of her mind.

Chapter 69

"We must be getting close to catching up with Halverson, boss," said Darren, driving his Harley next to Michael K.'s.

"Unless he stole a car," said Michael K. "He could have found an abandoned car with the key in the ignition on the road."

"I still think they can't be far away. Our hogs can drive around all the vehicles abandoned in the road. Halverson can't if he's driving a car."

"We'll get him. It's only a matter of time."

"What are we gonna do with him when we catch him, boss?"

"Give him a trial for first degree murder. We're not a bunch of thugs."

"Right."

Michael K. scoped out his bikers. "Well, not all of us are."

"Boss?"

"Am I going too fast for you? The jury will find him guilty, and we'll execute him and his partner in crime."

"Yeah," said Darren, pumping his fist. "He's guilty as sin."

"Nobody but nobody gets away with murdering one of my brothers. *My last remaining brother*. I'll hound Halverson to the end of the world."

Darren stared down the road. "It looks like we're heading for DC."

"Birdy said Costello has a brother who lives there."

"Costello?"

"Halverson's accomplice. They both work for the government."

"Then why did they assassinate the president?"

"Ask them."

"I will. Do you think DC is his destination or just a detour?"

"A detour, according to Birdy. Raven Rock is Halverson's real destination—if Birdy was telling us the truth."

"I don't trust anybody who works for the government. Birdy could have been lying."

"His life was on the line when he told us. I'm betting he told us the truth."

Michael K.'s necktie got caught in the wind and started flapping behind him as he rode his Harley.

"This is the life," he said, the wind rushing against his face as he drove, the sun beating down on him. "Free as a bird."

"Born to be wild, huh, boss?"

"Yeah. Steppenwolf. That's the smartest thing you've ever said."

Chapter 70

As Halverson drove the Fiat away from DC, he picked up on a fortysomething brown-haired man wearing an untucked red and black checked flannel lumberjack shirt standing near a grey Toyota parked in the road. He looked like he had recently gotten a haircut, not a very good one but serviceable. He was bending forward and trying to pull a thirtyish brunette out from under the car. She was dressed in jeans and a pink sweatshirt and looked to be in pain as she lay under the sedan chassis.

Halverson braked the Fiat. He knew he had no time to dawdle here, but he couldn't pass by someone who needed help. The two could be ghouls, but he doubted it. He couldn't see their eyes to be sure, but the man's reflexes didn't look shot like a ghoul's.

"Can I give you a hand?" said Halverson out the Fiat's open window.

The man turned around to eyeball him. "Hello, pardner."

They weren't ghouls, which couldn't talk as far as Halverson knew.

"What seems to be the problem?" he said.

"My wife got trapped under the car. She dove under there when the ghouls attacked us. She got stuck."

Halverson swung open his door and got out. He glanced back at Marta. She still looked out of it.

"My name's Max, by the way."

"Halverson."

"Thanks for helping us," said Max, extending his hand.

Halverson shook it. "No problem."

"Is your wife OK?" said Max, glancing at Marta. "She doesn't look well. Is she concussed?"

"She's not my wife. Her name is Marta. She's a bit under the weather." Eager to change the subject, Halverson said, "What seems to be the problem with your wife?"

"Her name is Selma. She's a mechanic."

Hunkering down, Max held out his hand under the chassis. "Take my hand, honey."

Halverson crouched down and peered under the chassis to see what was wrong with the car. He didn't notice anything untoward.

She grabbed Max's hand. He pulled her out from under the car.

Her sweatshirt and face were grimy, noticed Halverson. Grease stains from the undercarriage.

Brushing herself off she got to her feet.

"This is Halverson," said Max. "He was kind enough to stop and help us."

"Thanks so much," said Selma, turning to Halverson.

"It seems I wasn't needed," said Halverson, about to repair to the Fiat.

"We're from California," said Selma. "The whole state's on fire. Wildfires everywhere. After the government nuked San Francisco and Los Angeles to kill the infected ghouls, the fires that erupted couldn't be put out. The air is toxic with smoke. People are leaving in droves."

"Our car broke down," said Max, eying the Toyota that Selma had crawled out from. "The crankshaft's broken." He turned toward Halverson. "Are you from around here?"

"I'm from all over the place. I spent time in California, Arizona, Vegas—"

"That must be a good car to travel that far."

"I don't have time to chat. I need to get going."

Max whipped a concealed Ruger SP101 revolver out from his waistband that was concealed under his untucked lumberjack shirt and trained it on Halverson.

"Throw down that fancy hardware slung around your neck. Your hand goes anywhere near that trigger and you're dead."

Grim-faced, sweating, Halverson ducked, lifted the strap over his head, and shrugged off his MP9. It slid to the tarmac.

"We're gonna need your car," said Max.

"*We* need the car," said Halverson. "Marta is in critical condition. She needs to be taken to a hospital."

"Did one of those things bite her?"

"She's in shock."

"You'll have to walk. We need your car."

"You can't have it."

"I think your friend is turning into a ghoul. You best shoot her."

"She's fine. You need to reconsider your actions."

"Why?"

"Carjacking is illegal."

Max laughed. "Illegal? Do you really think we still have laws in this country?" He eyed Marta. "Tell her to get out of the car. I'm not getting in no car with a zombie in it."

"You're right about one thing. You're not getting in that car."

"You talk tough for a guy looking down the barrel of a .38."

"Time for you to push off."

"That car isn't even yours in the first place, is it? You jacked it on the road. Of all people you shouldn't be the one lecturing me about carjacking."

"It's ours now. Good-bye."

"I'm getting annoyed by your bad manners."

Max cocked the Ruger .38 and drew a bead on Halverson's forehead.

"Why are you sweating?" he said with a lopsided grin.

"I'm concerned about your health."

"Are you an idiot?" said Max, puzzled. "Look at what's pointed at your head."

Halverson whipped out his SIG from his rear waistband and blew Max's head off. Before Max knew what hit him he sprawled on the tarmac dead.

"It was his idea to jack your car," cried Selma, white-faced, and bolted down the road, glancing over her shoulder in terror at Halverson as she fled.

He put away his SIG, scoffed up his MP9 from the tarmac, and sprang back into the Fiat driver's seat. Marta continued to stare ahead in an unseeing daze.

"Are you OK?" said Halverson.

She didn't answer. She kept staring through the windshield.

He wondered if he should take her to a hospital. The problem was he didn't know the location of the nearest hospital. The doctors at Raven Rock could treat her.

He fired the ignition and drove away from the zombie-infested wreckage of DC.

Chapter 71

Standing on the cargo bed of an abandoned, beat-up pickup, Michael K. gripped a battery-powered mic and was lecturing his gang as they gathered around him and rested on their bikes in the middle of the road.

"It's time for us to take a break," he said. "We will be catching up with Halverson any minute now, but it's best to be well rested when we meet up with him. Go ahead and munch on some beef jerky and drink beer—not too much beer. I don't want a bunch of alkies riding with me. You'll end up getting yourselves killed when we reach the serial assassin Halverson."

Popping cans of beer the crowd laughed and unwrapped their jerky.

"And maybe we'll have an orgy later," he said, glancing at his harem of ten leather-clad girls who sat astride their Harleys and watched him with lecherous admiration.

A couple of them fixed their hair, flirting with him.

The gang hooted and cheered and proceeded to munch on their jerky.

Michael K. paced around the cargo bed, eyeballing everybody as he spoke.

"Life isn't just about hunting down our enemies. It's about having a good time as well. We can't let our enemies go on living, but we can't let them stop us from enjoying our lives. We weren't put here to suffer. We were put here to enjoy ourselves, to eat, drink, and make merry." Michael K. pumped his fist. "You know I'm right."

The High Rolerz cheered him on.

"In the end we have nothing to fear, so why worry? Nobody really dies. Everybody gets reincarnated. You come back as a muskrat or something. Death is nothing to be afraid of. Bureaucrats—I'm talking about the government agents running this country into the ground—all they care about is a steady paycheck. But we are gamblers. High rollers. We believe that the bigger the risk the bigger the reward. It's all about taking risks. Am I right or what?"

The gang cheered and pumped their fists.

"High Rolerz. High Rolerz," they chanted.

"We, not the bureaucrats, are the inheritors of the earth because we dare. Dare to be happy. Dare to do what we want. We will not be stopped. The stinking ghouls can't stop us, and the yellow-belly bureaucrats cowering in bunkers can't, either."

"High Rolerz. High Rolerz," came the chant.

"We will dare to kill and take what we want. We will dare to snort blow and speed. To smoke crack and weed. We will dare to drop acid. We will dare to take any goddam drug we want. Am I right?"

The gang cheered. Several of them snorted blow off the backs of their wrists.

"We are not bound by the outdated moralities of negativism. Thou shalt not do this. Thou shalt not do that. What's that nonsense all about? *We'll do anything we want.*"

"Tell it like it is," yelled a grinning woman with spiked red hair as she sat on her parked Harley.

"You know the saying, he who dies with the most toys wins. Well, I say, he who dies having the most fun wins."

The enthralled listeners screamed with delight.

"Am I right or am I right?" said Michael K., egging on the crowd.

"Yeah," they cried. "We want to have fun."

"We control our own destinies by daring to do whatever we want. We will rule the world with our belief. Our belief is the one true belief, and it will conquer all the rest. We fear nothing. Death is nothing. When you're dead you become reincarnated. You come back and go on living. We will rule forever. We are the High Rolerz."

"We are the High Rolerz," cried the ecstatic bikers.

"As long as we fear nothing, we cannot die," said Michael K., pumping his fist. "If somebody hits us, we *destroy* them. *There will be hell to pay.*"

"Fight, fight, fight," cried the crowd, carried away by Michael K.'s hell-raising speech.

"Who do you see when you look at my face?"

"You," they cried.

Michael K. pointed at his face. "When you see your own face instead of my face, you will become enlightened and freed from outdated moralities."

"Free," yelled the crowd.

"You are chained by outdated moralities."

"Free."

Pleased with himself, Michael K. chewed on a strip of beef jerky as he scoped out the cheering crowd below. He saw three ghouls emerge from the woods and approach the bikers.

"Barry, get the flamethrower and barbecue those zombies," he said.

Happy to oblige, Barry parked his Harley, booted the kickstand, and retrieved the flamethrower from the back of his bike. Holding the flamethrower, he approached the ghouls. When he was twenty feet from the creatures, who kept lurching toward him, he fired the flamethrower. A lance of flame tore across the grass verge of the forest and torched the ghouls, who flared like matchsticks.

"Zombies aren't alive," said Michael K. "Therefore when we kill them, we really aren't killing them, because they're already dead. They can't reincarnate after you destroy their diseased brains. They're nothing. Killing them is nothing. They're freaks of nature. They shouldn't even exist. Every other living thing in this world reincarnates after it dies, which proves zombies aren't living. They are dead things that kill, and they must be destroyed."

With satisfaction he watched the three ghouls burn and squirm as they caught fire.

"We're doing the world a favor by destroying these monstrosities," he went on. "This world is for the living, not for the dead. Zombies are abominations." He turned to Barry. "Make sure their brains boil and explode inside their skulls, or they will go on devouring all living creatures."

Writhing silently, the three ghouls fell to the ground and flailed their charred arms as if swimming. Barry continued training the flamethrower on them until they stopped moving, their charbroiled brains oozing out their ears in a black, bubbling paste.

"We will waste every zombie we see," said Michael K. "Nature hates dead things that can't reincarnate. Zombies are outcasts of nature. Every last one of them must be put down like rabid dogs." He glanced at his wristwatch. "Time's up. Break time is over. Time to hunt Halverson."

"Kill Halverson," chanted the High Rolerz, revving their Harleys, preparing to give chase.

Chapter 72

Vivian scooted to a stop next to a black Tesla. She waited for Freddie and Buzz to catch up with her. Their tongues were hanging out, lower to the ground than usual. She knew they were tired from running after her, but she had to catch up with Michael K. She wouldn't be able to do it by walking. It was the scooter or nothing.

She hunkered down in front of them.

When they caught up with her, they wagged their tails happily. She ruffled the fur on their necks.

"I'm gonna miss you guys," she said.

They could tell from the sound of her voice and the look in her eyes that something bad was going to happen. They whined.

"I'm gonna have to part with you two soon."

She gave them some beef jerky to chew to lighten the bad news. They stopped whining and chewed on the jerky.

"I don't want to leave you guys. In fact, it's the last thing I want to do. But I'm going to meet a bad man. I don't want him to meet you two."

She would die if anything happened to Freddie and Buzz. They were her only friends at this point. The High Rolerz had killed all her other friends. She knew they would kill Freddie and Buzz too. She couldn't let that happen. She wondered what to do with them.

She scoped out the area. Could she hide them somewhere until she got back? Who was kidding who? The chances of her coming back were nonexistent. She knew what she was walking into, and she wasn't going to walk out of it. But it had to be done. She couldn't let Michael K. get away with massacring her friends.

But what was she to do with Freddie and Buzz?

She supposed she could tie them to a tree and leave some water and jerky with them, but unless someone found them, they would eventually die of starvation or be eaten by ghouls. If she locked them in a car, the ghouls wouldn't be able to kill them. But they would still starve. She couldn't count on someone coming along and saving them. Life didn't work that way—not in these end times, anyway. Crazed murderers like the High Rolerz were running rampant across the country. Somebody who was starving and came across the dogs might even eat them. Perish the thought. But these were the times they lived in. People didn't know where their next meal was coming from. What was unthinkable twenty years ago was permissible now. The cops weren't gonna bust you for eating a dog, not these days. Cops? What cops? There was no law, and no cops to enforce it. And justice? Justice was a gun.

She flogged her back, trying to think of a way to leave Freddie and Buzz safely behind.

She couldn't leave the dogs locked in a car. There had to be a better way. She would have to think of it later. Seeing that Freddie and Buzz had finished their jerky, she mounted her scooter and resumed her journey to confront Michael K.

Freddie and Buzz woofed with joy and bounded after her, happy now that the three of them were still together, though they had no idea what she was talking about. They only knew it was bad.

Gnashing her teeth Vivian flailed her back. Why did life have to be so hard?

She flogged herself again in response.

She scooted faster to divert her attention from the pain racking her body.

Watching her, Freddie woofed at her in confusion.

"Don't mind me, boy. You don't have enough consciousness to know what I'm doing, and you don't need to know."

For some reason he seemed content with her answer.

"Pain is the name of the game. That's what you would learn with a human-sized brain." She paused. "You're probably better off without it."

Chapter 73

"Has anyone heard anything from Purdy?" said Uriah, agitated, standing beside his desk in his office.

"Not that I know of," said Dr. Morrow, who was the only other person in the room.

Uriah checked his watch. "He should have reported by now."

"Comms are down."

"I know, I know. Do you think I'm an idiot? Why couldn't he send one of his men back to tell us what's going on? This not knowing is killing me."

"How do we know he's not dead?"

"Why do you say that?" said Uriah, fixing his gaze on Morrow.

"There are ghouls all over the place. Maybe they got Purdy and his squad."

"That's negative thinking. Put it out of your mind this minute. If you think the worst, the worst will happen."

"I'm a doctor. I always think positive. I believe I can keep my patients alive forever."

"Good. Then we both know Purdy will return with Halverson's head in his hand."

Morrow looked uncomfortable.

"You look ill, Doctor. Are you all right?"

"Do we really need to kill the man? Why can't we just put him in jail for the rest of his life?"

"Because he assassinated a president of the United States. An unforgiveable crime. He and his coconspirator must be executed."

Worked up, Kowalski burst into the office, flinging the door open.

Uriah and Morrow started.

"I couldn't stop him, Mr. President, without hurting him," said the suit-clad Dakota who had been guarding the office door.

He grabbed Kowalski and made to eighty-six him from the office.

Uriah waved Dakota off. "You were right not to hurt him. We don't want to hurt our national heroes. Let him stay."

Releasing Kowalski, Dakota stood down.

"I lost another person," cried Kowalski, flushing, shaking off Dakota. "There's no end to those things."

"Calm down, Kowalski," said Uriah. "I don't want you to lose your shit in here."

"We're not gonna have any people left if you don't let us back into the bunker ASAP."

Uriah turned to Morrow. "How is the air, Doctor?"

"It's getting better, but we still don't have enough oxygen in the bunker to make the air breathable. Inhaling the current air will continue to make us weak and/or ill."

"When did you last check?"

"Five minutes ago."

"Did you hear that, Kowalski? You'll have to hold your position outside a little while longer."

"How many more people do we have to lose before you let us back in?"

"You're doing fine. Just hold on."

"None of us volunteered to go out there in the first place."

"You agreed to participate in the lottery like everybody else. It was a fair lottery. Everyone in this bunker appreciates the sacrifice you are making for us."

"It's a living hell out there, sir."

"I sympathize with what you're going through," said Uriah, placing his hand on Kowalski's shoulder. "Go down to the armory and get all the guns and ammo you want. As long as I'm president, you will get every gun and bullet you need."

Grudgingly Kowalski moved toward the door, his face grim.

"We couldn't have a better man defending the air vent outside," said Uriah. "Everyone in your team outside is a true hero, and all of you will be treated as such when you reenter the bunker."

"I hope we're still alive."

"Has anybody heard anything from Purdy?" said Uriah, eager to change the subject.

Nobody answered.

"On your way then," said Uriah. "Dakota, close the door behind you."

Dakota obeyed and vanished from sight along with Kowalski.

Uriah paced around the office. "Should I send a team after Purdy? I'm concerned about him. He should have found some way to report back to me by now."

"Maybe it's taking him longer than he expected."

Uriah coughed. "The air's still bad in here. I better not suffocate."

"The oxygen level is rising incrementally every half hour, Mr. President. We will be out of the woods soon."

"You need to make it rise faster."

"It's out of my hands. There are too many ghouls in front of the air vent blocking the oxygen intake."

"How do you know? Have you been outside to view the air vent?"

"I can tell from my measuring instruments that the increases in oxygen are too negligible to make the bunker air healthy for us to breathe at this point in time. The outside air has to be purified of radiation after it comes through the vent, which takes time. The bottom line is we're not getting enough oxygen, Mr. President."

"No wonder I feel like shit," said Uriah, holding his stomach. "I feel like I'm gonna puke."

"Vomiting will not improve your oxygen intake."

Uriah's eyes flared. "If people start dying of suffocation in this bunker, they're gonna blame you."

Morrow put on his sunglasses and said nothing, keeping his thoughts to himself.

Chapter 74

"It's only a matter of time before they catch up with us," said Halverson at the wheel of the Fiat.

Marta looked blank in the shotgun seat.

"I wish you'd snap out of it," said Halverson.

The Fiat began jerking. He checked the odometer. They were running out of gas.

They were entering a small town. He picked up on a gas station. Relieved, he drove into it. The Fiat barely reached the pumps before it came to a complete halt.

Halverson hopped out of the driver's seat, unscrewed the gas cap on the Fiat, retrieved a gas nozzle from the nearest pump, and inserted the nozzle into the fuel tank. He squeezed the trigger on the pump to unleash the flow of gas.

Nothing happened.

He squeezed the trigger again with the same result.

He threw down the gas nozzle in disgust and tried the other pumps. None of them worked.

He peered into the gas station office. It was deserted.

He faced Marta. "The gas pumps must be empty."

She stared straight ahead without acknowledging him.

He opened the passenger's-side door and let her out.

"We have to decide what to do," he said.

She looked at him, her face blank.

A thirtyish dead man in grease-stained coveralls lay prostrate in front of the open gas station garage, lying on his cheek with a bullet hole in his temple, a pistol lying three inches from his left hand on the asphalt.

Marta gazed at the body.

"Declan," she cried, her eyes wide.

"It's not your brother," said Halverson.

Marta shook her head as if to clear it of spiderwebs. "Where are we?"

"We left DC. Our car ran out of gas."

"The last thing I remember is Declan's body with a bullet in his forehead."

"You were out of it for a while. Are you OK now?"

"OK? That's a matter of opinion," she said, spotting more corpses with bullet holes in their heads sprawled among the abandoned cars in the strip mall parking lot adjacent to the gas station. "How can anybody be OK in these times?"

"The gas jockey must have shot the ghouls in the parking lot then killed himself after getting bitten," said Halverson, picking up on the gas jockey's mauled right hand.

"I hope he got all of them."

"Without a car we can't outrun Michael K." Halverson scoped out the town. "Maybe we should hole up here and wait for him and his gang to pass."

"I'm at the point where I don't care if they do catch us."

"I killed his brother."

"How do we know he's even chasing us?"

"If *he* isn't, a government squad is. They think we assassinated President Mims."

"Which we didn't do."

"Uriah didn't believe us. He wants us dead. I still think he had something to do with Mims's assassination. He's the one who wants the bunker purged so he can be president. To remain president he can't let anyone at Raven Rock know what he's doing. We're the greatest threat to his presidency because we're gonna tell Raven Rock what's going on at Mount Weather."

Marta nodded. "Another good reason for him to have us killed is so we can't keep telling everyone we're innocent."

Halverson strode to the street, Marta beside him. "Let's see if we can find a good place to hide."

"How does everyone know where we're going?"

"There's nothing in this area except DC."

"But we're leaving DC."

"Without a car we can't get far from here. In any case, Uriah fears we're heading for Raven Rock to contact the speaker of the house and tell him he's the real president. Uriah can't let that happen. For sure he sent a hit squad after us."

"Then let's go somewhere else."

"I can't let Uriah get away with stealing the reins of power. He's not the rightful president as long as the speaker of the house is alive at Raven Rock."

"Why do you care?"

"I'm still a CIA agent. We have to reach Raven Rock."

"Then we have no chance of escaping," said Marta, heaving a sigh. "How can we do anything with all this pressure on us?"

"Intense pressure turns carbon into diamonds."

"Did you learn that gem in the CIA?"

"Let's think this out. It's best to let Uriah's hit team and the High Rolerz get ahead of us. Then we won't have to worry about them coming at us from behind. They'll never expect us to be behind them. It's the safest place to be."

On the road they walked past an abandoned wreck of a Honda with its driver's-side door hanging open. The hood had telescoped after colliding with the car in front of it. The head of a fortysomething blonde lying on her back dangled out of the doorway, her mouth agape and crusted with tacky blood, her blue eyes rolled up in her head, her skull cracked open from crashing through the shattered windshield, her wounded brain exposed.

"At least she can't turn," said Halverson, stone-faced.

He saw a movie theater across the street and made for it.

"Do we really have time to go to a movie?" said Marta, catching up to him.

"It might make a good hiding place while we wait for our enemies to blow through town."

"What if they don't come this way."

"Then we'll rest here. If they see us in the road, we're dead. Michael K. could have over a hundred gang members easy. We wouldn't stand a chance against them."

Marta's face fell. "I don't really care. I don't even know what I'm doing now. My brother's dead. Where am I supposed to go now?"

"We need to get to Raven Rock."

"I could care less about Raven Rock. Don't you understand? I lost my brother. The bottom's fallen out of my life."

"We have to hope things will get better. In the meantime we need to survive."

"How much longer do you think we have?"

"It doesn't matter. We're still alive, so we go on."

Halverson scoped out the theater. The marquee was broken. Half of it was hanging perpendicular a foot above the sidewalk. The other half publicized the name of the movie they were showing. Dan Curtis's *Burnt Offerings*.

"I guess they show old movies here," said Marta.

"A grindhouse theater."

They entered the carpeted lobby, which was filthy, threadbare, and mantled with dust. Trash, including empty paper cups and empty popcorn buckets, was strewn on the carpet, which was torn in several places. Somebody had looted the food behind the counter and had trashed the shelves on the wall behind it. No candy or popcorn in sight. The soda machines were dry.

Feeling thirsty at the sight of the soda machines, Halverson pulled a plastic bottle of water out of his knapsack, unscrewed it, and drank from it.

He heard a noise coming from the auditorium. Clutching the water bottle he reached the entrance and parted the dark maroon curtain. Incredibly, *Burnt Offerings* was being projected on the screen.

"I can't believe they're still showing movies," said Marta at his side. "Aren't people too scared to go to them?"

"Maybe the movie's on some kind of loop. It just keeps running automatically."

"Look. There are people sitting in the front row," said Marta, pointing at them with amazement.

Halverson could discern the backs of heads of fifteen or so people sitting up front.

"I guess this town isn't deserted, after all," he said.

"Maybe we should go ask one of them for help."

"I don't see how they can help us."

"Maybe they have a car we can borrow."

"Why would anyone lend us their car?"

"It's worth a try."

"I still think we're better off holing up here and waiting for the hit squad and the bikers to pass. Let's rest here for a while. After they're gone, we can follow them without worrying about getting caught."

They removed their knapsacks and sat down in the back row.

Halverson yawned. He reached into his knapsack, withdrew a strip of beef jerky, and chewed it while watching Oliver Reed go nuts on the movie screen.

Marta gobbled down trail mix she had gotten from Adam.

Chapter 75

Michael K. and the High Rolerz roared to a halt in the road when they spotted an old white-haired woman carrying a shopping bag, wearing a heavy black coat, and wandering among the abandoned cars. The coat reached down to her knees, exposing her thick calves mottled with varicose veins. Her nylons were bunched around her ankles.

"Is she a ghoul?" said Darren, riding up to Michael K.

"She looks like one, but I don't think so."

Darren raised his pistol to shoot her. "There's no reason to take any chances."

Michael K. grabbed Darren's arm and lowered it.

"Have you seen Halverson?" he asked the bag lady.

The woman looked at him with washed-out crazed eyes that looked like they had seen too many suns and empty promises. "What?"

"Did Halverson and his woman pass this way?"

"You bums," she wailed. "You pieces of crap. You can't even get jobs."

"Do you know who you're talking to, crone?" said Michael K.

"Pieces of crap. Give me some food."

"I'll give you some food. Do you want to munch on a bullet?"

Michael K. withdrew his Colt Python from his hip holster and leveled the barrel at her.

"Listen to me," he said. "I'm gonna ask you a simple question. You don't have to think too hard about it. Did you see a man and a woman pass this way?"

"You're a piece of crap and you can't keep a job."

"Are you blind, hag? There's a gun pointed at your face. Answer the question. Did you see a man and a woman pass this way?"

"I seen a guy and a woman in a janky midget car the color of pea soup."

"That's better."

Michael K. saw a knot of four ghouls plodding out of the woods, drooling on themselves, flies swarming around them. The lead ghoul, a male fireplug, opened his mouth to growl, and a rat scrambled out, leapt to the ground, and scampered away, squealing.

"Now wasn't that easy?" Michael K. asked the bag lady.

"You pieces of crap—"

Michael K. shot her in the stomach.

She shrieked in pain and slumped on the ground.

"Why did you shoot her in the stomach?" said Darren. "If you don't shoot her in the head, she'll come back as a ghoul."

"Can't you figure it out?"

Darren scratched his head. "No."

"I want her to come back so I can kill the hag twice."

The ghouls shambled onto the tarmac to feast on the bag lady.

"Don't anybody shoot the ghouls," said Michael K., holding up his hand.

The ghouls crouched over the screaming bag lady and fell to consuming her. One sixtyish male ghoul ripped her arm off and gnawed on the bloody limb.

"How can she stand being eaten alive?" said Darren, watching the spectacle with disgust, the blood draining from his face.

A teenage ghoul tore out the bag lady's carotid artery, unleashing a fountain of blood. The bag lady stopped screaming soon after.

"She's dead," said Michael K.

He proceeded to gun down the four ghouls that were feasting on her, blowing out their brains. Their mouths stuffed with flesh and soaked with blood, they sprawled motionless on the tarmac.

Gun in hand, Michael K. waited, watching the mutilated bag lady. Five minutes later, minus one of her arms, she rose to her knees, stood up, and gazed at him with milky eyes. Drooling, she growled at him.

He shot her in the head three times until parts of her skull flew into the air behind her like pieces of coconut and she dropped dead.

"How did she ever live to be as old as she was?" he said, holstering his Colt.

"Bad news," said Darren, leering at her corpse.

"You heard her, everyone. Halverson passed this way. He jacked somebody's car. We're hot on his trail. He couldn't have gotten too far from here."

Michael K. gunned his Harley.

He ran over the crone's neck, cutting her head off.

"Darren, you take point," he said. "If you see a pea green compact, let me know."

Darren's Harley roared to the front of the biker gang.

Chapter 76

Vivian scooted toward the tunnel that had three corpses hanging from it. She was breathing heavily.

She passed an abandoned ambulance and stopped her scooter beside a white pickup, parked it, dismounted, and sat on the pickup's lowered tailgate.

"Let's take a breather here," she said as Freddie and Buzz caught up to her.

She didn't like the looks of the tunnel ahead, but she saw no way around it. She believed Michael K. had gone in this direction.

The two dogs sat in front of her.

"I guess you two want to hear my life story."

They cocked their heads at her.

"There's not much to tell. I had a nightmare childhood. My mother was a drunk with kidney cancer, and my stepfather abused me as a child. He inflicted terrible pain on me and treated me like dirt. I don't know how I stood the abuse and suffering for so long. One of the worst things about my nightmare childhood was that my mother knew about my stepfather's abuse and did nothing to stop him. She was as bad as he was in my eyes. It's a testimony to the human spirit that I survived under his reign of terror. I don't think I would have, though, if I hadn't run away from home. Not that either of my parents cared. They had ruined their own lives, and they were bound and determined to ruin mine.

"I didn't know what to do with myself. I was only thirteen. I had no idea how to survive in the world. I wandered around on the streets alone. Nobody cared, except a couple of men named Tom and Jimmy who tried to convince me to become a hooker for them. I didn't trust either one of them. However, I was desperate to survive. I had no way to make a living. My body had already been defiled by my stepfather. Why not defile it some more and get paid for it this time? But the thought repelled me. I didn't want to meet more men who were gonna abuse me. I had to do something to support myself, though. Being on your own when you're thirteen is terrifying. I had nowhere to turn, nobody to turn to. The pressure to make a living was driving me crazy. I didn't want to eat rotten, bug-infested food out of garbage cans and sleep in a cardboard box in an alley for the rest of my life.

"Before I had made up my mind that I was gonna join those two cads, I was lucky enough to meet Dmitri and his group of self-flagellators. He was a sad man but very nice. I asked if I could join him. He said yes, but he told me he was the leader of a movement that was very painful for its followers. He explained how I had to constantly flog my back like all of the other members. I thought he was the leader of a strange movement, but he seemed very kind, and I trusted him.

"I knew I didn't want to get mixed up with the pimps Tom and Jimmy. They would abuse me like my stepfather and sell me to other men who would also abuse me. I didn't like the idea of whipping myself. Dmitri called it 'scourging yourself.' He explained that life was all about pain. If you wanted to go on living, you could not escape pain and suffering. Scourging yourself cleansed your soul, according to him. Naturally I was hesitant to join his group because it meant I had to scourge myself. But I decided I'd rather inflict pain on myself than have someone else inflict it on me. At least, when I whipped myself I was in control. When others inflicted pain on me, I felt like a slave and I felt debased because I had no say in the matter.

"Dmitri said the group didn't have much food, but they managed to get enough from alms. It wasn't the life of luxury I dreamed of as a kid. I knew that such a life would never be mine, because I had grown up poor in a house of evil people who hated me. When you get kicked around all the time, you feel worthless. I decided joining Dmitri's group must be my destiny. Dmitri was a kind man, and I would be glad to whip myself in order to belong to his group of self-flagellators. I would never be glad to be abused by my stepfather or by anybody like him."

Vivian looked at Buzz.

"I know your story, Buzz. Your horrible master was like my stepfather. Anybody who would name a dog Buzzard has to be sick."

She eyed Freddie. "I wish I knew your story, but I'm sure it was full of suffering and pain like mine. I could tell when I first met you that our lives had much in common, that we were kindred spirits."

Freddie woofed in agreement.

Vivian craned around and set her eyes on the tunnel.

"I don't like the looks of that tunnel, but we need to go through it to catch up to Michael K. First, let's drink."

She set down the dog bowl and filled it with water.

"You first, Freddie."

Freddie greedily lapped the water until the bowl was empty.

Vivian refilled the bowl and set it in front of Buzz.

He lapped the water until the bowl was empty.

Meanwhile, Vivian took a long pull on her water bottle. She wiped her mouth clean and screwed the cap back on the bottle, which she reattached to its makeshift shoelace holder on her belt.

She stood up, mounted her scooter, and scooted toward the tunnel.

"Expect trouble in the tunnel, boys," she said, glancing up at the three cadavers hanging over the entrance.

Chapter 77

She didn't like the idea of entering an unlit tunnel, especially without car headlights to light the road in front of her, but she was sure Michael K. had passed this way. She had no other goal in life other than to confront him with his crimes.

A mephitic odor permeated the tunnel. She wished she could block the stench from entering her nostrils. She figured ghouls were foraging for humans inside. She heard them shuffling in the darkness. Freddie growled behind her.

"Quiet, boy," she whispered. "Don't let them know we're here."

Freddie stopped growling.

Buzzard loped behind him.

Vivian kept scooting down the road. Careful not to run into any abandoned cars, she had to move slowly, picking her way through the curtain of darkness.

Her palms sweaty, she couldn't wait to get out of this dungeon. She hoped the ghouls couldn't see her in the pitch dark. For sure she couldn't see them. She could only hear their scuffing and smell their stomach-turning putrescence.

She told herself not to succumb to panic.

She thought about lighting a match to see where she was going, but she feared the tunnel might blow up because of the miasmic stench surrounding her. It reeked of methane and some other equally noisome odor that smelled like sulfur.

She kept scooting forward, gripping the handlebars. How long was this tunnel? It seemed to be going on for miles, or was that her imagination? She peered ahead but saw no light at the end of the tunnel. She scraped her knuckles against the side of a parked vehicle on her left as she scooted by it.

She let out an involuntary cry of pain.

She thought she heard the ghouls changing their direction, shambling toward her.

She kept scooting forward.

She had no idea how far the exit was, but she wasn't going to turn back. She would either find the exit or die trying. She could die here as well as anywhere else. In any case, her mother and stepfather wouldn't be going to her funeral. They could care less if she died. She couldn't forget the nightmare memories of the pair of them that haunted her. She wanted to forget them and move on with her life, but the memories plagued her.

She sometimes wished her mind was a blank slate. But without memories her life was nothing. She might as well be a zombie. No matter how painful they were, at least the memories were hers. Like Dmitri had said, life was full of pain and suffering.

She ran into a rock or some kind of debris in the road and had to jump off her scooter when she lost control of it. She heard a growl beside her. She reached toward the sound and felt clothing hanging on a bony figure.

Her heart in her mouth, she realized she was standing next to a ghoul. She whipped out her knife and thrust it toward the creature. It was a blind thrust, because she couldn't see the thing in the impenetrable dark. She felt the blade cut through clothing and glance off a hard substance she took for a rib.

She knew she would never kill the ghoul with a chest wound. She had to target the head. But where was the head? She couldn't see anything. She could smell the creature's rotten stink, which was overpowering thanks to its close proximity to her. Knowing she had stabbed the creature in the chest, she could tell the thing was quite tall.

She felt a liquid on the back of her hand that gripped the knife. The liquid was drool from the creature that was lowering its head to bite her face. Appalled, she yanked her knife from the ghoul chest and thrust it toward the area where she expected the temple to be. She could only guess without visual confirmation. The blade struck bone but didn't penetrate. If she had hit the temple, the blade would have penetrated easily into the brain. She must have missed the temple.

She reared her hand and thrust again, this time closer to herself because she thought she had struck near the back of the skull previously. Meanwhile, the ghoul was lowering its head closer to her, growling and slavering. She hoped the thing was as blind as she was in this darkness. Her arm muscle was strong on account of her constant flogging of her back. She plunged the blade into the creature's head and felt it penetrate the skull and impale the brain.

The ghoul fell forward, stopped growling, and slid down her body till it sprawled on the tarmac. She reeled from the thing in disgust and bumped into a car behind her. She needed to recover her scooter. Crouching, she felt around the tarmac until she touched the fallen scooter and stood it up.

She heard Freddie growling beside her. He must have been sniffing the ghoul she had dispatched.

"Let's get out of here," she whispered.

She scooted toward the exit but not going too fast. She wanted to avoid running into another rock and taking a fall.

At last she saw light at the end of the tunnel.

She felt like crying for joy, but she kept her mouth shut to avoid making any noise that would attract the famished ghouls that prowled inside the tunnel.

As she neared the exit she saw an upended Suburban, which she approached circumspectly because she saw a bomb crater near it. She climbed the chassis and peered inside the windows. She saw four corpses with bullet holes in their foreheads. She wondered who these people were. There must have been a fight at the end of the tunnel. Who had killed them? Could it have been Michael K. and his gang? They took out everybody in their path.

The four passengers in the Suburban must have driven by her when she was unconscious from Michael K.'s bullet to her head and lying in the road among her massacred friends.

The bomb couldn't have gone off too long ago. The Suburban's hood was still warm. Which meant she was catching up to him.

She scooted around the two-foot-deep crater and outside the tunnel into the welcome warmth and brightness of sunlight. Freddie and Buzz trotted after her.

Chapter 78

After Michael K. and the High Rolerz left the devastation of DC, they drove through a small town.

Michael K. halted his Harley at the edge of town and held up his hand to signal the High Rolerz to stop.

"Remember the hag we met before we drove through DC?" he asked Darren, who had stopped his Harley beside him.

"She was a messed-up skank."

"But she said she saw a man and a woman drive by her in a midget green car."

"She had a couple screws loose if you ask me."

"She said it was pea soup green."

"Bonkersville," said Darren, drawing an air circle around his ear with his forefinger several times.

"Not so fast. I saw a pale green Fiat at the gas station we passed when we entered this town."

"I'm telling you she was out of it. What's a midget car? There's no such thing."

"She meant a compact car like a Fiat. Let's head back."

Michael K. and his gang made U-turns in the middle of the street and returned to the gas station.

Michael K. halted at the gas station where Halverson had tried to get gas for the Fiat. Michael K. dismounted from his hog and inspected the vehicle. Darren accompanied him and peered through the driver's-side window.

"The gas tank's empty," said Darren, watching him. "It could have been sitting there for a year for all we know."

Michael K. felt the hood. "The engine's warm. This jalopy hasn't been here long."

"If Halverson was driving it—and that's a big if—he must've jacked another car when this junker broke down."

Michael K. picked up the gas nozzle that lay on the ground. He squeezed the nozzle trigger with no result. He dropped the nozzle.

"These fuel pumps are dry," he said.

"So the driver jacked another car and took off."

Michael K. thought about it. "Males sense, but how do we know he was able to find another car in workable condition with gas in it?"

"Look at all these abandoned cars. He had a good selection to choose from."

"Maybe," said Michael K., gazing at the corpse sprawled in front of the service station garage.

Chapter 79

Halverson was relaxing and watching *Burnt Offerings* when he saw one of the filmgoers in the front row pass a hot dog to the person sitting beside him.

"They brought their own food," said Marta, noticing the same thing.

"Why did they pick the worst seats in the house when they're the only ones here?"

"Some people like sitting as close as possible to the screen."

"It makes me dizzy whenever I sit in the front row. I have to keep looking up all the time."

Halverson watched the filmgoers pass more hot dogs down the row.

"They brought a lot of franks," he said.

"Where are the rolls?"

"You can't get fresh bread nowadays. You can't get anything fresh."

"I'm starting to get hungry watching them," said Marta, reaching for her beef jerky in her knapsack. "I wish we had some popcorn."

A pair of latecomers entered the darkened theater and sat near the front row.

"I don't know how they can see in the dark to walk," whispered Halverson. "The lighting in here is terrible. The only light is from the movie screen."

A middle-aged guy with long grey hair in the first row passed a hot dog back to the couple who had recently entered.

"Do you smell something?" said Marta, turning up her nose.

"Yeah. This place. They probably haven't cleaned it in years."

"I can't believe they're still showing movies. How does the theater owner make money when there's nobody at the ticket window?"

The middle-aged guy got up from his front row seat, bent forward, and dragged something into the aisle close to the couple who were sitting behind him. Halverson couldn't tell what the object was on account of the dark. It had to be almost six feet long.

"What's going on down there?" whispered Marta.

"I can't see," said Halverson. "It's too dark."

He was burning with curiosity, though.

The middle-aged guy withdrew a hoselike thing out of the object, raised it to his mouth, and bit the end off. He handed the end, which looked like a hot dog, to the couple.

"What are they eating?" said Marta.

"I don't think it's hot dogs," said Halverson, squinting, trying to discern what the filmgoers were consuming.

He needed to get a better look.

He stood up and stole down the aisle toward the front row. He started when he made out what the object that lay on the floor was. A corpse with its stomach ripped open. The middle-aged ghoul was dredging out intestines from the cadaver's stomach, biting them off, and handing tubelike sections to his fellow ghouls.

Halverson dry-heaved at the sight. He turned around to go back to his seat. A ghoul had just entered the auditorium and was staggering toward him, sticking her arms out in front of her in anticipation of grabbing Halverson.

Halverson whipped his knife out of its leather sheath strapped to his ankle and stalked toward the twentysomething ghoul who had dyed blue hair. Growling, she lurched toward him. Hearing a noise Halverson craned around.

The other ghouls must have heard her, because they turned around in their front seats and spotted Halverson. As one they got to their feet and schlepped up the aisle toward him.

Facing forward Halverson thrust his hunting knife through Blue Dye's milky left eye into her brain. She dropped at his feet in a heap. He skirred back to Marta.

"Why don't we just let them have it?" she said, her MP5 at the ready.

"Waste of ammo."

"I can't believe we were watching a movie with a bunch of ghouls in the audience."

"A bunch of ghouls eating human entrails."

"Why did you have to tell me?" said Marta, the blood draining from her face.

"They're scarier than the horror movie."

Halverson snatched his knapsack from the seat beside his, strapped it to his back, and strode toward the exit. Marta followed his example.

A crewcut ghoul pushing thirty shuffled across the carpet in the lobby toward them, baring his teeth and snarling. Jerking his head from side to side, he flailed his arms at his sides, unable to control them like he had Parkinson's.

Halverson prepared to attack the creature with his knife.

Before he had a chance to make his move, Marta lunged in front of him and thrust her knife through the ghoul's ear into his brain. He slumped at her feet.

Halverson and Marta burst out of the theater.

And froze in their tracks when they saw Michael K. cut his eyes toward them as he stood at the service station surrounded by the High Rolerz straddling their hogs.

Chapter 80

The bikers raised their weapons and trained them on Halverson and Marta.

"Are you Halverson?" said Michael K., striding toward him.

"No," said Halverson.

"That's odd. You fit the description I was given of the slimeball who murdered my brother Bobby K."

"You must be mistaken," said Halverson, sweating with anxiety.

He knew he and Marta wouldn't stand a chance against all of these bikers.

"By the way, slowly drop your guns," said Michael K.

"We were attacked by ghouls in the theater," said Halverson.

"Drop your guns or you will die where you stand," said Michael K., raising his voice.

Halverson and Marta shrugged off their machine pistols and dropped them to the sidewalk.

Michael K. gazed at the weapons. "Those are pieces Special Forces would use. Why do *you* have them?"

"We found them," said Halverson.

"You're not gonna find guns like that just lying around."

"We live in strange times."

"We do indeed. Are you Special Forces?"

"No."

"You're not Special Forces, and you're carrying a Brugger and Thomet MP9? And your friend is carrying a Heckler & Koch MP5? Hard to believe."

"We live in—"

"Shut up," cut in Michael K. "What kind of idiot do you take me for?"

"A regular one."

"Are you trying to be funny? You're not gonna be laughing when we try you for the cold-blooded murder of my brother." Michael K. paused. "I hear you've been a busy man. Not only did you waste my brother, you assassinated the president of the United States."

"I did not."

"That Special Forces guy said otherwise."

"What Special Forces guy?" said Halverson, pricking up his ears.

"Ah—I think he said his name was Birdy or Turdy. Something like that."

"Where is he?" said Halverson, surveying the gang, trying to find Purdy.

"We joined forces for a while."

"Bloodlust makes strange bedfellows."

"True. The only thing we agreed on was your death."

"I don't see him."

"We had a falling-out."

"Where is he?"

"Dead. He wanted you as bad as I do. Except he's not gonna get you. You should thank me for eliminating him. You have one less enemy hunting you."

The filmgoer ghouls commenced jerking like marionettes out of the theater entrance.

"Take those things out," said Michael K.

The High Rolerz blasted their heads apart. Flying fragments of skulls bathed in brain matter sliced through the air as the herky-jerky ghouls fell dead, their strings cut.

"Cease fire," said Michael K.

The gunplay ended.

He turned to Halverson. "You're lucky I believe in justice and giving everybody a fair trial. You will have your day in court before we execute you."

Halverson snickered. He knew the so-called fair trial would be rigged.

"You should be thankful I'm giving you a trial," said Michael K. "Otherwise, you'd be dead where you stand."

"Your brother was in the process of murdering innocent people. I stopped him before he could murder more."

"It sounds like you're gonna plead guilty."

"Guilty of stopping murders in progress."

"Guilty of murder in the first. I will make sure you get the death sentence. My brother will not rest in peace until you're dead."

"Homicidal maniacs never rest in peace."

Michael K. withdrew his Colt Python from his hip holster and trained the muzzle on Halverson's face.

"I ought to shut you up here and now," he said.

"What are those two red lines under your eyes? Are you trying to look like an Indian in warpaint?"

"My two brothers' blood is forever etched on my face," roared Michael K., distraught. "Oran and Bill. Their blood's on me." He contorted his face with the pain of their memory.

He moved the Python closer to Halverson's face.

"It will be on me for the rest of my life," he said.

He continued drawing a bead on Halverson's face with the Python.

Halverson didn't doubt Michael K. would pull the trigger. His nerves taut, fear-generated sweat slicking his face, Halverson awaited the crack of the gunshot. He knew the man and his gang of cutthroats had massacred Dmitri and his cult of self-flagellators.

Seeing Halverson cowed, Michael K. felt better about himself.

"Do you know who I remind most people of?" he said, puffing out his chest with arrogance.

"Mr. Magoo?"

"No," snapped Michael K. "Valentine Michael Smith. That's right. *Stranger in a Strange Land.* A man with a plan. A born leader. My people lead this country now, because we're the only ones with the balls to come out of hiding. My beliefs resonate with the people who are still alive and trying to survive in this wasteland created by your dead president."

"The last I heard the president is still alive."

"Birdy the Turdy said you assassinated him."

"The secretary of state replaced him."

"So what? Do you think anybody trying to make a living in this godforsaken wasteland gives a damn who the president is?"

"For your information, I *didn't* assassinate the president. Marta and me were framed."

"Isn't that what Lee Harvey Oswald said?"

"He said he was a patsy."

"I heard the CIA were the ones who set him up to take the fall for taking out JFK."

"I don't know anything about the CIA."

"Of course not. Why should I believe the murderer of my brother?" Michael K. signaled to Barry. "Frisk these two and cuff them. They're professional assassins so I'm sure they have more weapons on them."

Barry obeyed, patted down Halverson, and threw down his handgun and knife. He did the same for Marta. Then he cuffed their wrists behind their backs.

Chapter 81

Vivian flogged her back as she scooted down the car-congested road. She knew she had to make a decision soon. There was no way she was going to expose these dogs to the peril of meeting up with the homicidal maniac Michael K.

She became alert as she spotted a woman riding a bicycle toward her. The woman couldn't be a ghoul. They had no motor skills. The next question was, was she friend or foe?

"Hello," said Vivian.

"Hi," said the woman in her midforties, stopping her bike near her.

"I'm Vivian."

"I'm Carla. Nice to meet you. I suggest you turn back if you're heading in this direction. Ghouls are everywhere."

"They're everywhere behind me too."

Carla pulled a face. She had short chestnut hair, sunken cheekbones, and an aquiline nose. Five six, she wore horn-rimmed glasses with round lenses. Her pale blue eyes twinkled when she saw Freddie and Buzz.

"You have nice dogs," she said.

"Meet Freddie and Buzz."

Carla got off her bike, lowered its kickstand, and approached the dogs. Hunkering down beside them, smiling, she patted their heads.

Vivian watched her. Carla had a nice smile. Vivian didn't want to part with Freddie and Buzz, but she knew she must prevent them from meeting the butcher Michael K. He would kill them if he saw them accompanying her when she confronted him with his crimes.

"Actually, they're not mine," she said. "We found each other. They're strays."

"They look very happy. You must treat them well."

"I prefer animals to people if you must know the truth."

"I was taking a nap in the woods when a gang of motorcyclists woke me up. I let them pass before I came out of the woods and resumed my journey."

Michael K. and the High Rolerz. Vivian was on the right path.

"Where are you headed?" she said.

"Out of DC. It's lying in ruins," said Carla, her voice breaking. "Millions of ghouls are infesting the wreckage. I couldn't wait to get out of there. So sad. The ghouls got both my mother and father. I was in the garage when the filthy things attacked our house. I tried to help Mom and Dad, but there were hundreds of ghouls inside the house, preventing me from entering and helping." Her voice broke again as emotion overcame her.

Freddie started whimpering next to her.

"I returned to the garage, shut the door, and climbed into the driver's seat of our car. I was planning on turning on the ignition and killing myself with carbon monoxide poisoning—"

"Oh no," said Vivian.

"But the car wouldn't start. Our electrical devices wouldn't work at home."

"That's lucky or you would have killed yourself."

"Where's the justice in the world?" said Carla, her eyes swimming with tears. "My whole family killed by godforsaken creatures."

She scratched Freddie's neck, which helped soothe her.

Vivian flogged her back and groaned.

"What are you doing?" said Carla, appalled at the sight of Vivian's lacerated and scarred back.

"I'm a self-flagellator. We believe we are doomed to suffer in agony while we walk this earth. Whipping ourselves reminds us we're alive."

"I never heard of such a group. I doubt I could live like that."

"We must suffer if we want to live."

Chapter 82

Carla took in the plastic water bottles hanging from Vivian's waist. "I'm dying of thirst."

Vivian handed her a bottle.

Carla took a long pull on it. "Thanks so much. Is it safe to drink the tap water around here?"

"Probably not, thanks to radioactivity from nuclear fallout."

"What a mess," said Carla, observing the dead bodies strewn in the road and at the edge of the woods. "We're probably inhaling radiation every time we breathe. Best not to think about it. Sometimes I feel powerless to do anything."

She returned to her bike.

A blonde ghoul in her late thirties with her fine hair tied back with a tortoiseshell barrette stumbled out of the woods as she was staring at a cell phone in her hand, her once-creamy complexion now a papier mâché consistency. A brown earthworm crawled out of her putrescent button nose and entered her open, slavering mouth.

"I guess I'd better be going," said Carla, looking away from the ghoul in disgust.

A fiftyish statuesque black woman with a snake writhing through her blue rinse hair shambled and staggered after the blonde.

"Where are you going?" said Vivian.

"I'm going down to Georgia to visit my daughter. Hopefully, things are better there. I don't know how people are surviving in these dreadful times. I have no way to contact her. I don't even know if she's alive."

Carla worried her lower lip.

"I'm sure she is," said Vivian.

"The last time I was able to contact her was three years ago. She said she had a baby."

"Congratulations."

"I don't know if I'd want to have a baby during these horrible times." Carla stared into space. "There's no future," she added in a monotonic voice.

"No future."

"We could be nearing the end."

"As long as we're alive there's a chance things will get better," said Vivian, not believing it wholeheartedly, but this conversation was getting too depressing. She needed to lighten the mood.

"Maybe there aren't so many ghouls down in Georgia," said Carla, becoming upbeat.

"There's only one way to find out."

Carla eyed the dogs and smiled. "You're lucky to have these two fellas with you."

"Do you want company?" said Vivian.

"You want to go to Georgia?" said Carla in surprise. "You're heading in the wrong direction."

"Not me. I have business to take care of with the bikers."

"I would avoid them at all costs."

"I was talking about Freddie and Buzz."

"You want me to take your dogs?"

"They're not mine. I just found them wandering around."

Vivian thought the safest thing for the dogs was for them to go with Carla. Vivian feared for their lives if she took them to Michael K. She needed to part with them so they could go on living.

"I couldn't do that," said Carla. "I'd feel terrible taking your dogs from you. They probably wouldn't even go with me. You're their master."

"Only for the last few days. To be honest with you, I fear for their lives if they remain with me."

"I wouldn't want anything to happen to them. Are you sure it's all right if your dogs go with me?"

"Positive."

"The question is, how am I gonna get them to go with me?"

"If only we had a pair of leashes. The dogs both have collars as you can see."

Vivian started inspecting the cars around her.

"What are you doing?" said Carla.

"Trying to find a car with the keys in the ignition."

"Even if you do, the car will probably be out of gas. Why else would the owners abandon it?"

"Who knows? Maybe the ghouls got them. Or cannibals."

"Cannibals?"

"I've heard rumors that cannibals are roaming around in the ruins foraging for food."

"What next?" said Carla, her face gloomy.

"Remember the Donner Party? When people are starving and there's no food in sight, they resort to cannibalism."

"No way would I do that. I'd rather starve," said Carla, shivering at the thought. She changed the subject. "If I had a pair of leashes, the dogs could run alongside my bicycle."

"Easier to find a working car than a pair of leashes," said Vivian, continuing to inspect car dashboards.

She rooted through the junk strewn in a pickup truck. She didn't expect to find dog leashes, but maybe she could stumble upon some rope. She dug through a pile of empty beer cans and found a coiled length of clothesline, which she withdrew.

"Here are your leashes," she said, holding up the clothesline.

Carla shrugged. "Why not?"

Using her knife, Vivian cut two eight-foot-long sections of clothesline from the coil.

"All-purpose clothesline," said Carla. "What would we do without it?"

She tied the lengths of clothesline to the two dog collars.

"I can tie the other ends to my bike's handlebars," she said.

Vivian felt sad that Freddie and Buzz were going to leave her. But she knew it was best for them, and it needed to be done.

Sitting, Freddie and Buzz looked at her and whined. They sensed something was up with the clothesline hanging from their collars.

"As much as I hate to say this, we're gonna have to say good-bye, old friends."

She felt like she was going to cry. She flogged her back and grimaced in pain, cutting off the tears.

Carla tied the two lengths of clothesline to her bike handlebars, one to the right side, one to the left. She mounted her bike.

"I better be going," she said.

"Be careful when you reach the tunnel. It's infested with ghouls."

"In the direction you're going there's a huge bomb crater in the road and a bunch of human skulls scattered everywhere. You're better off not driving a car. It won't get past the crater."

Carla started riding her bike. But the dogs sat down and refused to budge. They stared at Vivian.

"They want you to come with us," said Carla.

"Out of the question." To the dogs Vivian said, "Carla's nice. She'll be good to you. Go with her. I'll catch up to you guys later."

She would never leave if she kept looking at their sad eyes. Fighting back tears, she turned away from them and scooted down the road on Michael K.'s trail. She turned a deaf ear to their barks and ululations. Even so, she felt tears stream down her face. If she stopped and went back now, she would never leave them. They didn't understand that it was for their own good that she was giving them to Carla.

Chapter 83

"Throw them in the pickup," said Michael K.

"Where are we going?" said Halverson.

"To your execution."

Halverson sneered.

Darren and Barry frog-marched Halverson and Marta to the said pickup, lowered the tailgate, and told them to climb into the back.

Halverson was in no position to refuse what with being disarmed and having his wrists cuffed behind his back. He managed to sit on the tailgate and scooch into the cargo hold.

Leering at Marta, Darren lifted her into the cargo hold, where she scrambled next to Halverson.

"Everybody has the right to a speedy trial in this country," said Michael K. "And that goes for you two. We'll start your trial in a few minutes."

"Who's the judge?" said Halverson.

"I am."

"What a surprise."

"I'm tired of your mouth. Do you *want* me to find you guilty? You should be going out of your way to flatter me."

"I already know what the verdict's gonna be with you as judge."

"Do you want a trial or not?"

Halverson figured any kind of delay in his execution would benefit him. Maybe it would give him time to devise a means of escape.

"Yeah," he said. "Who's the prosecuting attorney?"

"I am."

"Are you the jury too?"

"That wouldn't be fair."

"Is this supposed to be fair?"

Michael K. ignored him. "Twelve members of the High Rolerz will serve as jury."

This was getting more ridiculous by the moment. Halverson knew his execution was assured. He dreaded to ask, but he had to know.

"Who's my lawyer?"

"The court can appoint one."

"Who's the court?"

"Me." Michael K. paused. "Or you can represent yourself."

"Fine. I'll be my own lawyer."

For all the good it would do him. But maybe it would allow him to buy time.

"How do you plead?" said Michael K.

"Not guilty by reason of self-defense—"

"Wait a minute. I have to round up the jury." Michael K. turned to his gang who were idling their Harleys around the pickup. "I need twelve volunteers for the jury."

Twenty members on their hogs roared up to the pickup.

"I only need twelve of you. I appreciate your service, but eight of you have to leave."

Eight motorcyclists grumbled and drove away.

"Kill Halverson," said one of them as he retreated from the prospective jurors.

"Don't you need substitutes?" said Halverson.

"This trial won't take long," said Michael K. "You don't have to worry about a juror getting sick."

"I'm sick already," said Marta.

"OK, I count twelve," said Michael K. "Jurors, gather around the pickup."

Astride their chugging Harleys, they parked in a circle around the pickup and idled their machines.

Michael K. stood in front of the pickup tailgate.

"Can everybody hear me?"

"Yeah," said several of the jurors, who were composed of seven women and five men, all dressed in black leather.

Five of the women were from Michael K.'s harem.

Michael K. confronted Halverson. "Is your name Halverson?"

"Yeah," said Halverson, sitting in the back of the pickup, his wrists secured behind him.

"Stand when you address the judge."

Sneering, Halverson stood with difficulty courtesy of his bound wrists.

"I will charge you with contempt if you don't stand," said Michael K.

"I *am* standing."

"You are being charged with murdering my brother Bobby K. in cold blood. The charge is murder in the first. How do you plead?"

"Not guilty."

"This is a court of law. When speaking to the judge, say *Your Honor* or I will hold you in contempt."

"You're not a judge."

"I'm gonna have you executed right now for being in contempt. How do you plead?"

This was no win. Halverson decided to play along.

"Not guilty, Your Honor," he said with disgust.

"Sit down."

Halverson sat.

"One of the group of self-flagellators told me she witnessed you murder my brother Bobby K."

"I want to cross-examine the witness, Your Honor," said Halverson.

When he said *Your Honor* he gagged like there was a bunch of old copper pennies lying on his tongue.

"You can't."

"Why not, Your Honor?"

"She's dead."

"How convenient."

"Our of order. I will charge you with contempt if you make another outburst."

Halverson said nothing.

"Describe in your own words what happened when you murdered Bobby K.," said Michael K, acting as the prosecuting attorney.

"I shot him in self-defense. He killed an unarmed cult member. I thought he would kill more, including me, so I shot him."

"What gives you the power to read another person's mind?"

"I saw him murder an unarmed cult member, which he did for no reason. I believe he did it because he liked committing murder and would gladly do it again."

"Are you saying you can read a person's mind? Because if you can, you'd be quite unique," said Michael K., appealing to the jurors.

The jurors laughed.

"In fact, you'd be the only person on earth who can read minds," went on Michael K.

"He was a loose cannon waiting to go off. I saw him commit murder once and knew he would do it again. Even if he didn't, the fact remains he killed an unarmed person in cold blood. It was my duty to punish him."

"You're a self-appointed killer of other killers. Is that it?" snickered Michael K.

Several of the jurors laughed.

"You took the law into your own hands, is what you did. Isn't that right, Halverson? You judged my brother guilty and executed him."

"I shot him in self-defense. I have the right to defend myself from an armed assailant."

"This trial is a joke," Marta said under her breath to Halverson.

"I want to call one of the self-flagellators to the stand, Your Honor," said Halverson.

"You can't," said Michael K.

"Why not? They witnessed my killing your brother. The court needs to hear their testimony, Your Honor."

"None of them can be called on to testify, because they are all dead."

Halverson gaped. "How could they *all* be dead?"

"We executed them for taking part in the murder of my brother. They were as guilty as you are, because they were your accomplices in crime."

"You're the one who should be on trial for mass murder—"

"Order. Order in the court. I don't want to have to cite you for contempt, but I will if you continue to interrupt the court."

"I'm not dead," said Vivian, scooting toward Michael K, a whip in her hand.

Dumbfounded, he stared at her with wide eyes.

She flogged her back and winced in pain. "I am Vivian. I'm one of the self-flagellators, and I witnessed the killing of your brother, who was about to murder more of my people before Halverson shot him. I also witnessed you and your gang massacre my people. I demand justice. I demand you confess to your crimes."

Michael K. stood nonplussed, his face chalk white.

Halverson admired Vivian for managing to catch up with the bikers with only a scooter. In point of fact, she did not witness his shooting of Robert K. He was thankful, however, for her testimony. On the other hand, she was on a foolhardy mission since she had nobody with her that he could see. Not only that, she was unarmed.

"This can't—this—you're dead," Michael K. managed to utter at last in befuddlement. "You can't be alive. I shot you dead."

The High Rolerz backed away from her in awe, not believing their eyes.

"She's a ghoul," said one biker.

"Ghouls can't talk," said Darren. "She's no more a ghoul than you or me."

"You're a liar," Michael K. told Vivian. "You did not witness Bobby K.'s murder. I met you after we punished your comrades who helped Halverson kill Bobby K. You were with a different faction of your cult when I met you. There are laws against perjury."

Staring at her, Michael K. commenced removing his black tie.

Chapter 84

His face flushed, Johnny Romano burst into the president's office, followed by Dakota, who had his SIG drawn.

"Kowalski and his squad are all dead in front of the air vent," cried Romano. "Ghouls are swarming around the vent."

Sitting behind his desk, Uriah thrust to his feet.

"Romano," he bellowed. "You went AWOL. You're a deserter. How dare you barge into my office screaming and shouting at me?"

"Fucking A. You killed Kowalski."

"A deserter has no right to speak to me like that. I'm the president of the United States of America, the greatest country in the world."

"Do you want me to arrest him, Mr. President?" said Dakota, gun in hand.

"Not yet. I want to hear him out."

Dakota holstered his gun and patted down Romano, who was unarmed.

"I didn't desert," said Romano. "I came back. I'm here."

"You were absent without leave. I never authorized your departure."

"I found out my wife was having a baby. I had to see her," said Romano, wrought up.

"You. Didn't. Have. Permission."

"Permission to see my own baby?" said Romano, indignant.

"Dakota, throw Romano in the brig," ordered Uriah.

"If you even care, they were both dead. Ghouls got them," said Romano, his face working, his eyes tearing.

Dakota grabbed Romano's arms, pinned them behind his back, and hustled him into the hallway, shutting the office door behind him.

"He said Kowalski and his team are dead," said Dr. Morrow, his face wan.

"Horrible news," said Uriah. "God bless all of them. They sacrificed their lives so the rest of us could live."

"Couldn't we have let them inside, Mr. President?"

"You said we don't have enough oxygen for all of us to breathe in the bunker. That's why they volunteered to go outside."

"That doesn't mean we should let them die at the hands of the ghouls."

"I gave them all the guns and ammo they needed."

"Apparently not."

Uriah rounded on Morrow. "I don't like being second-guessed. I did the right thing. It's not my fault that Kowalski and his team didn't know how to defend themselves. He was a professional soldier, a SEAL, for Chrissake. How could he not know how to defend himself? I don't hold it against him, though. Their sacrifices will never be forgotten. God bless them."

"Don't you understand? You sent them to their deaths."

"How dare you? They volunteered to leave the bunker and protect the air vent so the rest of us could breathe."

"They didn't volunteer. They lost the lottery."

"There's no difference. I'm not gonna stand here and split hairs with you, Doctor. In the end you're the one who's guilty of their deaths. It was *you* who told me we didn't have enough oxygen to support everybody in the bunker. That's why I held the lottery."

Morrow clasped his brow. "This is a terrible tragedy." He flung his hand away from his face. "But I'm not the one who told them to go outside. I refuse to accept blame for their deaths."

"Of course not. *It was their own fault they died*. They weren't up to the job of defending the air vent from the ghouls. But let us not forget they made the greatest sacrifice a person can make. They sacrificed their lives for this country. They died heroes. They will live on in our hearts," said Uriah, putting his hand on his heart and bowing his head.

"I hope we're not gonna have more lotteries."

"That would depend on the nature of the situation. If people don't volunteer, we have to resort to lotteries."

"Has it come to that? Are we all victims of chance?"

"Not as long as I'm in charge. I'm the one making the decisions for this country, not blind chance. And where the hell is Purdy? Has he sent back any news regarding Halverson?"

"I haven't heard anything."

Uriah brooded. "Halverson must have reached Raven Rock or Purdy would have returned by now with his decapitated head. This is horrible news."

"Why?"

"Because Halverson must have told Speaker Smirnoff that I assumed the presidency," said Uriah, pacing rapidly around the room. "Which means Smirnoff will challenge my authority. We cannot let that happen. It will tear the country in half and foment another Civil War. In its present state the country will not be able to endure it. We must forestall Smirnoff from attempting a coup."

"How is it a coup? The constitution says the speaker of the house is the rightful president, according to the rules of succession."

"You're forgetting one thing," said Uriah, coming to a halt and staring at Morrow.

"What's that?"

"I have the football. I have total control of the nation's nuclear arsenal." Uriah paused. "And it may be time for me to use it against Smirnoff to prevent him from challenging my presidency."

He pressed the intercom switch on his desktop.

"Adriana Copper, report to the president's office," he said.

The better part of three minutes later Copper flung open the door and barreled into the office.

"Yes, sir," she said. "Reporting for duty."

"The valiant heroes guarding the air vent outside have perished at the hands of the ghouls."

"How awful."

"I want you to go outside with select Army Rangers and make sure Kowalski and his team are all dead. In other words, put bullets through their brains. I don't want them resurrecting as ghouls."

"Yes, Mr. President."

"Be quick about it. People can turn rapidly if their brains remain intact after infected ghouls bite them. Make sure you take care of Kowalski's entire team."

"Sir," said Copper, saluting Uriah, her body stiff as a board. She bolted out of the office.

"The idea of Kowalski coming back as a ghoul turns my stomach," said Uriah.

"He was a good man," said Morrow. "He didn't deserve to be devoured by ghouls."

"Nobody deserves it. Turning is an obscenity. Our mission on earth is to prevent any other humans from becoming infected and turning into ghouls."

"We failed that mission with Kowalski and his team," muttered Morrow.

"I didn't catch that. Did you say you're volunteering for the next lottery?"

"Nothing, sir."

Uriah's mind was elsewhere, his visage hard. "I believe I'm gonna have to fire ICBMs equipped with nuclear warheads at Raven Rock to deter Smirnoff from mounting an attack against us now that Halverson must have told him I have assumed the presidency."

Chapter 85

Vivian was terrified, but she didn't let on. She knew the High Rolerz might take her life any second.

"There's no way you could have survived our attack against your cult," said Michael K., running his tie through his hands, staring at Vivian. "Every last one of you was dead. I saw your corpses with my own eyes."

"Yet here I am. I demand an apology for your egregious crimes."

"Maybe she's a ghost," said Darren with concern.

"I'm no ghost," said Vivian. "I'm alive and well, thank you."

"I don't trust cults. They practice black magic. Her cult might know how to bring people back from the dead."

"Impossible," said Michael K. "You can't come back from the dead as the same person. When you reincarnate, you come back in a different life form like a kangaroo or a wombat."

"Then how can she be standing there?" said Darren.

"Our bullets must have missed her. She played opossum and scammed us."

Vivian scourged her back and screwed up her face in pain.

"I demand an apology for the atrocities you committed against my friends."

"Come here," said Michael K.

"Why?" said Vivian, suspicious.

"Your survival instincts impress me. I want to make you one of my group."

"Getting me to join your group won't erase your heinous crimes against my friends."

"You have nowhere else to go. Why not join us?"

"First, you need to apologize."

"Come closer, and we can discuss my offer."

"I don't want your offer. I want your apology."

"That will be part of my offer if you come closer."

Her heart pounding off the charts as she trembled with fear, Vivian knew she must confront the murderer.

She stepped toward him.

"When you look at my face, who do you see?" he said.

"I see a mass murderer."

"When you look at my face and see your own, you will be free."

"I still see the face of a mass murderer who owes me an apology."

"Look closer."

"Your words are lies."

"How am I any different from you and your cult?"

"We don't believe in killing fellow human beings."

"That's too bad. I was gonna ask you to join us. We are not limited by religion or anything else. We are free."

"I am not limited by my beliefs. I am guided by them."

"Do you see your own face when you look at mine yet?"

"No way."

He grabbed her, wrapped his tie around her neck, and proceeded to strangle her. She tried to pry the tie away from her throat, but she couldn't get her fingers underneath it because it was too tight against her flesh.

"How dare you demand anything from me. Your cult helped murder my brother. You and they are as much to blame for his death as Halverson."

Grinding his teeth Michael K. continued to strangle her.

"This time you're gonna die for real," he said. "You're not gonna rise from the dead again. I'm not letting go of this tie until your dead body is limp in my hands."

Vivian kept trying to stay alive, but she was losing her strength. She knew she could not last much longer. But she would do everything she could to stay alive. She reached behind her and tried to gouge out his eyeballs.

"Whoa," he said. "Whoa."

When that failed, she tried to head butt him. But he was too tall. She couldn't reach his head with hers.

Feeling faint she fondly recalled Freddie and Buzz and was glad she hadn't brought them with her. They would continue to live after she perished. It made her feel good knowing she had saved their lives by handing them off to Carla. As for her own life, Vivian knew she had nothing to live for now that all of her friends in the cult had been massacred.

Nevertheless, she continued to struggle to survive, trying to rip the tie from her throat—until her strength was no more.

Her mind blacked out.

"I guess she's not a ghost after all," said Michael K., feeling her body go limp.

"Are you sure she's dead this time, boss?" said Darren, uncertain.

"Positive."

Michael K. let Vivian's lifeless body slide to the tarmac. He felt for the pulse in her neck. Nothing.

"Why did she come after us?" said Darren. "She doesn't even have a gun."

"Fuckin' freak, man," said Barry, approaching Vivian's corpse and leering at it.

"She was nuts," said Michael K. "All those cult types have screws loose. Look at those welts and scars on her back. What kind of person would do that to themselves? Only a self-loathing psycho."

Chapter 86

Halverson was repulsed by the sight of Michael K.'s murder of Vivian. He was furious that there was nothing he could do about saving her with his wrists in cuffs.

He admired her courage. Vivian must have known Michael K. would kill her when she approached him and yet she did not let her fear deter her. She did what she thought was right.

Halverson ached to kill Michael K. He swore Michael K. would not get away with yet another cold-blooded murder of a defenseless person. Yet the reality was Halverson would probably be the next person on Michael K's list of victims after this kangaroo court judgment was handed down.

"Get her out of here and feed her to the ghouls," said Michael K.

Straddling his motorcycle Darren drove up to Gayle, the blonde with a mohawk, who lifted Vivian's limp arm so he could snatch it. Clenching Vivian's arm he dragged her across the tarmac to the edge of the woods and deposited her corpse in the grass, where the ghouls would find it and turn her if she had inhaled their spores earlier.

Darren drove back to the pickup.

"Let's resume our trial now that the crazy woman is dead," said Michael K.

"What did she hope to accomplish by coming here?" said Darren.

"Who knows what goes through the minds of demented people?"

"How did she ever find us?"

"Never underestimate the luck of fools and psychos."

Michael K. eyeballed the twelve jurors who sat astride their Harleys around the pickup.

"Do you all understand your jobs as jurors?" he said.

"We do," said several of them.

The rest nodded their assent.

Michael K. turned to Halverson and Marta. "You two are being charged with the murder of my brother Bobby K. We are trying you for murder in the first, which carries the death penalty. How do you plead?"

"Not guilty," said Halverson.

"Not guilty," said Marta.

"She had nothing to do with your brother's death. You can let her go."

"Why should the court believe anything you say?" said Michael K.

"Because *I'm* the one who pulled the trigger of the gun that killed your brother."

"You just said you were pleading not guilty. Are you changing your plea?"

"No. I'm pleading not guilty by reason of self-defense."

"The cult members I interviewed said they saw you blow away my brother. Is this true or not?"

"Where are these cult members? Defendants have the right to view their accusers."

"Not in my court they don't."

"Because you and your gang killed them."

"Out of order. Did you kill Bobby K.? True or false?"

"I shot him to stop him from killing more people—"

"The court instructed you to answer true or false," cut in Michael K., scowling. "No editorializing. Answer true or false. Did you kill Bobby K.?"

"True."

"Let the jurors note that the defendant has admitted he murdered my brother." Michael K. turned to Halverson. "Do you wish to call anybody to the stand?"

"I wish to call Marta."

"Do you swear to tell the truth, Marta?"

"I do," she said.

"Did you witness the deceased, Bobby K., behead an innocent cult member, Marta?" asked Halverson.

"I did. Bobby K. was preparing to behead another cult member when you shot him."

"Objection," said Michael K. "Marta is giving an opinion. She can't read minds." He paused and answered as the judge. "Objection sustained."

"And Bobby K. was gonna shoot me and Halverson if Halverson didn't kill him first."

"She's giving an opinion again, Your Honor. Objection sustained."

"This court is a travesty of justice," said Halverson.

"Out of order," said Michael K.

"We feared for our lives," said Marta. "Halverson shot him to save ourselves and the cult members."

"Our of order. Out of order. You are both in contempt of court." Michael K. turned to the jury, who were idling their Harleys as they parked in a circle around the pickup. "Jurors, I submit to you that Halverson and his cohort, Marta, killed Bobby K. in cold blood. We are asking for a verdict of murder in the first degree. How say you? I will poll you individually. Rev your hogs once for not guilty, twice for guilty. Let us proceed. Juror One?"

Snarling, Juror One revved her Harley twice.

The rest of the jurors followed her example. The roar of Harleys combined with their exhaust suffused the air.

"The verdict is unanimous," said Michael K. "Halverson and Marta are guilty of murder in the first degree. The penalty is death. Do the defendants have any last words?"

"This court is a joke," said Halverson, outraged. "The judge is a murderer. He just strangled an innocent person in front of hundreds of witnesses."

"She wasn't innocent."

"What crime did she commit?"

"She was born. Court is adjourned."

Michael K. withdrew his Colt Python and trained it on Halverson. "We will now proceed to the execution phase of the trial."

A cacophonous noise filled the sky.

Everybody started.

Chapter 87

Halverson jerked his head up to look at the source of the racket. A helo was descending rapidly above them and angling for the woods, leaving a trail of thick fuscous smoke in its wake.

Michael K. peered up at the damaged helo.

"Military chopper," said Darren, gazing at its swift descent.

"It's a Boeing CH-47 Chinook," said Halverson.

His eyes wide, Michael K. eagerly watched it heading for a crash in the woods.

"It's a military transport chopper," he said. "It has to have guns and ammo on board. We need as much guns and ammo as we can get."

Flying at speed, the Chinook grazed the top of the tallest oaks in the forest then turned vertical and plummeted to the ground and exploded into a massive fireball that spewed a column of black smoke into the sky.

"You stay here and guard the prisoners, Darren," said Michael K. "The rest of you are with me. We need the weapons on that Chinook."

"Why do I miss out on all the fun?" said Darren, leveling a glare at Halverson.

Michael K. mounted his Harley and, burning rubber, peeled off in the direction of the smoke pluming from the woods.

"Nobody could have survived that blast," said Gayle, brushing back her mohawk and taking off after him.

"You heard him," said Barry, driving up to her. "We need the guns."

He passed her and had to slow down when he reached the woods.

Michael K. had already stopped at the edge of the woods.

"We're gonna have to walk through there," he said. "Our hogs are gonna get stuck in all the underbrush. There aren't any dirt trails in the woods that I can see. Let's go."

He dismounted, parked his Harley, and strode into the woods, keeping his eyes on the fire and smoke of the burning Chinook. The rest of the High Rolerz followed his example and belted into the woods after him.

"I didn't know any planes or helos were left," said Barry. "I haven't seen any in so long."

"The military still has them," said Michael K. "They have the advantage of controlling the skies."

"They don't give a damn about any of us."

"We need to reach the crash site before anybody else. The first ones there are gonna loot the Chinook."

Michael K. stepped up his pace between the overarching trees. He tried to avoid the underbrush but when he had no choice he trampled through it, blazing a path to the Chinook. Cringing, he heard another explosion at the crash site.

"They must have bombs on the chopper," said Barry.

"For sure they got ammo," said Michael K. "We gotta have ammo."

"I hope you guys know where you're going," said Gayle.

"We're heading straight for the smoke and fire. We don't need a map for the obvious."

"You might need one for the way out," Gayle said to herself.

"Is everybody packin'?"

"Yeah," came a chorus of voices.

"Never leave home without it," said Gayle, patting her Ruger pistol in her waistband.

Chapter 88

Halverson felt relief at his reprieve from a bullet to the head. He knew he and Marta had to get out of here before the High Rolerz returned. Now was his best chance to escape with only one guard watching him.

The problem was the handcuffs binding his wrists behind his back. They prohibited him from jumping Darren and disarming him.

Halverson spotted the handcuff keys hanging from Darren's leather belt next to his holstered Staccato HD P4.

"Got a problem?" said Darren, remarking the direction of Halverson's gaze.

"Why'd they make you stay here?"

"I dunno. I wish I was with them."

"It's not too late to catch up to them."

"You'd like that, wouldn't you? Then you two would escape. Do you think I'm an idiot? You're both gonna die when Michael K. gets back. Don't think you won't."

"We need a distraction," Halverson whispered to Marta.

"What'd you say?" said Darren.

"I wasn't talking to you."

"No keeping secrets. I want to know what you said."

"I told her you got screwed because they made you stay here with us."

"Next time you say anything, say it loud so we can all hear it or I'm gonna make you eat the muzzle of my Staccato," said Darren, patting his piece. "Do you understand?"

"Sure."

Fuming at Halverson's blasé attitude, Darren whipped his Staccato out of its holster and hammered its butt against Halverson's knee.

Halverson yelped in pain.

"You're gonna regret that," he said.

Darren hammered the Staccato on Halverson's knee again.

"Shit," said Halverson, grimacing in pain.

Darren trained the Staccato on Halverson's face. "I oughta do you right now. The boss would thank me when he comes back."

"Or he'd whack you for stealing his fun from him. He wants to see the look on my face when he blows me away."

Darren thought about it and holstered his Staccato.

Marta ogled him. "I like strong men."

"You got good taste," said Darren, smiling cockily.

They all jumped when they heard another explosion from the Chinook downed in the woods. The pickup vibrated from the blast.

"That bird must be loaded with ammo," said Darren, gazing into the woods in the direction of the smoke hovering over the treetops.

"Don't tell me you prefer explosions to girls," said Marta.

Darren faced her. "Whatever gave you that idea?"

She raised her eyebrows and smiled coyly.

"Be careful or I'm gonna come up there," he said.

"What's holding you back? You look like someone who does what he wants. I'm not gonna stop you."

Darren whipped his head behind his back to make sure nobody was watching. He ogled Marta, who was sitting on the pickup's steel bench and licking her lips.

She opened her mouth and stuck her tongue lasciviously at him.

"I'm coming up there, baby," he said.

He sprang onto the flatbed and, standing above her, leered down at her.

Halverson kicked up his legs, scissored them around Darren's throat, and flung him down. Darren smashed his head into the side of the pickup, rolled over the open tailgate, and crumpled on the tarmac, blood seeping out of his ear.

Halverson bounded to his feet. He knew he had to act fast before Darren came to.

Halverson jumped off the tailgate, landed next to Darren, who was lying motionless on the tarmac, and picked up on the handcuff key attached to Darren's belt loop. Halverson squatted beside

Darren's waist. Without the use of his hands he would have to retrieve the key with his mouth.

Darren groaned.

"Hurry," said Marta.

Halverson leaned over Darren's waist, chewed on the key ring and yanked it, trying to break the cotton belt loop and free the key. The fabric didn't break. He kept yanking on the key ring with his teeth until the fabric broke.

The key ring in his mouth, he stood up and faced Marta.

"I'll free you first then you do me," he said.

She stood up and approached him as he stood in front of the open tailgate. She knelt down with her back toward him.

Using his mouth he tried to insert the key into the left handcuff lock.

Not easy.

The metal key tasted bitter in his mouth. It was difficult to grip with his teeth.

He heard Darren groan again.

Halverson redoubled his efforts. At last he inserted the key into the lock and twisted it with his teeth. The cuff fell off Marta's left wrist and dangled from her right.

She wheeled around to face him and snagged the key from his mouth. She unlocked the cuff on her right wrist and tossed the handcuffs on the tarmac. She leapt off the open tailgate and unlocked the cuffs binding Halverson's wrists behind his back.

Halverson cuffed the unconscious Darren and seized the Staccato.

He strode toward the forest, gun in hand.

"What are you doing?" said Marta, whipping out a knife from a sheath on Darren's belt. "We need to get out of here before they come back."

"I'm gonna take out Michael K.," said Halverson with grim determination.

"His gang will kill you," she said, aghast, running after him.

"He's evil. He needs to be whacked. I have no choice. I saw him strangle Vivian, and there was nothing I could do to help her. It burned in my craw to watch the murder and not be able to stop it."

She latched onto his elbow and brought him to a halt. "You need to calm down and think straight. Your mind's not clear. *They will kill you*. There must be at least a hundred of them versus one of you."

"He massacred Vivian and all of her friends. He can't be allowed to go on living."

He broke away from her grasp and made a beeline for the woods. Before he reached them he grabbed a key from the ignition of one of the Harleys. The High Rolerz had left so quickly for the Chinook crash site that some of them had left their keys in the ignitions.

"You're committing suicide by going after him," she said, chasing him. "He has surrounded himself with professional killers."

"Grab a hog key."

"You have no chance," she said, snagging a key from the nearest Harley.

"The CIA trained me to kill."

"When the odds are a hundred to one against you?"

"He's gonna kill more people if I don't take him out. He's an evil messiah who kills whoever he wants dead."

"Clear the cobwebs out of your mind and think what you're doing. You're committing suicide."

"When we get back, we'll need to get out of here like greased lightning. We'll drive straight to Raven Rock and tell Speaker Smirnoff about the illegal goings-on at Mount Weather."

"Why don't we do that now while we're still alive? Michael K. almost blew your head off a couple minutes ago. That chopper crash saved our lives."

"Nothing's gonna save *his* life."

"How do you expect to get close enough to him to shoot him without him or his gang spotting you?"

"Don't forget. We have surprise on our side. He thinks we're handcuffed in that pickup. He's not gonna expect anybody to be following him."

Halverson bopped into the woods.

Marta sprinted after him.

Another explosion from the downed Chinook rocked the forest.

"All these explosions are gonna attract the ghouls," said Halverson.

"Cheer me up, why don't you?" said Marta.

"I don't see how anyone could have survived the crash unless they parachuted out of the helo earlier."

"Is there any way I can change your mind about Michael K.?"

"None."

Chapter 89

Halverson tore through the forest, his eyes focused on the smoke and fire of the burning aircraft.

He tripped in the underbrush as his big toe got caught on something. He landed on his stomach in brambles. He heard growling behind him. Something clasped his leg. He looked to see what it was. A ghoul lying in the underbrush had tripped him and was attempting to take a bite out of his leg.

Halverson tried to kick the creature to get him to let go of his leg. Eager to devour Halverson, the twentysomething ghoul with snarly hair down to his shoulders hung on. His blond mustache was moving on his face. It turned out to be a bunch of pus-smeared maggots. Halverson couldn't risk using his gun on the creature lest it warn Michael K. and the High Rolerz that a gunman was behind them.

Sweating, hoping to fend off the creature from chewing his calf, Halverson fell to clubbing the ghoul in the head with the Staccato he had commandeered from Darren, but he couldn't crack the skull with the compact pistol.

Marta bounded over to him and thrust her knife into the ghoul's neck just beneath the back of his skull and drove the blade up to the brain all the way to the hilt, making sure she penetrated the infected brain and killed it.

Halverson nodded at her in gratitude, shook the dead creature off his leg, and scrabbled out of the brambles, scratching his arms on thorns.

He didn't care. He had to kill Michael K. A few scratches weren't going to stop him.

"Maybe this is a sign for us to turn back," said Marta.

"I don't believe in signs," said Halverson, resuming his pursuit of Michael K.

Marta shook her head but kept up with him.

"Do you have any idea how you're gonna kill this guy without being killed by his gang?" she said.

"Not yet," said Halverson, not breaking stride.

"The smell of the smoke is becoming stronger."

Breathing hard, he halted, leaned forward, and picked up a long object.

"What is it?" said Marta.

"An M16. One of those explosions must have flung it here."

He examined the M16 to make sure it was loaded. He could hear yelling and hoots of joy up ahead.

"They must be finding plenty of guns on the Chinook," he said.

"Then it's stupid for us to attack them."

"I'm not attacking *them*. It's only Michael K. I want. As soon as he's dead, we're outa here."

M16 in hand, Halverson jogged toward the crash site, on the lookout for guards that Michael K. might have posted. Halverson didn't see any. Michael K. must not have expected company while he plundered the Chinook.

Halverson did spot ghouls drawn by the ruckus plodding toward the smoking crash site. Several of them looked more like skeletons than ghouls with barely any flesh on their moldering bones.

"Graveyard ghouls," said Marta, watching the skeleton creatures with dismay.

"We're not the only ones who want him dead," said Halverson. "We need to hold down our voices now. I can see the gang up ahead."

He darted behind a wide-girthed oak to keep out of their sight, Marta in tow.

"Do you see him?" she whispered.

"It shouldn't be too hard to spot him with his shiny head and black tie."

Halverson peeked around the oak.

The High Rolers were cavorting in front of the crashed Chinook, rooting through the debris, casting around for weapons and ammo. There were plenty of M16s strewn around the smoldering, smoking chopper.

Distracted by their joy at finding the ordinance, the gang didn't notice a ghoul that shambled up to one of their own as he lifted a Glock from the wreckage. It was Barry handling the Glock with a smile on his face. The tall middle-aged ghoul lunged toward him from behind and bit the side of Barry's neck, tearing out a huge chunk of flesh and scarfing it down, blood jetting from Barry's severed jugular. Clutching his mauled neck, Barry screamed in agony and emptied his Glock into the ghoul's face, whose mouth was stuffed with a bloody hunk of flesh.

"Shit," cried Barry in agony, white-faced, blood gushing from his shredded throat.

Seeing his plight Gayle approached him and, screwing up her face in revulsion at what she had to do, shot him in the head, felling him.

Aroused by Barry's scream, Michael K. emerged from the damaged Chinook fuselage, holding a stack of M16 magazines in his arms.

"What the hell?" he said.

"A ghoul got Barry," said Gayle, her face drawn as she pointed at Barry's mutilated corpse that lay on the grass.

Hidden behind the oak, Halverson could see everything from his coign of vantage. He hoisted his M16 to his shoulder and trained it on Michael K.'s head as the dumbfounded High Rolerz started to drift toward the scene of carnage.

"You think the gang is just gonna stand there after you shoot him?" said Marta, incredulous.

"Cut off the head, and you kill the body," said Halverson.

Halverson couldn't waste time. As the bikers approached Michael K., Halverson would lose sight of his target standing among them. He squeezed the trigger, firing a three-round burst at Michael K., whose head burst into a cloud of pink mist.

"Let's beat it," said Halverson, gripping the M16 in one hand.

He and Marta barreled away from the crash site and the High Rolerz, who were staring in stunned disbelief at Michael K.'s motionless body sprawled on the grass. Overcome with shock, they were trying to assimilate what had happened.

Gayle was the first to recover her senses.

"Over there," she said. "I saw a muzzle flash near that humongous oak."

She bundled toward it, clutching an M16 she had commandeered from the Chinook.

The others were slower to react as they stood in a circle around Michael K.'s corpse and took it in with somber faces. Confusion and bewilderment etched several of their visages. All of the High Rolerz were having trouble accepting his sudden death. To many of them Michael K. had seemed immortal.

Realizing she was alone Gayle came to a halt, slewed around, and favored the lot of them with a glare.

"Snap out of it, morons," she cried. "We got work to do. Nobody gets away with whacking our leader. What did he tell us? There's nothing better than the *sweet* taste of revenge."

Letting out a whoop she pumped her fist.

The bikers roared belligerently and charged after her, brandishing their weapons like maniacs gorged with bloodlust.

Chapter 90

Now you've gone and done it, decided Halverson, hearing the bloodthirsty eldritch wails chasing him and Marta like banshees from a necropolis.

"The body's doing quite fine without the head," said Marta, gasping for breath as she raced after him.

His lungs on fire, Halverson pumped his legs beneath him for all he was worth, beads of sweat popping from his face. Fear was a great motivator.

"We have to reach the hogs," he said.

"It sounds like there are a million of them behind us."

She tripped on a root and went flying. She landed on her face in a clump of bushes the size of a recliner.

Halverson heard her go down. He stopped, turned around, and belted to her. He helped her get to her feet.

They tore through the woods, making for the road.

Halverson started at the crack of a gunshot behind him. Running, he craned his neck around but saw no one behind him. A plethora of gunshots followed. The biker gang was still out of sight. They were shooting their weapons into the air to fill him and Marta with fear.

"Can you see them?" said Marta.

"No. We're almost there," he said, catching a glimpse of the road as he blasted through the trees, trampling pine duff littering the ground.

A black twentysomething five-five female ghoul with a Prince Valiant haircut sidled out from behind a tree in front of Halverson. Her face riddled with maggots weltering out of its pores, she blocked Halverson's path. She bared her snaggle-teeth at him and vomited a bilelike fluid on his face, preparing him for digestion. Halverson smashed her upside the head with the stock of his M16 without breaking stride. Her skull cracked audibly as his blow sent her reeling. He used his arm to wipe the noxious sickly green fluid off his face with disgust

He didn't know if he had killed her, but he wasn't going to hang around to find out.

Seeing the road he burst out of the woods, gasping for breath, and sought the motorcycle he had the key for. Slinging his M16 over his shoulder, he straddled the Harley and waited for Marta, his pulse racing.

She blew out of the woods, her face flushed from all her running.

"Grab your hog and let's go," he said.

She flew toward the motorcycle she had chosen then stopped in her tracks.

"We got a problem," she said.

Halverson fired the ignition and revved his Harley. "Let's talk about it later."

"This can't wait."

"We don't have time."

She stared at him. "I can't drive a motorcycle."

Prince Valiant wasn't dead. She had only been stunned by Halverson's blow. She staggered out of the woods with her cracked skull and homed in on Marta, groping toward her with withered, grimy fingers with broken nails, her throat covered with the green fluid she had barfed on Halverson.

"Sit behind me," said Halverson.

Marta shot toward him and mounted the hog. She embraced his chest.

Halverson peeled out, leaving a trail of burnt rubber in the shape of a comma in his wake. He slammed down the road, the Harley roaring between his legs.

"Where'd you learn to drive this thing?" she said, the wind buffeting her cheeks as she looked over his shoulder at his face.

"At the CIA. I can drive anything." He hung fire. "Except a dirigible."

"A dirigible? One of those hot air balloon things?"

"Yeah. I missed that class."

"Do you know where you're going?"

"Raven Rock."

"Are you still determined to go there?"

"Speaker Smirnoff needs to know he is the rightful president, not Uriah."

"Aren't we supposed to be wearing helmets?"

"Do you think any cops are gonna bust us?"

Chapter 91

President Uriah stood in his office studying the football he had placed on his desktop.

"It's almost time to exert my power as the president," he said.

Dr. Morrow watched him, picked sleep from his eye, analyzed it, then flicked it across the office.

"You're not really considering using that?" he said with a healthy dollop of skepticism.

"And why not?"

"Do the circumstances warrant it?"

"Halverson and Marta must have reached Raven Rock by now. They're gonna tell Speaker Smirnoff that he is president. That is a lie. *I* am the president because I have the football. Whoever has the football is president."

"Then why worry about it? There's nothing Smirnoff can do even if he knows you have declared yourself president."

"He can stage a rebellion. We're heading for the second Civil War if I allow him to go on living."

"Is it that bad?"

"That's why I told Purdy to terminate Halverson with extreme prejudice. If Halverson hadn't told Smirnoff about my rise to the presidency, Smirnoff never would have known, and there would be no problem of Civil War II."

"Maybe Halverson never reached Raven Rock."

"He must have. Purdy would have reported back to me by now if he had taken out Halverson," said Uriah, studying the buttons on the football. "Halverson must have taken out Purdy and his squad."

"The whole squad?"

"Halverson is a CIA-trained black ops killer. Hundreds of people have tried to kill him, and none have succeeded. I know for a fact that Special Forces–trained agents have tried to take him out for many years and failed."

"If he's that bad, we should never have let him back in the bunker after he failed his mission to get the vaccine for the zombie plague."

"I wasn't president at that time. For sure *I* wouldn't have let him in. He's a mole trying to destroy the American government."

"Why?"

"I have no idea. I'm not a psychiatrist."

"I dunno. A lot of people in our government idolize him."

"He's a first-rate con artist. I can't let him tell Smirnoff about me. I have no other choice but to launch nuclear-armed ICBMs at Raven Rock. Smirnoff cannot be allowed to incite a revolt against me."

"You'll be killing our own people," said Morrow, aghast, realizing Uriah's threat was for real.

"Smirnoff must be considered an insurgent. It is my duty as president to take him out."

"Consider all the collateral damage you'll be inflicting on the people who live in Raven Rock and in the surrounding area."

"Like I said before, and I'll say it again, uneasy lies the head that wears a crown . . ."

"You can't seriously be considering nuking fellow countrymen."

"We're talking about the very survival of our great country. This is an existential moment in our nation's history. We can't have two presidents. We tried that in the first Civil War with Abe Lincoln and Jeff Davis. Do I need to remind you how that ended?"

"We're talking about innocent people's lives, Mr. President."

Uriah gazed at Morrow. "Are you not a patriot, Doctor?"

"Of course I am."

"Then why can't you understand that what I'm gonna do is for the good of the country?"

"Because you're gonna kill boatloads of people when you press those buttons on the football."

"The lives of insurgents mean nothing to me. They are the enemy. They are the cancer that wants to destroy this great country and turn it into a shadow of itself."

"If you press those buttons and fire ICBMs at Raven Rock, you have crossed the point of no return."

"Did Julius Caesar have doubts before he crossed the Rubicon? Of course, he did. And I have doubts too, but in the end I, like him, must do what I think is best for our country. Our country is more important than any individual that comprises it."

"On your head be it," said Morrow, distancing himself from Uriah's actions.

"I'm the president, Doctor. I'm the one who makes decisions around here. It's always on my head."

"Of course. I meant no disrespect, sir."

Uriah set his fists on his desktop. "Don't you understand? Halverson forced my hand. He's to blame for this fiasco. I can't let Smirnoff split the country in two. I'm sure you're familiar with the term *divide and conquer*. We will be destroyed by another country if he succeeds in creating a schism in our great land and thereby weakening the US."

"I'm a doctor. I see each human life as important. You see them as pawns on a chessboard."

"I see Smirnoff as a threat to democracy. He will challenge my rule, and he will take up arms against me. I must forestall him to prevent another Civil War where many American lives will be lost. If I don't attack him first, he will attack me. He who attacks first has the advantage."

"Why do you have such a low opinion of human life?"

"My father always taught me to stand up for myself. He told me if I didn't stand up for myself, nobody else would. I'm not gonna let Smirnoff stage a coup d'état."

Morrow lowered his head. "We're doomed."

"The time for arguing is over. I'm the one who makes the decisions here, and no force on earth can stop me once I've made up my mind."

Uriah started pressing buttons on the football.

Morrow hoped it wouldn't work thanks to the beating it had taken when President Cole had nuked himself. Morrow's hopes were soon dashed. With dread he heard the football whirring and saw its control panel lighting up.

"I want you to stand witness that I am launching ICBMs equipped with nuclear warheads in order to save the country from the insurrectionist Smirnoff."

"OK," muttered Morrow, his face blanching.

"I didn't hear you. I need a witness for this momentous event I am about to enact in order to keep this great country free."

"OK."

Morrow watched with horror as Uriah's fingers flirted over the football control panel preparing to set the steps into motion that would launch ICBMs at Raven Rock and forever change the face of the country, taking it down a dark and unknowable path.

"Bless me, Doctor. I know what I do is righteous."

"I'm not a priest. My job is to save the flesh, not the soul."

"You'll thank me for this later," said Uriah, his face beaming like some kind of demented wizard in the wash of the colored lights flashing on the football control panel.

Chapter 92

Halverson's jacked Harley thundered down the road toward Raven Rock. He felt Marta's arms embracing him, her body pressed against his back.

Scores of chugging hogs ridden by the High Rolerz were catching up to him.

He saw the closed blast door of the Raven Rock bunker the better part of a mile up ahead. He was hoping the crew inside the bunker would open the door when their facial recognition equipment picked up on his face and ID'd him—if the equipment was working.

Ghouls lumbered down the road in front of him foraging.

They were the least of his problems. The gang on his tail were closing in. Halverson zigzagged to avoid their incipient bullets, knowing he could not outstrip the bikers at this point. Several of them opened fire on him, steering their bikes with one hand and firing their guns with the other. Which, luckily for him and Marta, threw off their aim thanks to the movement of their bikes and to his evasive maneuvers.

Gripping his Staccato, he craned around and exchanged shots with his pursuers, hoping it would slow them down. Wearing fingerless black leather driving gloves, Gayle returned fire, narrowing her eyes and twisting her lips into a sneer.

They were picking up ground on him as he backed and filled. The blast door was rising as he approached it, but it wouldn't be high enough for him to drive under it when he reached it.

"We're gonna have to jump off the Harley before we reach the door," he said. "When I count down from three, we jump. Then we roll under the door."

He couldn't hear her answer what with the deafening roar of his Harley and the others behind him.

"Three, two, one, jump."

He turned the hog away from the blast door and when it was low to the tarmac he jumped off the seat, feeling Marta draped on his back. She slid off his back as he rolled toward the bunker door. His head was spinning from all his rolling when he came to a stop. He cleared his head and looked back at Marta, who lay motionless on her stomach on the tarmac, her back soaked with blood from the bullet wounds in it.

"No," he cried, and hammered the tarmac with the bottom of his fist until the skin was bloody.

Out of the corner of his eye he glanced a fiery streak tearing through the sky, arcing like the band of a rainbow.

"Incoming, incoming," somebody cried inside the bunker.

The bunker door started closing.

Halverson saw Marta move her arm. She was still alive. Fifteen feet away from him.

He estimated the distance between him and the bunker and watched how fast the door was closing.

If he scrambled to the bunker, he might make it to safety before the ICBM warhead struck. On the other hand, if he ran to Marta and helped her to the bunker, he figured the door would be shut by the time he got there with her.

Two bullets fired by the approaching bikers sang past his head. The bikers had slowed their approach ever since they had spotted the ICBM warhead hurtling through the sky. They had stopped in the road, not knowing what to make of the warhead.

Halverson wasn't going to save himself and leave Marta outside to die. He would do everything he could to save her. He had to act on a dime. He bolted to her bloody body, the ICBM warhead emitting a deafening shriek as it split the sky and homed in on the bunker at almost two thousand miles per hour.

He helped her to her feet. Weak from loss of blood, she could barely stand. He draped her arm over his neck and, gritting his teeth with effort, set out for the bunker door as fast as he could manage with her additional weight.

"I coated my bullets with zombie drool," cried Gayle, watching him, her MP5 in hand.

Looking skyward, her mouth agape, her arms spread out at her sides, she let out a maniacal guffaw as she sat on her hog. She had figured out what the blinding streak was.

ABOUT THE AUTHOR

Multi-award-winning author Bryan Cassiday writes horror fiction and thrillers. His postapocalyptic horror thriller *Horde (Zombie Apocalypse: The Chad Halverson Series Book 6)* won both the Independent Press Award for Best Horror Novel 2022 and the American Fiction Award for Best Horror Novel 2021. His Scott Brody thriller *Threads* won the Independent Press Award for Best Thriller Novel 2023 and the American Fiction Award for Best Hard-Boiled Crime Novel 2022. He lives in Southern California.